QUEEN OF THE ISLAND SKIES

AJ BAILEY ADVENTURE SERIES - BOOK 6

NICHOLAS HARVEY

Copyright © 2020 by Harvey Books, LLC

All rights reserved. This book or any portion thereof may not be reproduced or used in any manner whatsoever without the express written permission of the publisher except for the use of brief quotations in a book review.

Printed in the United States of America

First Printing, 2020

ISBN-13: 979-8667871484

Cover design by Wicked Good Book Covers

Beechcraft Model 18 photograph courtesy of Tim Felce

Mermaid illustration by Tracie Cotta

Author photograph by Lift Your Eyes Photography

This is a work of fiction. Names, characters, businesses, places, events and incidents are either the products of the author's imagination or used in a fictitious manner unless noted otherwise. Any resemblance to actual persons, living or dead, or actual events is purely coincidental.

DEDICATION

For Cheryl, my mermaid.
These novels, and this existence, would not be possible without you.

1

CARIBBEAN SEA – APRIL 1958

It wasn't about the money.

Rod 'Dingo' Doyle laughed out loud. He was the only one in the Beechcraft Model 18 he piloted, so there was no need to explain his sudden outburst of humour. He had been flying for almost five hours, mostly over water, his backside ached, and his mind wandered in search of distractions to pass the time. It was always about the money, to some degree, he thought. Without the money he couldn't fly, and flying aeroplanes was life itself to Dingo. He looked out of the side window at the Caribbean Sea creeping underneath him 9,000 feet below, and pulled at the collar of his rugby shirt. He would be shedding the cotton jumper in a hurry when he landed on Grand Cayman for fuel, but cruising at 176 mph almost two miles up, he was slightly chilled. He looked over his shoulder, where the seven passenger seats had been replaced with four long wooden crates. The thirty-one-year-old Australian didn't give a damn about politics, but running guns for Cuban rebels was probably a short career, and who was he kidding, this trip was all about the money. He sighed and looked out front again, instinctively scanning the skies for other aircraft. He was one and done with this deal, he said to himself. Again.

His nickname, 'Mad Dingo' Doyle, was given to him by the RAF lads when he trained to fly fighters in England in 1945. A month before his eighteenth birthday, he had set out for England determined to fight for the Commonwealth. Son of middle-class parents who owned a flourishing jewellery shop in Sydney, his father had paid for his flying lessons as a sixteenth birthday gift, and Dingo had found his life's passion. By the time he reached England, he had turned eighteen and was old enough to enlist. The RAF were happy to take a young man with hundreds of flight hours' experience and Doyle quickly adapted to the training planes. An inverted fly-by a few hundred feet above the grassy airfield earned him the 'Mad Dingo' moniker, the Pom's Australian twist on 'mad dog'. Disciplinary action for the stunt also held him back four weeks. He was assigned to a squadron of Hurricanes the week the war ended in Europe, and never flew a combat flight.

Dingo looked across the gauges of his beloved twelve-year-old, twin-engined plane. Temperatures all looked good, fuel level showed half full, and both fuel and oil pressures were stable. She was a beauty. Polished aluminium fuselage, distinctive twin tail design and a pair of radials that sang sweeter than Elvis himself. Her name, 'Queen of the Island Skies', was painted on both sides of her nose, with a scantily clad young beauty, and a couple of palm trees. His thoughts wandered once more to the money. For several years he had been flying tours out of Acapulco as the beach destination had grown and become the place to be seen by Hollywood's stars. The movie elite were happy to pay his prices to be flown around by a good-looking former RAF pilot, but the local officials and other tour operators were not so keen on Dingo's popularity. They found plenty of ways to keep the Queen of the Island Skies planted firmly on the ground. From bogus inspections to the aviation fuel supplier suddenly running out of petrol when it came to Dingo's plane, they had made it hard for him to make ends meet. He needed to find a new base to operate from, one with less hostile competition. He could have stopped and topped off with petrol on the Yucatan peninsula then made the hop to the Sierra Maestra mountains where the Castro brothers and their men were hiding out and training. But, he had decided on Grand Cayman, for two reasons. The first, it meant he would have plenty of petrol to get the hell out of Cuba as he had no clue what he would be facing there. He was supposed to be landing on a makeshift runway in a field at the foot of the mountains, but he was sure Batista's government troops would be keen to seize his cargo, and Queenie, if they spotted her. Secondly, he could take a look at the island as a possible new location for his business. He had heard the rich liked to spend their holidays there, and some had built themselves little getaway mansions. Using the range of the Beechcraft, with its 318-gallon fuel capacity, he could reach Miami, Atlanta, maybe even Houston without a fuel stop. The island was governed by the British authorities on Jamaica, so he figured there had to be business between the two islands to boot.

The left engine spluttered, and Dingo's mind left Grand Cayman in a hurry as he worked the controls to square the plane back up. The motor seemed to clear again and a quick check of the gauges showed nothing untoward. But when he stared at the fuel pressure a little longer, he swore he could see it flicker for a fraction of a second. The fuel level was showing just under half, plenty to finish the 150 miles to the recently constructed George Town airfield. He flew on without further incident for several minutes, but he could feel a subtle change in the vibrations through the yoke and his seat. The rhythm in the smooth, methodical drone of the Pratt & Whitney radial motors had shifted. Queenie was an extension of Dingo's own body. He knew every rattle, harmonic and sound as though she was a part of his flesh and blood. Something wasn't right. He saw the needle flicker on the fuel pressure at the same moment both motors spluttered. His heart leapt into his throat. Both motors. He was over wide open ocean, with Grand Cayman the nearest land, still thirty minutes away. If he lost both engines, he was going to be ditching in the water. He eased the mixture levers forward to enrich the fuel, and they both recovered.

He breathed again, but noted with concern he had already lost a thousand feet of altitude.

Dingo's mind shot back to that morning and the argument he'd had with the man selling fuel at the airfield in Tuxpan. He had flown the 300 miles at first light from Acapulco, on the Pacific coast, to Tuxpan on the Caribbean coast, where he had picked up his cargo. The man had started by swearing on his mother's grave that the petrol he had in his regular tank was 100 octane AvGas. Dingo didn't believe him; he'd seen the man topping up his own car from the pump a little earlier when they had been loading the crates in the plane. Finally, the man conceded and apologised, telling Dingo he had two barrels of AvGas in storage he had been saving for a customer, but he would sell him some of it. Without a way to check the octane level, Dingo had to take the man at his dubious word. He had topped off his tanks, which were two thirds full when he arrived from Acapulco. The existing fuel would have sloshed around and mixed with the new fuel he had added and by now he had stopped worrying about the octane level, as the motors had seemed fine. It had to be something else. He thought back to watching the man pump the fuel from the barrel. He had asked if the pump had a filter, and the man had indignantly told him of course it did. Dingo figured it was unlikely the fuel was 100 octane, but worse than that, he'd been lied to about the filter. If the new petrol was riddled with debris from the old barrels, it was now clogging his fuel filters. All he could do was pray the filters wouldn't become completely blocked before he reached the island.

He didn't get to do much praying. Both engines spluttered and misfired in unison. Dingo dipped the nose to keep his airspeed up as he lost thrust from the propellers, and hung to the hope he could glide in if only they would keep running for a bit longer. He moved the mixture levers again but with the filters not letting enough fuel to the engines, it was having no effect. Grand Cayman had to be just over the horizon, and he felt his backside lift out of the seat to stretch his neck optimistically. A cloud bank in the distance suggested it might be hovering over the island, but he couldn't see land. The left motor cut out first and the right motor followed a few seconds later as Dingo stared out of the left side window, listening to the sickening sound of his engines winding down. He quickly pressed the two buttons to feather both props, which would stop them spinning uselessly and creating more drag. All he could do was glide in a steady descent to keep his airspeed above stalling. He would either reach the island and land, or ditch in the ocean, which currently appeared to be the more likely scenario. If he dropped below stall speed of 77 knots, he would plummet from the sky and punch a hole through the water. Dingo scanned the horizon and frantically checked between his compass heading, airspeed and altitude. The plane had an eerie quiet without the deep-throated drone of the radials, leaving silence except for the whistling rush of the wind. He squinted through the front windscreen. Way out there, up ahead, he could see something. For a moment he let himself hope it was the island, but it was too small to be a land mass. Even one as small as Grand Cayman. He continued gliding and was under 5,000 feet of altitude when he could finally make out the fishing boat – but still no land ahead.

Dingo had to make a decision. Keep flying straight for the island and ditch as close as he could get, or set down in the water near the only other human beings he had seen for the past few hours. It felt like he was deciding between being shot or blown up; the result was likely to be the same. He looked down at the water, now only a few thousand feet below him. Water always looked calm from the air. It was once you flew down low that you could see whether it was indeed flat, or had five-foot swells that would destroy Queenie the moment she touched. If Dingo committed to descending now, there was no turning back or choosing plan B; he was going in the water whatever the conditions were.

He glanced at the left-hand prop, now slowly rotating, and swung his head around to check the right propeller. It was still spinning much faster.

"Bugger me, come on Queenie, not now," he groaned.

He worked the pitch lever for the right-hand propeller back and forth and tried the feathering button again, with no effect. It must be the hydraulics that varied the pitch of the prop, he thought; perfect timing.

With the added feathering problem, he opted for human contact. He lowered the flaps as he continued to slow and began a banking turn to circle the fishing boat. He needed to set down into the wind which was coming from the east. That would allow him a lower ground speed, his goal being to stall the moment he skimmed the ocean to land – or crash – at the slowest speed possible. The other thing he needed to do was catch the attention of the fishermen. The whole exercise would be a waste of time if they didn't see him go in. He figured they would notice a plane crashing in the same piece of ocean they occupied, but without power he couldn't control precisely where he would be at the moment he would need to turn into the wind and set down. Hitting the fishing boat would also be an ironic disaster.

Dingo wagged his wings at the fishing boat as he swept past at 500 feet above the water and saw two men looking up and pointing at him from the deck.

"At least they'll witness this spectacle," he mumbled to himself, as he made his final bank, turning into the light breeze and pulling the nose up slightly to shallow his descent. He flirted with the stall speed of the plane as the water came closer and closer and he noted with relief that the sea was almost flat calm.

"Come on Queenie, my love, nice and easy," he coaxed, as the Beechcraft flashed across the ocean at 85 knots airspeed, figuring his stall speed would be higher with the right-hand prop still spinning.

Dingo felt the controls go light and the wings shudder as they teetered at the edge of stalling. It seemed like he was right on top of the water, but he knew he was still 20 feet above it. If he stalled from here the nose would plunge under and the plane would be torn apart. Against all instinct, he eased forward on the yoke, knowing the ground effect from the ocean's surface would help his lift when he got close, and he desperately needed a few more knots airspeed. Just as he was sure he was skimming waves, Dingo pulled back on the yoke to lift the nose. The whole plane shuddered as the wings stalled and dropped to the ocean, a loud swishing sound coming from the belly of the fuselage as it skipped across the water. He heard a terrifying thwap as the spinning propeller caught the ocean, buckling and shearing a blade at the clamp which flung itself through the side of the cockpit, before all went silent.

2

GRAND CAYMAN – JULY 28, 2020

Annabelle Jayne Bailey lay sprawled across her sofa with her laptop computer open on a dining chair next to her. She smiled at her boyfriend, Jackson, who was telling her about the week he'd had since they were last able to speak. His soft voice and Californian accent made his story about tracking down illegal fishermen in South America sound like a regular, average occurrence. Which it was for the Sea Sentry marine conservation organisation which Jackson worked for as first mate on one of their fleet of ships. His long black hair was tied back in a ponytail revealing his tanned, lean face and neatly trimmed beard.

Jackson finished his story and smiled, his blue eyes lighting up. "What? You're just sitting there grinning."

AJ laughed. "Yeah," she said, her English accent a contrast to his American.

Jackson shrugged his shoulders. "What? Do I have something in my teeth?"

"No. I just like seeing you," AJ said quietly. "You realise if it wasn't for this damned pandemic you'd be here now?"

Jackson sighed. "Yeah, believe me I've been thinking about that.

But hey, if I can't be there, at least I got back aboard for another tour where I can do some good."

"Sure, you get to do good, and it means you're doing something," she exclaimed. "I'm going insane not working. At least we can get out a little more now and take the boat out, if we fish." She leaned her head on her arm and stared at the screen. "I just wish I'd been able to come with you. You are doing something good and worthwhile, while I'm sat on my arse being useless."

"I was just fortunate with the timing – one more week and I would have been ashore and heading to San Francisco to my family. Then I would have been stuck there and still not able to come to Cayman. But, yeah, it would be great for you to do a tour with us," he smiled. "And at least we'd be together."

AJ nodded. "Yeah. Together would be good."

He leaned a little closer to the screen. "This too shall pass. We've made this work for a year, my love, we'll get through this too. And then you'll see me so much, you'll be begging me to leave," he said, laughing.

She shook her head. "Not a chance. Besides, I'm making a job list of all the stuff you can do around here. I'll make sure you're useful, don't you worry," she said, raising her eyebrows.

He beamed back at her, "I'll do my best to keep you happy." His smile faded. "I gotta go."

"I know," she replied. "Go save the world, I'll just sit here and wait for my man to come home one day."

Jackson laughed. "It wouldn't kill you to take it easy for a while, you know. You've had your fair share of thrills since I've known you."

AJ waved her hand at the computer screen. "All in the day's work of a dive boat operator."

It was his turn to shake his head. "You're crazy. But I do love you, and I do have to go."

"I love you too," she replied. "Talk to you next week – be safe."

"Sounds good, and you be safe too." He clicked his computer

mouse and the image of his smiling face disappeared from the screen.

"I think I'm a lot safer than you my love," she said out loud, looking around her tiny cottage.

She adored her little home in the grounds of a large house on Seven Mile Beach, but she was tired of being shut away during the lockdown. The Cayman government had reacted quickly and closed off the island to any visitors shortly after a cruise ship passenger unwittingly brought the COVID-19 virus onto the island. Since then a tough stay-at-home policy had kept the spread under control. They were finally easing restrictions and allowing islanders to get outside more, go to the beaches and take their boats out to fish. AJ had been inventing various workouts she could do in the large garden between the main house and the beach, but she was much happier getting back to her regular run on the beach. The landscape company was considered essential, so fortunately they had been allowed to keep the grounds in good shape; no easy task maintaining a lawn with the tropical weather and thin soil. AJ's cottage, which she rented from the family who owned the property, was at the south end of the garden. Rent was cheap in exchange for her keeping an eye on the house and the grounds, plus some diving thrown in when they travelled down from Atlanta, Georgia. Between the beach and the garden was a low wooden fence, dissuading anyone from wandering onto the property, and a line of palm trees to throw a little shade over the garden without blocking the beautiful view.

AJ closed her laptop and walked to the door. She picked up her mobile phone and earbuds from the tiny dining table next to the door before stepping outside. It was mid-morning and the heat and humidity hit her like a hot blanket after the air-conditioned cottage. She had put on her running shorts, sports bra, tank top and barefoot shoes before her Internet call with Jackson, knowing she'd be sullen after saying goodbye. Speaking to him was the best part of her week and saying goodbye sent her into a funk for a few hours. She had found her best therapy was to turn up the rock music and furiously work out. Her toned, athletic body missed her daily regimen of carrying dive tanks around, working the boat and being active, so she did her best to replace the missing activity with extra workouts.

A welcome breeze blew from the ocean and rustled the palm fronds lining the edge of the beach. The sky was a brilliant blue with a sprinkling of wispy clouds breaking the azure palette. Something caught her eye in one of the upstairs windows of the main house and she squinted against the bright sunlight. A pretty blue and white tree swallow flew from the balcony down to the lawn and alighted at the base of one of the palms. The bird looked curiously over at AJ with its head cocked to one side.

"Hello there, birdie," she said and chuckled at herself. This seclusion had reduced her to talking to the birds, she thought. She remembered she had forgotten to put on sunscreen and stepped back inside the cottage. She smothered on the lotion to protect the tattoos that adorned both her arms and dabbed a little across her nose and forehead. Satisfied, she went back outside and was just putting in her earbuds when her mobile rang. She looked at the caller ID which read 'Roy Whittaker'. She wondered why on earth the detective would be calling her. She hadn't seen or heard from him since the lockdown began. She accepted the call and put her mobile to her ear.

"Hi Roy, how are you doing?" she said.

"Hello, AJ, I'm well, thank you. I'm not disturbing you, am I?" the Caymanian policeman asked politely. Their paths had crossed various times over the ten years AJ had been on Grand Cayman, sometimes social, and unfortunately sometimes business. They'd formed a friendship, but it was unusual for him to call her unless it was a police matter.

"No, I was just going for a run, but I hadn't left yet so it's good timing. Is something wrong?" she asked.

He paused. "Well, not really wrong, no. In fact in a way, it's wonderful news," he said cryptically.

"Okay, you can deliver my football pools winnings to the cottage then." She chuckled.

"Not that good I'm afraid," he laughed. "Do you recall the sailboat that went missing earlier this year? The one from Crystal Harbour?"

"Sure, I can't remember what make it was, but I remember it was a really nice ocean-going type, wasn't it?"

"A Jeanneau Sun Fast 3200." Whittaker replied.

"Right, that's it. It went missing right after that whole business with those poor girls and the International Fellowship of Lions resort, didn't it?" AJ asked, becoming more intrigued.

"That's correct, and the good news is, the sailboat is back," he said with a tinge of humour in his voice.

"It's back? Like someone left it lying around somewhere and just remembered where they put it?" AJ asked.

"Exactly." Whittaker chuckled. "It showed up the same way it went missing; it just appeared again. The owners aren't on island, they live in the States, but their neighbour is a resident and called them to say their sailboat was back this morning. Tied up at the sea wall in front of the house where it's been missing from for months."

"Bloody hell." AJ wasn't sure what to say. "No sign of who's had the boat or where it's been?"

"We're dusting for prints, but so far they tell me it's wiped so clean it's more sterile than a hospital. Seems to be in perfect shape, no damage, clean and tidy just as the day it was taken."

"Are they sure a family member didn't borrow it without asking? That's so strange it would just reappear. I'm guessing thieves don't usually bring things back." AJ chuckled again.

"Indeed, it would be a first. There was an investigation into the disappearance, not just by us, but by the insurance company as well. They concluded it was stolen and paid the family the insurance value. Got a bit of a problem now, whether to give back the money, or the boat. Fortunately, they hadn't bought a new one yet."

AJ wondered when Whittaker would get around to asking her

what he had really called for. She let her silence on the line give him the chance to get to his point.

"Have you heard from Nora, the Norwegian girl, by any chance?" he finally asked.

AJ laughed. "Figured that's where you were going with this, Roy."

"I'm not as subtle as I think I am, huh?" he said lightly.

"Not this time, Sherlock," she ribbed him.

There was another pause. "Well? Have you?" he asked.

"Oh. No, of course not, I would have told you. They still want to talk to her in Norway I presume?"

"They do, I'm sure. But I'd be interested in chatting with her about the sailboat. If it was her that stole it, we need to address that."

"Borrowed it," AJ said.

Whittaker laughed. "Nice defence, barrister, but I'm afraid it's still theft if it's taken without consent, even if it's brought back."

"I suppose," AJ conceded. "I received a postcard in the mail a few months back; it was stamped from one of the leeward islands and postmarked from a different island. It was addressed to me and all it said was thank you, with a smiley face. I thought it might be from Nora, but I had no way to tell exactly. But no, other than that, I've not heard a word from her."

"I figured it was a long shot, but I had to ask," Whittaker said. "Would you mind if I took a look at that postcard, maybe dusted it for prints?"

"Of course not, it's stuck on my fridge door, drop by anytime," AJ replied.

"I'll come by later today on my way home if that's okay?"

"See you then, Roy."

They hung up and AJ thought about the young Norwegian girl she had helped save from a human trafficking ring. A Brazilian woman had set up a resort on the island providing the company of underage girls to wealthy clients. The girls were kept for a year at the resort under the promise of money and a new life at the end of their term. What they actually received was a heavy weight around their ankles as they were tossed overboard in deep water. The culprits were now in prison and one of the girls, Hallie, a local orphan and relative of AJ's co-worker, Thomas, now lived safely with his parents. AJ had pulled Hallie from the water at the same time Nora had disabled the resort's boat, enabling the police to apprehend two of the resort's ringleaders.

AJ opened the door to her cottage and grabbed a set of keys from a hook. She closed the door and walked over to the main house, crossing the concrete patio decorated with exotic potted plants and statues of dolphins. She unlocked the back door and waited for the alarm to beep. There was no beep. She closed the door behind her and took a few steps to the high-top breakfast table in the middle of the open-plan kitchen.

"Hello?" she called out.

A tall, young woman with long blonde hair, wearing jean shorts and a Bob Marley tee-shirt, stepped around the corner from the living room.

"Hello, AJ."

3

CARIBBEAN SEA – APRIL 1958

Edmund had spent his life on the water. He had worked on a fishing boat since he was fourteen and built the twenty-eight-foot wooden vessel that he and his sixteen-year-old son, Isaac, worked every day except Sundays. He had weathered storms, broken down, found things floating he couldn't identify, organic and man made, but he had never seen anything close to what he had just witnessed.

"What do we do, Pa?" Isaac said in his sing-song island accent as he looked at his father.

Edmund slipped his cloth cap off and scratched his balding head. "Figure we go over and see if there's anyone left to help."

He turned and slipped the old diesel motor into gear. The prop spun and the boat slowly began to ease forward as Edmund cut the wheel to port, circling around towards the downed plane. They both stared in disbelief at the Beechcraft floating in the water a quarter of a mile from them. The forty-year-old Caymanian had seen an aeroplane up close before, but only the Caribbean International Airlines PBY Catalina seaplane that used to fly people to and from the island before the airfield was built in '53. Since then, he had only seen other planes in the air. The PBYs were odd-looking birds with a fat body, an overhead wing with twin engines, and a belly like a boat hull. The plane he was looking at through his wheelhouse window was much prettier.

Earlier, about mid-afternoon, he had been ready to give up on the day and head home, when their lines began going tight and the fish decided to bite. It had been thin pickings until then, so they had stuck around and hauled in a fine catch of tuna and wahoo. It was 5:30pm when Edmund helped Isaac pull their lines in, ready to start the five-hour trek back to Grand Cayman. In calm seas, the diesel would chug them along at 12 knots, 14 if he pushed it, but then she would complain by billowing black smoke. Edmund preferred to make the run home in daylight, but with sunset only an hour away, he would be navigating his way back in the dark this day. He had made the sixty-eight-mile run plenty of times before and hadn't missed the island yet, so he figured he'd manage it again. That was when the plane had circled their boat.

Edmund looked behind him at the deck.

"Push our catch to the side and clear the deck some, son – we'll be putting some people back there."

Isaac nodded and began shoving the heavy wooden boxes full of fresh fish to the gunwales.

"What if they're, you know, Pa, what if they're…" The boy trailed off, unsure if he should say the word.

"If they dead?" his father replied with a grim look. "Then they coming aboard anyhow, ain't right to leave them out here."

Isaac nodded, sweat beading down his dark skin. "No sir, guess that's right."

Edmund piloted his old boat alongside the plane and hesitantly peered in through the small windows, unsure what he would see inside. The shiny, polished aluminium plane appeared to be intact and undamaged until he cleared the starboard wing and saw the hole in the side of the fuselage. He could make out a figure slumped over the controls in the left side pilot's seat.

"Come here, son, take the helm and keep us in close but try not to bump the plane now. I'll step over and take a look."

Isaac took over the wheel as they idled slowly beside the front of the wing to the nose. They both stared at the gaping hole torn through the side of the fuselage. The side window was gone, the aluminium below it was a twisted mess and part of the sloped windscreen was smashed. Edmund looked back at the wing-mounted engine and realised one of the propeller blades was missing, the other one bent around the engine cowl. He walked around the boat's narrow cabin to the bow, and carefully stepped over to the wing of the plane.

"That's a pretty picture," Isaac said, looking at the nose art of the girl. "Queen of the Island Skies," he read aloud.

"Yeah, I'm afraid she ran out of sky today," Edmund replied. "Ease back a bit, Isaac, I'll see if I can get inside."

Isaac slipped the fishing boat in reverse and idled away a few feet. Edmund leaned forward and looked inside the cockpit through the hole where the side window used to be.

"Oh my Lord," he mumbled.

He turned to Isaac. "He dead I believe, son, but I don't know how to get inside this thing, it ain't got no doors."

Edmund turned back and looked at the pilot. The man had blood down the side of his face with his head hanging limply and the belts the only thing stopping his body falling forward. Holding the body pinned to the seat was the remains of the metal propeller blade. It had speared into the floorboards between the two front seats and torn a gash in the ceiling as it came to rest embedded in the side of the pilot's seat. The man's right trouser leg was covered in blood and the limb was kinked at an unnatural angle above the knee. Edmund shivered at the sight. He looked back inside the plane in search of a way in, and noticed the long wooden crates in the back. Finally, he spotted a door towards the rear on the left side.

"There's a door in the back, on the other side. Come back over and get me," he shouted to Isaac, who idled back towards the wing. "We'll see if I can get in through there."

"Anyone else in there, Pa?" the boy asked.

"Nah, just the pilot is all I see. Part of the propeller came in through the side and got him. Not sure I can get him clear anyway, but I guess I'll try," Edmund replied as he stepped back over to the bow of his boat.

Isaac manoeuvred the boat around to the other side of the plane and eased in beside the rear door his father had located. Edmund reached over and tried the handle. The door fell outward and swung down on bottom hinges until it banged against the bow of the boat.

"Back up some, son," Edmund called out and Isaac gently idled in reverse until the door swung the rest of the way down and splashed into the water.

The door had steps on the inside creating a stairway into the plane and Edmund jumped from the bow to the steps and grabbed the inside of the door frame. The whole plane rocked under his weight and water washed into the rear of the fuselage. The Beechcraft appeared to be floating on its wings and underbelly in the calm seas, but Edmund realised with the sealed door open it wouldn't take much wave action to sink the plane. He stepped between the wooden crates, and hunching over in the cramped space, he moved forward to the cockpit. He had seen a dead body or two over the years and blood didn't bother him too much, as long as it wasn't his. But he still tentatively leaned over between the seats to examine the pilot. He looked at the battered metal of the prop gouged into the sheet metal. He moved behind the co-pilot seat and heaved on the broken blade to see if it would move. It creaked and small pieces of debris sprinkled down, but it didn't budge. He put a foot against the side of the pilot's seat to gain a firm footing and pulled as hard as he could. More shards rained down and the prop finally inched back in the jagged slot it had made in the ceiling.

Edmund jumped and hit his head on the ceiling as the man's arm moved. He cussed under his breath and shook his head. Of course the body moved, he realised, it's pinned by the prop, which finally budged a little. He set up again with his foot on the seat, cupped both calloused hands around the propeller blade and heaved with all his might. The metal groaned and creaked and the prop juddered a few more inches towards him. And the hand moved again.

"Hey, man, are you not dead?" Edmund stammered, taking his foot from the side of the seat and pinning himself back against the fuselage.

A gap appeared in the streak of blood down the side of his face, as the man opened an eye.

"Not yet, mate," the man whispered.

4

GRAND CAYMAN – JULY 28, 2020

Nora held AJ's embrace tightly and it felt like she didn't want to let go. AJ knew some of what this eighteen-year-old girl had been through, and doubted she trusted anybody. It made AJ's eyes moist to think that maybe she was one person Nora did feel comfortable with. When she finally let go, AJ held her at arm's length and looked her over. She seemed well. She was tanned, her tall slender figure appeared fit and strong, her Scandinavian blue eyes sparkled, but also held a hint of the sadness and worry someone her age shouldn't know. She smiled at AJ, but her joy seemed shallow, or short lived. A fleeting moment in the arms of a friend before returning to her own darker place.

"We need to go over to my apartment. Turning off the alarm in here triggers the security cameras so we're being recorded." AJ said, stepping back.

Nora grinned sheepishly, "No, it's okay, I turned the cameras off too," she said in perfect English with a Norwegian accent.

"How on earth do you know how to do that stuff?" AJ said, shaking her head.

Nora shrugged her shoulders. "You pick up a few tricks along the way."

"Well, anyway, can you reset everything? We should get out of here in case the alarm company checks on why everything is turned off."

Nora nodded. "Ja, they may do that. Just set your code and everything will be good again."

AJ locked the house back up with the alarm system safely reset, and the two walked over to AJ's little cottage, Nora bringing her rucksack with her. AJ guessed the young woman's sole possessions were likely in that one small bag.

"Are you hungry? When did you get back here?" AJ asked. "I have a lot of questions, actually," she added.

Once inside the cottage AJ made Nora sit at the dining table and dragged the other chair over from next to the sofa, putting her laptop aside.

"I'm starving," Nora replied, looking towards the kitchen area a few feet away.

"Stay there, I'll fix you something." AJ started towards the kitchen and wondered what she had in her cupboards. She was ten days into her attempt at shopping only once every two weeks during the pandemic. She pulled a loaf of bread out and rummaged for peanut butter in the larder.

"When did you get here?" AJ asked again.

Nora hesitated. "Well, who's to say I haven't been here all this time?"

AJ laughed and took the postcard from the fridge door, holding it up for her to see. "Postmarked BVI. And, by the way, Detective Whittaker called and is coming by later today to borrow this. He seems to think you might be back."

"What did you tell him?" Nora asked nervously.

AJ pinned the postcard back to the fridge door. "Everything I knew." AJ turned back and smiled. "I got a postcard a while back and didn't know for sure who it was from, but otherwise I hadn't heard from, or seen you. He called a few minutes before I came over to the house."

"Why did you come over to the house?" Nora asked.

"I thought I saw something in the window upstairs, and then once Whittaker said he suspected you were back, I took a guess," AJ replied, bringing the sandwich over and setting it in front of Nora.

"Thank you," Nora said, looking up at AJ, "for, you know, everything."

AJ nodded and went back to the kitchen to get them both a drink. "All I've done is make you a sandwich; you saved yourself back on the Cova do Leão. Besides, Whittaker wants to check the postcard for fingerprints, so don't thank me too soon. They're dusting the sailboat too."

Nora stayed deadpan. "There are fingerprints on the postcard, but not mine."

AJ looked at her, trying to read her expression as she set the glasses of orange juice down. Nora looked up from her sandwich, which she was eagerly devouring.

"What sailboat?" Nora added, between bites.

AJ sat down and her mouth opened but no words came out – she didn't know what to say. Nora looked at her quizzically. And then the edges of her mouth crept into a slight grin. They both burst out laughing.

"We shouldn't be laughing, stealing a boat is a serious thing," AJ said, once she had regained her composure.

"Borrowed," Nora corrected.

AJ shook her head. "I tried that line with Whittaker; he and the Royal Cayman Islands Police Service don't see it that way, I'm afraid."

Nora shrugged. "There's no trace of me on that boat. Like I said, what sailboat."

"Fair enough," AJ conceded. "I'm just glad you're okay."

Nora smiled, and AJ saw that same look of buried pain. The girl had maturity way beyond her years.

"How is Hallie?" Nora asked before AJ could quiz her further.

"She's doing really well. She lives with Thomas's parents; they've taken guardianship of her. Do you remember Thomas?"

"Of course, he was with you on your boat when you rescued us. Hallie's cousin, right?" Nora said before finishing her orange juice.

"Do you want another sandwich, and some more juice?" AJ asked, having seen the way the slender girl devoured what had been put in front of her.

Nora grinned, with a hint of embarrassment. "Could I please have another sandwich? It's been a few days since I had food."

"Of course," AJ replied, standing and taking the empty plate back to the kitchen. "I assume you need a place to stay for a bit?"

Nora turned in her chair so she could see AJ in the kitchen. "If it's not too much trouble. If it makes a problem for you with the policeman, then I can go somewhere else."

"We'll figure it out," AJ responded, and wondered how to ask the question she really wanted to know the answer to. Why was Nora back on the island? She started to ask, but stopped herself. AJ knew she wasn't a patient person and tended to say, or ask, what was on her mind. Now, approaching thirty-one years old, she had learnt that sometimes it's best to let people take their time and tell you some things in their own way, and in their own time. She ventured into a different subject that had her curious.

"When was the last time you were home, in Norway?"

Nora frowned. "I haven't been back since I left, two years ago," she said, then added quietly, "It's a bit of a problem for me to go back there."

AJ brought her the second sandwich she had made, topped off her orange juice, and sat down.

"Whittaker told me you were listed as missing in Norway; do you still have family there?"

Nora chewed a bite of the sandwich before replying, "Ja, I do, and I feel bad because my family are good people, but I sort of have a complicated situation there."

She looked at the sandwich in her hand and then up at AJ. "It was easier for them to think I had drowned than to explain everything."

AJ thought for a moment. She couldn't imagine a situation so awful that she would rather let her parents think she was dead than explain or face up to whatever had happened. But she hadn't walked in Nora's shoes, and the girl had certainly had a traumatic time of things from the part of her life AJ knew about.

"That must be hard for you, and for your family," was the best response AJ could muster.

"I sent them a couple of postcards too – they should know I'm alive. I'm guessing the Cayman police contacted them too, after the resort stuff," Nora said. "One day I'll see them again and explain. None of it was their fault, it was mine. But I was just sixteen and I didn't know how to handle things then. I would have done it differently now. One day I have to stop running and sort everything out. I'm just not quite there yet."

AJ reached across the table and softly touched her hand. "You can stay here until you figure out what's next. We'll just need to hide you later this afternoon when Whittaker comes by. Other than that, with this whole pandemic business, people aren't socialising and visiting each other, so no one will know you're here."

"Thank you," Nora said and put her sandwich down on the plate. She looked at AJ. "And of course you're wondering why I am here, aren't you?"

AJ shrugged her shoulders. "I figured you'd tell me when you were ready."

She was silently proud of herself for having waited and not asked. Nora nodded, and her eyes searched AJ's face as though she was trying to gauge her reaction before she had told AJ her reasons.

"I need your help."

"Okay," AJ replied, wondering what she could possibly need her help with, beyond sheltering her for some time.

"You and your boat," Nora said, still watching AJ carefully.

"My boat? Didn't you just give back a boat? Why do you need my boat?"

Nora kept looking at AJ, the girl's blue eyes alive with determination. "Because we need to go diving."

5

CARIBBEAN SEA – APRIL 1958

Edmund's heart pounded in his chest when the dead man spoke to him. He finally recovered, and realising the man was in a bad way, set about trying to free him. Now the man was conscious, he could see he was in a lot of pain, which spiked every time Edmund tugged on the broken propeller blade. He had managed to move it a few more inches, but the jagged metal of the ceiling had now clamped it in place.

"I need to get my saw," Edmund said.

The injured man stirred. "You ain't gonna cut me leg off, mate," he mumbled, having leaned back in his seat where he could look up at the ceiling.

"No, no, mister, I mean for cutting through this here propeller thing," Edmund reassured him.

The man attempted to laugh. "You ain't cutting though that prop blade either, mate, unless you got a gas axe hidden on that boat of yours."

Edmund stopped heaving on the prop. Sweat poured from his brow from the effort and the heat inside the metal plane.

"I think you're right about that, and no I don't have me no

cutting torch." He looked down at the injured man. "What should I be calling you, mister?"

The man peered up at Edmund. His brown hair was tousled and messy, his face half covered in blood from a gash in his forehead, but he managed a slight grin.

"They call me Dingo," he said weakly. "But if you don't get me out of Queenie pretty soon, you can call me what you like and I won't know the difference, I reckon."

Edmund nodded. "Right then, I'll fetch some tools from the boat, see what I can do. Don't die on me again, Mister Dingo."

Dingo chuckled. "I'll do my best, mate. Bring some clean rags if you have some. We'll see if we can stop me leaking so much." He looked down at his own leg and quickly looked away again.

Edmund rushed back through the fuselage to the door in the rear, picking his way between the wooden crates and ducking to avoid hitting his head on the low ceiling. When he reached the open door he called to Isaac.

"Come back in closer, son, I need a crowbar from the toolbox."

Isaac brought the fishing boat back in closer until Edmund could reach out and touch the bow. Edmund leaned over and grabbed the bow line coiled on the foredeck and turned back to the plane, looking for a place to tie the rope. The outside of the plane was sleek and smooth with nothing obvious to loop the line around, so he ducked back inside. He reached down and tried lifting one of the long crates by the rope handle on the end. He was barely able to raise it off the floor. He tied the bow line through the rope handle to keep the boat lashed to the plane and ducked his head back out the doorway.

"Isaac, drop the fender tyres over the port side and you'll need to lower them so they keep us off the wing." He didn't know why he felt the need to protect the downed plane – he couldn't figure how it was going anywhere but underwater from here – but it was the most beautiful thing Edmund had ever seen, so it didn't seem right to damage it further. Isaac handed him down the crowbar.

"I need some clean rags or a towel," Edmund said, but he knew they didn't have anything sanitary aboard; it was a fishing boat after all. Isaac stared back at his father, clearly sharing the same thought.

"Get my spare shirt," Edmund said. "Probably best we can do."

Isaac nodded and returned a moment later with a stained but clean shirt in his hand.

Edmund once more made his way to the cockpit and was pleased to notice the water inside the plane didn't appear to be rising. He presumed airtight meant watertight, and as his boat was now tied to the plane he was relieved it didn't look to be imminently sinking. Dingo's eyes were closed when Edmund reached him, and for a moment he thought he was dead again, but his head moved and his eyes opened.

"What's your name, mate?" Dingo mumbled.

"Edmund, sir, and that's my boy on the boat, he's Isaac," Edmund said as he handed him the shirt. "Sorry, it ain't much, but it's all we have."

Dingo nodded and reluctantly looked down again. He tried to wrap the shirt around the open wound in his leg but groaned in pain and looked back at Edmund.

"You gonna have to help me here, Edmund, I can't lift my leg." He gritted his teeth and took a few breaths. "It don't seem to be working. We gotta get this tied off above the break, stop some of this bleeding."

Edmund peered over at the man's leg. It didn't look good. He took the shirt back and, taking one end, he tried pushing it under Dingo's thigh.

"Strewth, mate." Dingo clutched at his shattered leg, but when Edmund hesitated he urged him on. "Do it, mate, you just gotta do it."

Edmund took a deep breath himself, pushed his hand under Dingo's thigh until he could grab the end of the shirt from the other side and pulled it under the man's leg. Dingo's head fell to his chest and Edmund froze, terrified he'd just killed him. He waited until he heard the faint sound of breathing and let out a sigh. He quickly tied the shirt snugly around Dingo's thigh, hoping he had done it correctly, and picked up the crowbar. He prayed he could get the propeller blade removed before Dingo came to again, and set about levering the sheet metal away where it stuck through the ceiling. After the first few attempts he realised without much to lever against it wouldn't be as easy as he had hoped. He settled into a steady rhythm, preparing himself for a lengthy labour.

Dingo stirred and came to a few moments before Edmund finally loosened the aluminium around the blade enough to wiggle free of the ceiling. Edmund was doused in sweat, his grimy, fish-stained, cotton shirt soaked through. He laid the crowbar down and gave himself a few seconds to catch his breath before heaving on the lower piece of the blade. It didn't want to budge. He shook his head, picked the crowbar back up, and started again, working on the floor. He tried to ignore the grunts and groans from the pilot as the prop vibrated and juddered against his shattered leg. Out of breath and out of strength, he levered against the blade itself until it finally broke free, falling over towards him. He threw the remains out of the broken side window into the ocean. Dingo looked over through eyes barely open.

"Guess you'll have to drag me out the back. This ought to be a gas, mate."

Edmund nodded. He was not a big man; the broad-shouldered Australian looked to outweigh him by fifty pounds and he couldn't see how he would pull him out of the seat then over the crates.

"Wait there just a minute, Mister Dingo, I'm gonna fetch my boy to help."

Edmund patted Dingo on the shoulder and started back down the inside of the plane. Behind him he heard Dingo mumbling.

"Yeah, I'll be right here, mate."

Isaac wasn't too eager to get inside the plane and Edmund hesitated for a moment when he realised they would all be inside the downed aircraft. If the plane chose that time to sink they'd be going down with it, and dragging their boat along too. He looked around the inside of the fuselage and saw no more water had come inside.

"Hurry now Isaac, this man ain't gonna last much longer if we don't get him some help."

Isaac obeyed his father and hopped over into the doorway of the Beechcraft. They picked their way back to the cockpit and Edmund squeezed Dingo's shoulder again.

"Okay, sir, we gonna try and get you out now."

Dingo grunted, put his right hand over to the co-pilot's seat and tried lifting himself with his arms to ease over to the edge of his seat. He yelped in pain and his arms collapsed. Edmund reached in and supported Dingo under his right arm and nodded to Isaac to lean over the pilot's seat and help. Isaac had been hesitantly waiting a few feet back, nervous of the bloodied stranger, but he stepped forward and leaned over the seat to lift under Dingo's other arm. Between them they half lifted, half dragged Dingo over the backs of the two front seats. Dingo gasped as his broken leg twisted, and thankfully passed out again.

"Quickly now, while he's out we'll get him to the boat," Edmund urged, panting at the effort.

Between them, they hauled Dingo's limp body through the plane, over the crates to the back door, his broken leg twisting and flopping at grotesque angles.

"What's in the big boxes?" Isaac asked, catching his breath and looking at the wooden crates.

Edmund looked up at the bow of their boat and tried to figure out how they could haul the body up there.

"I don't know, son, and we don't have time to worry about that." Edmund pointed outside the door. "We gonna drag him onto the wing out there, then we gonna turn the boat so the stern's against the wing, then pull him onto the deck."

Isaac looked over at the wing several feet from the doorway. The door lay open, floating in the water like a walkway, but would undoubtedly sink under their weight. He shrugged his shoulders as he watched his father make the long step from the doorway to the wing with its flaps below the surface. Edmund slipped and almost fell in the water but managed to scramble farther up the wing and regain his balance.

"How we gonna get him to the wing, Pa?" Isaac asked.

Edmund scratched his head before resetting his cap.

"Gonna have to throw him in the water, son," he replied, "You get him in and shove him this way and then I'll pull him up the wing here."

Dingo's limp frame was draped across the crates with his head hanging forlornly over the edge of the doorway. Isaac stood over him, and with his hands under the man's armpits, he heaved him a few inches closer to the opening. He repeated the process and Dingo's head banged unceremoniously against the door hinges.

"He be a big fella, Pa, I reckon he don't much want out of his plane."

"Keep doing what you're doing – once his shoulders are out it'll get more easy, boy. Put your back into it now," Edmund urged.

Isaac flopped, banged and dragged Dingo's beaten body farther out the doorway and sure enough, the weight of his head and shoulders soon had him sliding into the water head first. His broken leg slapped and whipped out of the doorway, sporting an extra joint that shouldn't be there. Edmund stretched out and grabbed Dingo by the hair, lifting his head clear of the water and pulling him next to the wing. He reached down and hauled him up the wing, using the smooth metal as a ramp. Edmund flopped down on his backside and took a moment to catch his breath again. He looked to the west where the sun was low in the sky as the daylight began to ebb away. Guess I'll be making the whole trip back in the dark, he thought.

"Okay Isaac, take that line free and get back on the boat. Back the stern up to me here and we'll pull him aboard."

The boy did as he was told and after a few minutes had the stern bumping against the polished aluminium wing of the Beechcraft. He shut the engine down and rushed to the stern where his father had Dingo's 5' 10" frame dragged to the edge of the wing. Between them they pulled him over the transom and onto the rear deck. Edmund wiped his brow and stared at the injured man before him, sprawled between the fish they had spent the afternoon catching. Isaac looked back at the open door to the plane as the boat slowly drifted away from the Queen of the Island Skies.

"So, Pa, what about them boxes in there?"

6
GRAND CAYMAN – JULY 28, 2020

"We're in the middle of a lockdown, Nora, we're not allowed to go diving," AJ explained. Nora had finished the second sandwich and they both sat back in their chairs, sipping orange juice.

"I know. But you're allowed to go fishing. So, we go fishing," Nora replied matter-of-factly.

AJ smiled. "This is not a big island – we're likely to be seen by someone. And rightfully so, they're serious about the restrictions."

Nora leaned back over the table. "We wouldn't be diving near the island, we'd be out of sight."

AJ took a deep breath. "Okay, you'd better give me a bit more to work with here. Grand Cayman is an underwater mountain that just peeks out of the water. It's a big mountain too. All around us is 6,000 feet deep, or more. We can't dive any of that."

Nora nodded. "I know." She grinned. "But it's not all that deep is it? There's a few more mountains out there, like the one your submarine is sitting on."

AJ had discovered the hiding place of a scuttled German WWII submarine several years before, which was indeed resting on a pinnacle that didn't reach the surface, but was still at a depth they could dive. There were a handful more of these peaks scattered about in the ridge line of the mountains that ran from Cuba to Mexico across the Caribbean Sea. Or more accurately, below the Caribbean Sea.

"You're talking about one of the banks?" AJ asked.

"Sixty Mile Bank," Nora replied.

"Okay, well, I guess you're right, no one would see us out there," AJ agreed. "I doubt the local fishermen are going that far afield yet. But what's out there? Not many people have dived that bank, but a few have. I've never heard of anything out there."

Nora sat back and thought a moment before replying. "I will tell you some things, because I believe you will keep them to yourself. Then you can decide if you want to help me do this. If you decide to help, we must leave very quickly, and once we are on the way, I will tell you the whole story. All I can tell you now is a little piece of it, but it is the important parts." She looked over at AJ. "How do you say in English? The big picture?"

AJ laughed. "Yeah, that's more American English, but I get what you mean. This is all very cryptic and secretive. Is it illegal?"

"You said you're not allowed to go diving, so yes, I guess it is illegal, but what we would be diving for is not illegal," Nora clarified.

"Hmmm, okay, so tell me what you can then," AJ said.

Nora took another deep breath. "So, these are the things I can say. One, there is something valuable on Sixty Mile Bank, or near to the bank."

"As I was saying," AJ interrupted, "if it's near the bank, it's going to be in water too deep for us to dive, Nora. We don't have a side-scan sonar or anything like that to search for it either. We have a basic fish-finder-type sonar, but that's it."

Nora held up her hand.

"Okay, okay, I'm sorry, carry on," AJ said, reminding herself to let people tell their stories in their own time.

"Second, there is a good chance what we're looking for isn't there. But if we don't look, we won't know," Nora said. "Third, If we find these things of value, we will be giving them back to the family of the person who lost them. None of us should expect to make money."

She looked at AJ, but AJ made an effort to keep a poker face and not give away what she was thinking. Which was relatively easy as, so far, she didn't know what to think. Treasure hunt for no return, she thought, that's all the treasure hunting I ever seem to do.

"Why are you grinning?" Nora asked and AJ realised her poker face needed some work after all.

AJ laughed. "Some people get rich treasure hunting, but not me apparently."

"The submarine you found, there's much gold inside, no?" Nora asked.

"There supposedly is, yes," AJ answered.

"But from what I read, you weren't interested in cutting the submarine apart to get the gold?"

AJ shrugged her shoulders. "It was never about the gold, it was about following through on my grandfather's story and finding the wreck. It was for the families of the men from the submarine. Maybe one day we'll find a good way to get inside without destroying the submarine and, if it is in there, the gold can go back to the descendants of the people it came from. The victims of the Holocaust."

It was Nora's turn to smile. "So, you will be happy with the reasons we will find this treasure then, and maybe not happy, but okay with not getting paid."

AJ rolled her eyes and chuckled. "You're making this sound like a wonderful deal so far."

"I know," Nora said quietly. "I'm sorry to be so secretive, but that's about all I can say. It's not against the law, we may not be able to find it, and if we do, it goes back to the rightful owners. Oh, and I have a few hundred dollars I can give you towards petrol."

"Diesel," AJ corrected with a grin.

"Okay, diesel, petrol, unicorn droppings, whatever, I'll give you all the money I have." Nora laughed.

"And, you think it's on Sixty Mile Bank?" AJ asked.

"I know it was," Nora replied confidently.

"How long ago?"

Nora thought for a second. "Let's just say it's last century, so we're not on a crazy, pirate treasure hunt or anything like that."

"What's your connection to this? How are you involved?" AJ asked.

Nora thought again, this time for longer. She finally looked up, and AJ could see the sadness had returned in her expression. "It's for someone who means a lot to me."

"Would they be coming too?" AJ asked, carefully.

Nora's jaw clenched slightly. "No, they can't come with us."

AJ sat and thought, trying to think of what else to ask but realising she needed to be delicate about it. There was something behind all this that meant a lot to Nora, and was likely a big part of her sadness. Before she could come up with anything else, Nora spoke again and sounded more cheerful.

"You were going for a run, I think?"

"I was." AJ glanced at the kitchen clock, which read 12:40pm. "Do you mind if I go now? Running helps me think and I need to think about all this."

"Of course I don't mind," Nora replied. "Would it bother you if I came along? I'll be quiet so you can think. It's been a while since I could run."

"It's fine with me, but I don't think we should risk you being seen." AJ stood and walked to the kitchen. She hadn't eaten anything since breakfast and realised she usually would have had lunch by now. Pandemic lockdowns seemed to make mealtimes more like beacons on her journey through the day. She watched ahead for them constantly, and worried her figure was suffering for it.

"Don't worry, no one will recognise me. I'm used to hiding in front of everyone," Nora said, rummaging through her rucksack and pulling out some clothes.

AJ found an energy bar in the cupboard and ate a few bites. When she turned, Nora was stripped naked in the living room, about to slip some shorts on. She must have seen the surprised look on AJ's face and chuckled.

"I'm sorry, I'm used to either being alone or with the girls at the resort, I forget."

AJ blushed and immediately felt silly. She was the thirty-year-old woman of the world, and here she was embarrassed at the eighteen-year-old girl with no inhibitions.

"No, no, it's okay, I'm used to being on my own too much I suppose," she said and went back to nibbling the energy bar and getting a drink of water.

"See," Nora said after a few minutes, and AJ turned back towards her. She was wearing football shorts and a loose tee-shirt over a sports bra that flattened her small, but as AJ had just witnessed, perfect breasts. She had coiled her long, blonde hair up underneath a baseball cap and she hadn't been wearing any make-up anyway. There she stood, looking remarkably like a skinny, soft-featured, teenage boy.

"Okay then little brother, let's go for a run," AJ laughed.

Nora nodded and they headed out the door. As they walked across the garden to the gate in the fence to the beach, AJ glanced at the slender Scandinavian girl who was about five inches taller than her. She looked down at her own figure. She was in great shape and had an athletic physique, but she also had shapely hips, and while she wouldn't describe herself as buxom, her chest was not going to be flattened with a sports bra. She would never be a runway model, and she was fine with that. But Nora could be. She could be one of the girls in the magazines, modelling the latest fashions and styles. How the poor girl's life had steered her in such a different direction. Not that the life of a model would probably be a satisfying one for her, but she could have had choices, if things had gone differently. She was incredibly smart and surely could have chosen any path for a university education. AJ hoped that life would come around to some normality for the girl; at only eighteen, those choices could still be possibilities. She hardly knew her, yet she felt a bond, a closeness, and a friendship. Sharing life-threatening situations can do that to people.

"Ready?" Nora asked, putting her earbuds in.

AJ nodded. "You bet."

The two set off along the gently sloping beach, running on the hard-packed sand close to the water. The sun was overhead, fiercely beating down and the sand sucked much of the energy from each stride, conspiring to make an intense workout. AJ used to monitor her pace during her run with an app on her mobile, but lately she had turned the mileage alerts off and checked her stats after she was done. Some days the sand was harder going, or like this day, she was running in the blazing heat of the middle of the day. She was comfortable with the effort level she needed and knew her turn-around point for a six-mile run. Nora fell in step and appeared happy to match the pace AJ set as the two of them lost themselves in their own thoughts. Music pumping through their headphones provided a feeling of isolation and privacy, a virtual cocoon from the world outside.

AJ tried to sift through the small amount of information Nora had given her. It wasn't much to make a decision on. Maybe that was easier, she thought; the decision was more about the person than the task. Nora was wanted by the authorities in several countries, for questioning at least, but she sensed with all her heart that the young woman was not an evil or malicious person. AJ knew she had been coerced into the role she played at the resort, which after almost a year of working as an escort had led to her to being beaten and raped by one of the so-called guests. How the girl would ever have a balanced view, and sense of physical relationships with men, was hard for AJ to imagine, but she hoped one day it would be possible. Being around loving and caring couples would be an example of how things could be. AJ felt lucky that in a world of divorce and broken partnerships, her parents had remained together, and in love. Her best friends and mentors, Reg and his wife Pearl, were a further example of a loving couple who were committed and still completely besotted with each other after thirty-five years of marriage. Nora just needed some positive examples in her life, people she could trust that believed in her and truly cared for her. That had to start somewhere, AJ decided.

They reached AJ's turn-around point outside the WaterColours luxury condominiums, and she came to a stop. Sweat streamed down her body and her tanned skin glistened in the bright sunlight. She pulled out her earbuds and Nora did the same.

"You swear there's nothing illegal about this?" she asked.

"I promise you, there is nothing illegal about searching for and taking these things if we find them. Or where they came from and how they got there, for that matter. We would simply return them to their owners," Nora replied, catching her breath.

"Okay, I'll take you. But on one condition, and it's not negotiable," AJ said, her flat stomach heaving as she too caught her breath.

Nora peered out from under the bill of the baseball cap, her joy clearly guarded.

"What is the condition?" she asked, cautiously.

"There's two other people we have to take with us, and they'll need to know everything I know. If they won't go, then we don't go," AJ said firmly.

"You must trust these two people?" Nora asked.

"One hundred percent. They've both saved my life before. And we need them for a dive operation like this, out in the open ocean – we can't do this alone."

Nora nodded and bit her lip, clearly thinking it through. "Same deal as with you though, I can only tell them what you know, but I'll explain the whole story once we're on our way."

"You won't have to tell them anything. I'll speak with them. I'm not going to mention you, for your, and their, protection. They won't know more than I do, because I can't tell them what I don't know. But if they can't, or won't, go for any reason, I can't do it either."

Nora smiled. "I trust you."

AJ nodded and put her earbuds back in. She didn't know what exactly they would face out on Sixty Mile Bank, but the warm glow she felt inside told her she was doing the right thing.

7

CARIBBEAN SEA – APRIL 1958

Dingo slowly came to and was assaulted by the smell of fish. He blinked his eyes clear as the searing pain in his right leg brought his memory back into focus. He wasn't inside Queenie anymore, he thought, staring up at a clear but darkening blue sky. He heard Edmund's voice speaking quietly and the sound of wood splintering. He made out another voice and presumed it must be the son, who he hadn't seen yet.

"There's a million nails in these things."

"Lift that board as best you can, son, I nearly got it now," Dingo heard Edmund say.

He propped himself up on his elbows and sharp streaks of pain shot up from his leg. He still couldn't see the two Caymanians over the transom, but saw the top of his beloved plane and his heart sank. He may never see her again, and worse than that, the two men were about to see something it would be better they didn't.

"Well, I'll be…" he heard Edmund say.

"They guns, Pa?" the boy asked and Edmund quickly shushed him.

"Edmund," Dingo called out, lying back down on the smelly wooden deck. There was silence and he figured the man was trying to decide how best to handle this new knowledge. Dingo looked to his side where a dead tuna fish hung out of a box, staring blankly back at him. I might be in the same boat as you, he thought, and then groaned at the comedy of already being literally in the same boat as the dead fish.

"Edmund. Best leave them crates, mate. I'll tell you all about it as we head to the island. Pretty sure I need a doctor in a hurry here," Dingo called out.

The bleeding had slowed considerably since they had tied the shirt as a tourniquet around his thigh, but he knew he had lost a lot of blood, and his leg was in bad shape. He really needed something else from the plane, but until he could decipher Edmund's frame of mind since discovering his cargo, he couldn't risk bringing it up. He heard movement from the plane and Edmund's face appeared over the gunwale. He was frowning, but more in concern than anger, Dingo guessed. Or hoped.

"Mister Dingo, we were trying to save your cargo but they's too heavy to lift over, so we opened one." Edmund shoved his cap back over his sweaty brow and scratched his head. "Can't say we'd have stopped to help if we'd known what you was carrying, mister."

Dingo propped himself up on his elbows again and gritted his teeth against the pain.

"I understand you don't want to be involved in nothing like that mate, especially with your boy and all. But it ain't exactly what it seems, Edmund."

Edmund nodded slowly. "It seems like you're running guns for money," he said and stared at the Australian.

"Well, yeah, on the face of it, that's about what it is," Dingo conceded. "But, it's not what I usually do. I fly tours around the coast of Mexico, you know, sightseers and such. I've been a bit strapped lately..." He paused as he thought about how to explain all the struggles he'd had in Acapulco, then realised, why should this man care? "You know where Cuba is, right?"

"Of course," Edmund replied.

"That's where those crates were heading. I had to refuel on your island, then hop over to Cuba. Do you know anything about the government over there?"

Edmund shrugged his shoulders and Dingo couldn't tell if he didn't know, or didn't care. Or both.

"Yeah, so, the government over there are pretty corrupt, and the people are trying to overthrow them. Those crates are…" He paused and corrected himself. "Were, headed to the rebels, to help them get this Batista bloke, who's like a dictator, get him out of running Cuba."

Edmund looked towards the plane for a moment, then back to Dingo.

"We been to the trouble of getting you outta your aeroplane, guess we'll take you where we're going. Don't suppose you're in much shape to give me trouble." Edmund started to turn away.

"Edmund," Dingo called and stopped him. "I'm much obliged you stopped to help, mate. And, honestly, the last thing I'd do is cause trouble for you and your boy." He nodded towards the plane. "Do you think your boat could tow Queenie?"

Edmund laughed. "I got nothing to tow her with, Mister Dingo; besides, she'd pull my boat apart, and that boat is my life, mister."

"Fair enough, mate," Dingo replied, and thought carefully. "How deep is this water?"

Edmund looked at him with a puzzled expression. "A thousand fathoms. Most of the ocean between here and Grand Cayman is between a thousand and two thousand fathoms, so I'm told." Edmund looked out over the water. "Can't say I'd know for sure."

Dingo slumped back down with a groan. His beautiful aeroplane would end up thousands of feet underwater, where she'd be lost forever. The idea of her rotting away in the pitch-black gloom at the bottom of this vast sea was devastating. All because that swindling crook at the airfield in Tuxpan sold him contaminated AvGas. Now he had to decide. Explain to Edmund how to retrieve his hidden package, or say goodbye to his nest egg forever. Holding something like that in his hand could change a man. Edmund appeared to be a good fella, a simple fisherman, but put something like that in front of him, and maybe he'd flip Dingo over the side and head home. No one would be any the wiser, and Edmund and his family could live out their days as wealthy folks. Dingo had promised his father the small fortune would only be used in a life-or-death situation. He had made that promise the day he had left Australia for England, and the war. Apart from buying Queenie, he had kept that promise. Through his financial troubles in Mexico, he had kept that promise, and now, in a life-or-death situation, he couldn't use them to save himself. In fact, they may cause the opposite. He wasn't sure he would live through the next few days anyway, but he decided his odds shortened greatly if he told Edmund about the package. He resigned himself to the sad truth his small fortune would be lost.

"Course, where we's at right here is only sixteen or seventeen fathoms, that's why we come out all this way to fish," Edmund said as he disappeared from view.

"Wait!" Dingo shouted and ignored the pain as he propped himself back up. Edmund's face appeared over the gunwale again.

"Sixteen fathoms, that's, what, about a hundred feet, right?" Dingo said excitedly. Maybe there was hope yet.

"About that," Edmund said. "Why?"

"How long's your anchor chain, mate?"

"One I usually use is about 50 feet; we anchor in the shallow water around the island sometimes. Everything else is too deep to anchor anyway," Edmund replied, looking confused. "Why you asking about anchors?" His expression changed as he realised what Dingo was thinking. "I got more chain below though. I traded fish with a man for 200 feet of it. I only used fifty. Got a spare anchor down there too," he said excitedly. "You thinking we anchor that plane of yours and come back out with something bigger to tow it in?"

"That's exactly what I'm thinking, Edmund," Dingo said, forgetting the agony in his leg for a moment. Isaac appeared next to his father and looked between them both.

"What about the... You know... Them crates?" he said

nervously.

Dingo hadn't considered that. If they came back out with a bigger boat, possibly one owned by the authorities, they wouldn't take too kindly to a cargo of guns.

"Toss them out," Dingo said. "Pop the lids off the crates and toss them in the water."

Edmund nodded. "Alright." He looked at the setting sun. "Best we hurry, it'll be dark soon. Let's anchor the plane first, make sure we haven't drifted off the bank here; this shallow part ain't very big."

As the father and son walked around Dingo and their catch from the day, he wondered how on earth the fisherman could find this small underwater mountain in the vast sea. He watched the two drag the heavy chain up the narrow steps from below the cabin before Edmund took the end and stepped back to the wing of the plane.

"Where's best to fix this chain to your aeroplane, Mister Dingo?" he asked.

"That's a good question, she's not really designed to be chained to anything." He thought a moment. He had put down on the water with the landing gear up to keep a smooth surface under the plane, so they couldn't use the wheel assemblies.

"You'll have to use the tail, Edmund, loop the chain around the fuselage forward of the tail wing. Fix the chain back to itself if you can to form a noose."

Edmund nodded. "Isaac, fetch me one of them shackles we have," he called to his son then turned back to Dingo. "Gonna scratch up your pretty aeroplane some I'm afraid, maybe dent it too."

"Yeah, best we can do under the circumstances, mate. There's a large hole in the cockpit gotta be fixed before she'll fly again anyhow. That's assuming we can come back out and find her again."

Edmund smiled. "I'll find her for you, Mister Dingo, don't worry about that."

Isaac handed his father a steel shackle with a pin and Edmund scrambled over the wing to the fuselage where he pulled himself up onto the roof. The chain clanked and rattled as it fed out over the transom with Edmund shimmying along the relatively flat roof of the Beechcraft towards the tail. He let the end of the chain go over the far side of the tail just in front of the distinctively wide tail wing. With the shackle in his hand he dropped into the water on the opposite side and reached under the tail to retrieve the end of the chain. Pulling it under the tail he then shackled the chain to itself underneath the fuselage. When they dropped the anchor the tail wing would keep the chain loop from sliding off the rear of the plane. Edmund swam back to the wing and hauled himself out of the water.

"Take a depth here, Isaac, make sure we're still over the bank," he called to his son.

Isaac took a length of line with what looked like an old piston and con-rod tied to the end, and threw it over the side. He played out the line as the weight dropped towards the sea floor. Dingo noticed the knots in the line every six feet as they slid through the boy's hands.

"That's how you know you're over the shallow all the way out here," Dingo exclaimed.

Edmund stepped back onto the boat and nodded. "Yes sir, but we have to find the place first. Sounding line just tells us if we did or not."

Dingo recalled the lack of land within sight from the air when he had circled.

"How far are we from Grand Cayman?" he asked.

"Sixty miles, give or take," Edmund answered. "Be why they call this the Sixty Mile Bank."

"So, how do you find this all the way out here?" Dingo asked incredulously.

Edmund shrugged his shoulders. "I just know where it is. Been coming here my whole life, every week or so. My Pa knew where it was. Few years and Isaac will be able to find it alone too. I missed it a couple of times – when seas are rough it's harder to find 'cos we get blown around more on the way out. I have a compass I use."

Dingo couldn't believe the man's natural navigation ability. Sure, he had a compass, but that didn't help a man judge the drift from the winds and currents. The line went slack in Isaac's hands and Dingo noticed a ribbon tied by the next knot that hadn't gone over yet. He guessed it to be their depth marker for the bank. Isaac nodded to his father who quickly stepped over Dingo, picked up the anchor fixed to the other end of the chain and threw it over the transom. The chain rattled its way after the heavy anchor with Edmund helping throw sections of it over to save the metal grating on the wood of the back of the boat. Isaac wound in the sounding line, coiled it neatly in the cabin and then the two returned to the plane. Dingo could hear the splashes as his cargo of Castro's guns was deposited into the Caribbean Sea.

It was almost dark when Edmund and Isaac finished, tossing the empty crates in the water and struggling to lift the door up out of the water to seal it closed. They stepped back aboard their boat with the line they had tethered to the plane in hand.

"All set then, Mister Dingo, time we headed home."

Dingo felt weary and groggy from the constant pain. He looked up at the fisherman, silhouetted in the fading light.

"Thank you, Edmund, I'll find a way to repay your kindness."

"Don't need no pay, sir. I have to go with the best sense I get of a man, and I sense you ain't meaning no harm. So I'm glad we been able to help."

Isaac offered Dingo a rolled-up shirt to put under his head which he gladly accepted.

"Rest up as best you can now, be the best part of five or six hours back home," Edmund said as he started towards the helm. He paused alongside Dingo for a moment.

"Best we not make mention of those crates when we gets there."

"Much obliged, Edmund," Dingo replied weakly.

He let his eyes slowly close. The outline of Queen of the Island Skies was the last thing he recalled before drifting into fitful sleep.

8

GRAND CAYMAN – JULY 28, 2020

AJ had been operating Mermaid Divers for more than five years. Having started with a smaller rigid inflatable boat, she now operated a thirty-six-foot custom Newton dive boat, the standard of the Caribbean dive industry. She still kept the RIB, Arthur's Odyssey, for special projects and a second boat when needed, but Hazel's Odyssey was the boat she and Thomas Bodden, her first mate, fellow dive instructor and good friend, used every day. Thomas was a local twenty-two-year-old Caymanian who AJ had poached from Reg Moore three years before when he was interning for Pearl Divers, Reg's three-boat-strong operation. AJ and Thomas worked like two finely engineered gears meshed together, each finishing the other's thoughts and sharing the labour and the joys equally. Over the past three years, Thomas had first achieved his divemaster certification, and then his instructor rating, so between them they could perform any of the roles needed.

AJ had first tried scuba diving on a family holiday to Grand Cayman when she was just sixteen. The dive operator her father had chosen was Pearl Divers, and two seeds were planted that day. The first was AJ's love of diving, and the second was her family's close relationship with Reg and his wife. On the surface, Reg was a grumpy old sea salt, a veteran of the British Navy, and a hard hat salvage diver before he settled on Grand Cayman and opened his dive business. Underneath the straggly greying hair, unkempt beard and gruff tone was a big-hearted man who would do anything for someone he felt was deserving.

AJ had called Reg and Thomas and asked them to meet her on Hazel's Odyssey. Her boat was moored in the Yacht Club marina, located near the North Sound, on the opposite side of the narrow spit of land from Seven Mile Beach. She hadn't seen either of them in weeks with the stay-at-home advisories in effect and their businesses inoperable. They had all been carefully isolating with close family and felt no reservations in greeting each other with a big hug.

"Good to see you, girl," Reg said in his deep tone, as he clutched her in his broad-shouldered embrace.

"You're crushing me you big ol' bear," she managed to squeak out, and he finally released her.

She smiled up at his wind-worn features and mischievous eyes, belying his sixty-five years.

"Good to see you too, Reg. Hug Pearl for me. I talk to her every day, but I miss seeing you both," AJ said warmly.

"Aye, strange times these are, but like everything else in this world, it too shall pass."

"Jackson said the same thing this morning. Passing too bloody slowly if you ask me," she said, rolling her eyes.

Reg gave Thomas a hearty slap on the back and AJ hugged her friend.

"How's your mum and dad doing, Thomas?" she asked.

"They're good and said to say hello to you both. If I'd given her more warning I was coming here you'd be leaving with some fish pie or some sort of stew. She was mad at me about it, you know how she likes to make food for everyone."

They sat on the benches under the cover of the fly-bridge and AJ pulled two bottles of Strongbow cider and a Coke from a cooler she had brought along. She handed Reg a cider and Thomas the soda.

"It's great to see you both, but I'm guessing there's something more to this little gathering," Reg asked and took a long pull of the cool drink.

AJ nodded. "Yeah, I've got a little expedition I want to go on, but I need you two along to make it work."

She had barely got the words out before Thomas nearly jumped out of his seat. "When do we go?"

AJ and Reg both laughed. "You don't know anything about it yet," AJ pointed out.

"I don't care, man, one more day stuck in the house and I'll be crazier than a back-yard chicken. I been fishing some with Papa, now he can go back out, but I get all..." He waved his hands around trying to think of how to explain himself.

"Ants in yer pants?" AJ offered, chuckling.

"That about describes it right," Thomas said. "You know me, I can't be sitting still, and Papa, you know, he be happy just sitting there with his lines in the water. If they don't bite 'bout thirty seconds after that line goes in, I'm wanting to move somewhere and find them fish. He thinks them fish be spending all day looking for his boat; me, I reckon it works the other way round."

"Does he catch fish?" Reg asked with a grin.

"Sure, he catches lots of fish," Thomas admitted, "but it take him most all the day. If he'd motor about and fish here, fish there, till he find them fish, he'd be home before lunch."

AJ and Reg couldn't stop chuckling. Thomas was one of the hardest working people they knew and the island taking-it-easy gene had missed him by a country mile. Very few Caymanians worked in the dive industry – the people had made their living from the sea for centuries, but they preferred to stay on top of the water. Thomas was an exception to the rule and a great example to the local kids. More and more youngsters were beginning to show an interest.

"Well let me tell you what I can about this adventure, and then you can decide whether it's for you or not," AJ said, and Thomas shrugged his shoulders, indicating he was unlikely to change his mind.

"We'd be going fishing, out to Sixty Mile Bank," AJ started. "And by fishing, I mean we'd take some rods with us, but what we'd really be doing is diving. It's a long shot that it's still there, but what we're looking for is something that went down over the bank at some point in the last century. If we find it there's something valuable we'll attempt to retrieve. If we're successful, what we bring up gets returned to the heirs of the rightful owners."

"We're hunting treasure?" Thomas asked, his enthusiasm undampened.

"Essentially, yeah, I suppose it is, just not centuries-old treasure," AJ replied.

"How has this all come about?" Reg asked. "You're being all cloak and dagger about it. I mean, what is this wreck? You know there's some who have dived on that bank, and I've never heard anyone say there's a wreck there."

AJ thought a moment. "It's thin on details, because I don't know much about it. I don't know that there even is a wreck, I just know there's something valuable out there. We would all learn the whole story on the way out."

"So, someone else will be going with us?" Reg asked.

"Yes, but don't ask me who," AJ quickly replied.

"Not that bloody idiot Jonty Gladstone is it? I am not heading out to the deep sea with that bugger and you should know better by now than to contemplate the same," Reg growled.

AJ laughed. Jonty was a treasure hunter on the island she had helped a couple of times, and his projects always managed to fall apart, or become life-threatening calamities.

"Do you think I'd even talk to you about this if it was Jonty?" AJ retorted. "There's no way he'd come back if you got him out in deep water."

Reg grinned. "Probably true. Maybe we should take him along." He winked at Thomas, who laughed.

"It's somebody I care about, and I trust," AJ said softly. "We'd be doing it to help them out. They can't pay; I mean they've offered diesel money, but I won't take it. It's about helping out a friend and having a bit of an adventure."

"And it's legal, right?" Reg asked.

"Apart from the diving instead of fishing bit, yes, it's a legal recovery to the best of my knowledge. Again, I'm going on the word of someone I trust, and I'd be asking you to do the same."

"Alright, I ran out of projects at the house weeks ago; even Pearl's getting sick of me I reckon. Sounds like this might be the perfect escape for a few days. You do realise it'll take us a few days to get out there, search for a while and get back?"

"Yeah, I figure we'd leave before first light tomorrow and plan on two nights out there. I looked at the weather and we've got three good days ahead and then they're predicting stronger winds coming in."

"Tomorrow? Blimey, we better get cracking then, I hope we've got enough tanks filled 'cos you know we can't get mixed gas during this lockdown business," Reg responded, and scratched his beard thoughtfully.

Reg had a compressor he had fitted at his dock they both used in West Bay, just north of Seven Mile Beach, but it could only fill tanks with regular air. For the dives they would be doing they needed a custom mixed gas called enriched air nitrox, which contained a higher oxygen percentage, replacing some of the nitrogen. Nitrogen became a problem for divers on deeper dives for extended periods of time. If they were going deeper than recreational diving limits of 130 feet they'd need even more exotic gas mixes, using a portion of helium.

"I figure we'll take all nitrox, if we have enough, and then an assortment of trimix in case we end up deeper," AJ said. She looked at Thomas who had stayed quiet. "What do you think, Thomas?"

He grinned. "I already told you I'm in, just waiting for you to stop talking so I can go pack me a bag."

AJ shook her head. "Let's make a list of things we'll need first, then we'll meet back here before sunset and load the boat."

She pulled two more ciders and a soda from the cooler.

9

GRAND CAYMAN – APRIL 1958

The boat ride back to Grand Cayman felt like a long, painful dream to Dingo. He faded in and out of consciousness, or sleep, he wasn't sure which, but when he did wake, the world seemed hazy and hard to pull into focus. On the open ocean, clear of artificial light, the night sky was resplendent with sparkling stars, one of the few memories that clung to his mind. Edmund ran without any lights, the glow from the tip of his occasional cigarette the only evidence Dingo wasn't alone. He stirred to as the fishing boat bumped against something solid. Dingo's frazzled brain pictured his beloved aeroplane and he thought they were back alongside her. He heard voices. He felt the boat bumping some more, and then he drifted. He came to again while he was being carried, with more voices around him, but he felt too exhausted to stay with them.

The next thing he knew he was waking in a brightly lit room. He felt different. No pain for the first time in how long? He had no idea, time had lost all meaning and reference to him. He lifted his head slightly and saw a brown-skinned woman looking over at him.

"Hey there, decided to say hello, have you?" she said, in an accent that reminded him of someone he couldn't place.

She was wearing a white uniform and cap, and he slowly realised she must be a nurse. He was in a hospital. The thoughts were clearer, but coming to him in slow motion.

"Whar at... flay ta..." he heard himself say and gave up in confusion.

The nurse smiled and patted his arm. "Doctor has given you some medicine for the pain. You'll be going into surgery soon, he's just getting ready. Don't try and speak, just rest."

He let his head drop back into the soft pillow and noticed the tube running from a bandage in his forearm to a bottle hanging on a stand by the bed. A sheet covered him to his chest and he felt a strong desire to lift the cover. The nurse stopped his hand before he could pull the sheet aside.

"Don't worry about a thing, now. Doctor will fix you up just fine." She beamed. "You're a lucky man from what I been told. Ol' Edmund not been out that way with his boat, you'd still be strapped in that aeroplane of yours."

She tucked the sheet snugly under his body, making it harder to pull out, before continuing.

"Quite the fuss, getting everyone out of bed in the middle of the night. Not too often we get this kind of excitement on our little island now."

He wasn't convinced he shared her excitement, seeing as he was the one lying in a hospital bed, but things still weren't quite making sense in his mind yet. She mentioned an aeroplane and that struck a chord – he remembered flying. That's right, he was a pilot, he thought, but then he pictured his plane floating in the water and that didn't seem normal at all. She just said something about a fella and his boat, though, so maybe...

The door opened and a man in a loose white gown and an odd little hat covering his hair entered the room. Dingo wondered why patients were walking around the hospital.

"Hello there, I'm Doctor Polson," the tanned, white-skinned man with a bold moustache introduced himself in a soft Scottish accent. "We'll take you back and get you patched up in a few minutes."

They let patients perform surgeries here, Dingo thought with a feeling of panic that gently ambled rather than surged through him. The recognition of the doctor's words followed closely behind and Dingo nodded his head.

"Mer pain…" he said and quickly shut up again when he heard the babble he was producing.

"Yes, yes, I'm sure it's quite painful, dear chap, but I've given you all the morphine I can." The man patted him on the arm, and Dingo wondered if that was something they taught everyone in medical school. "You'll be fast asleep shortly, don't worry."

He had tried to ask about his plane but his tongue wasn't cooperating. Bits and pieces of the accident were coming back to him and he now recalled leaving Queenie in the middle of the ocean. There had been someone there who helped him. Had to be the man the nurse mentioned, she had said someone had brought him to shore. Edmund, that's what she had said. He needed to talk to Edmund. He needed to get back out to the plane. The doctor mumbled a few words to the nurse as he left the room, and then she moved back to the bed.

"Right then, let's get you on your way," she said, and released the brakes on the hospital bed. She pulled the bed away from the wall and wheeled it towards the door, somehow corralling the IV stand along for the ride.

Dingo tried his best to hang on to his thoughts, but they bounced around and eluded him once more. He felt an overwhelming concern for his plane that his brain had recently rediscovered. A desperation to return to wherever it was. He kept seeing her shiny aluminium body floating on the water. It struck him as strangely psychedelic, like seeing a fish in the sky, or a pig underwater. There was something more, a draw back to his Queenie that he couldn't understand or remember, but the pull was gravitational and relentless.

The sound of the wheels rolling down hallways had stopped

and the lights had got much brighter. He squinted up and saw what he guessed was Doc Polson, but now he had a mask over his face.

"Cheerio ol' chap, you have a bit of a sleep, and I'll see what we can do with this mess," he said, and before Dingo could ask what mess, he fell back to sleep.

10

GRAND CAYMAN – JULY 28, 2020

AJ glanced at her Rolex watch as she opened the door to her apartment. The watch was a thirtieth birthday gift from her parents and friends, and her concern over the time was based on expecting Detective Whittaker to show up at any moment. She stepped inside to an empty apartment.

"Nora?"

Nora stepped from the bathroom and smiled. "I heard someone coming and wanted to be sure it was you."

AJ set her keys on the hook by the door. "One of the good things about being tucked away in the garden here, people usually call or text before they come through the gate. But good thinking to be careful. Whittaker is likely on his way, it's quarter past five."

Nora stood still and looked at AJ expectantly.

"They're in. We leave early tomorrow morning," AJ said, realising she was leaving the girl wondering.

Nora flew over and threw her arms around AJ's neck.

"Thank you," she whispered, and let her go.

AJ smiled. "I guess you're already packed," she said, looking at Nora's rucksack sitting on the floor by the sofa. "Better hide that in the wardrobe," she added, pointing to a door next to the bathroom.

Nora picked up her rucksack and moved it to the tiny, built-in wardrobe.

"Do you think you could fit in there?" AJ asked. "Might be better than the bathroom, just in case he asks to use the loo."

Nora laughed and wiggled into the three-foot square wardrobe amongst the hoover, a small suitcase, and a slew of hanging clothes. Her muffled voice emanated from behind some shirts.

"Hopefully he won't stay long."

They both laughed and Nora burrowed her way back out. She reached into the pocket of her jeans shorts and held out a small wad of folded bills to AJ.

"I wish I had more, but this will cover at least some of the petrol… I mean diesel."

AJ waved a hand towards her. "We'll sort that out when we get back, hang on to it for now."

Nora hesitated and still held out the cash. "But you must let me pay what I can. I'm asking you, and now your friends, to go to a lot of trouble for me."

AJ gently pushed her hand away. "Hey, we're happy to get out of the house for a few days. But don't worry about it, we'll settle up when we get back."

Nora relented and put the money back in her pocket as AJ's mobile chirped. She read the text message aloud. 'Be there in 5 mins, okay to come through the gate?' AJ quickly typed back, 'Yup, see you in 5.'

"That's Whittaker, he's five minutes away, which likely means he's three minutes away. He's usually prompt."

Nora looked at the wardrobe and shrugged her shoulders, "I'll get back in my burrow then."

"Need to pee before you nest down in there?" AJ asked with amusement.

"I think I'm good as long as you don't keep him here for dinner," Nora replied as she wriggled back behind the clothes.

"Okay then," AJ said, closing the wardrobe door. "And resist the urge to burst out if he says anything you don't like."

She heard Nora chuckling inside the tiny closet at the same time as the gate opened across the garden. AJ walked to the door and opened it. Detective Roy Whittaker was a tall, slender man in his fifties, with close-cropped salt and pepper hair and a goatee to match. He was dressed, as usual, in a grey business suit with a dark-coloured mask across his face, as was expected during the pandemic. He waved to AJ as he walked across the lawn and she realised she had forgotten to don her own mask. She quickly ducked back inside and retrieved her mask from the key hook and slipped it over her face. Hers was sewn by Thomas's mother from material printed with sharks on it.

He stopped about eight feet short of the doorway. "Hello AJ, it's good to see you. Feels like it's been forever since we haven't been doing the Friday nights at the Fox and Hare."

Reg's wife Pearl was a regular performer at the local Fox and Hare pub in West Bay, and Whittaker was a big fan of her music. They were used to seeing each other every other week when she was playing. Restaurants and bars were starting to open back up, but as yet Pearl had not resumed her gigs.

"Yeah, good to see you too, Roy, how's your wife?"

Whittaker made no move to come closer and AJ couldn't decide whether to ask him inside or if he preferred to stay away in the garden. Having hidden Nora, she felt like she needed to show him her apartment was empty, but then realised she was being paranoid and probably had a guilty look on her face. Good job I'm wearing a mask, she thought, but could feel her cheeks blushing. She hated lying, and especially to Roy. She had hidden truths from him in the past to protect people she cared about, and when he had found out he had been somewhat understanding. If it became clear she had done it again, their relationship would likely deteriorate.

"She's well, thank you, and as I've been working this whole time she's not sick of me yet, fortunately."

AJ could tell he was smiling by the wrinkles around his eyes. So strange, she thought, trying to judge people's expressions when their faces are hidden.

"Can I get that postcard, please?" he asked after an awkward silence.

"Oh, of course, I'm sorry. Let me get it," she said. She turned to retrieve the postcard but stopped and looked back at Whittaker. "Would you like to come in for a minute?"

Whittaker held up a hand. "No, that's okay AJ, we're trying to respect people's space as much as possible. When this is all over I'll drop by for a coffee one day, when we can chat properly."

AJ nodded and stepped inside the apartment to get the postcard. She wondered what that meant, exactly, 'chat properly'. She pulled the postcard from under a small dive flag magnet on the door of the fridge and scolded herself for reading too much into every word the man was saying. She handed the postcard to him and he opened an evidence bag for her to drop it into.

"Thank you. I'll get this back to you once we've dusted it for prints." He sealed the bag and slipped it into an inside pocket of his jacket. He looked at AJ, who had stepped back into the doorway.

"I assume nothing has changed since we spoke earlier?" he asked.

"I went for a nice run on the beach," AJ answered, trying her best to avoid verbalising a lie. "Any luck figuring out anything from the sailboat that beamed back to its dock?" she asked, hoping he wouldn't notice she had ducked out of answering his question.

He shook his head. "Not so far. Whoever took it wiped it down thoroughly; there's no clear prints so far, not even the owner's. But we're not finished yet. Still some tricks we have up our sleeve. It's pretty hard to remove every strand of hair, which we can use for a DNA match. It all takes longer than they like to make it sound on TV though – it can be months before we get DNA tests back sometimes."

"Wow, that has to be frustrating," AJ replied, hoping they were close to wrapping up the conversation. "Well, my fingerprints will be all over that postcard, I'm afraid."

"That's okay, we have yours on file so we'll be able to eliminate them easily. Fingerprints we can do quickly as it's all in-house and we have access to a large computer database. I'll let you know what we find in a day or two," he replied.

"Great, thank you. I'd be interested to know," AJ said, and then realised if he came by or called in the next few days she would be missing. Where they were going cell phones were useless and even the VHF marine radio wouldn't reach the island.

"Reg and I are actually going fishing for a few days, so if you can't reach me just leave a message and I'll call you when we're back," she added.

Whittaker had appeared ready to leave but now he paused. "Oh, really? I didn't know you two were much into fishing. A few days, huh. Where are you going?"

AJ cursed herself; here she was back in a corner about to lie if she wasn't careful. "We're not really into fishing, but we're less into sitting around the house and not being on the water. Fishing's the only option to get out on the boat, so we talked about heading to one of the banks. If we go to Twelve Mile Bank we'll be back the same day but we were thinking about Pickle, or perhaps Sixty Mile. Make a little adventure out of it, you know."

There, she thought, she hadn't really lied, they were going to one of the banks. Whittaker looked at her for what seemed like forever but was likely only a few seconds. She felt her cheeks flushing again.

"Well, tell Reg I said hello, and you two have fun out on the water." He turned to leave but once more paused. "Thank you for the postcard," he said, as he looked back at her. "Stay out of trouble out there," he added with a nod before walking back across the garden.

"We will," she said sheepishly. "See you when we come back."

AJ ducked back in the house, closed the door, hung her mask back on the peg and slumped into one of the dining chairs.

"You can come out, he's gone," she called across the room.

Nora stumbled her way out of the wardrobe, bringing her rucksack with her and closing the door.

"I could hear most of that, did he seem suspicious?" she asked.

AJ rolled her eyes. "I have no idea. I'm bloody useless at this cloak and dagger stuff. I think he sees right through me like an X-ray."

She looked over at Nora. "Did you hear the part about looking for strands of hair on the sailboat?"

Nora bit her lip and nodded. "I did, yeah." She forced a grin, but AJ could tell she looked worried. "What sailboat is he talking about?"

AJ smiled. "Exactly, what sailboat."

11

GRAND CAYMAN – APRIL 1958

Dingo looked across George Town harbour as the 55-foot Chris Craft motor yacht tied up, and several men disembarked and said their farewells. What he didn't see was anything towed in behind the beautiful wooden pleasure boat. He let out a long sigh.

"That the boat you been waiting on?" the nurse asked, sitting on the stone sea wall above the water.

"Yeah, that's it," Dingo replied despondently.

The Caymanian woman, who he had first met the night he had arrived at George Town hospital, went to say something more, but closed her mouth and remained quiet. She reset her nurse's cap instead, the ocean breeze trying its best to relieve her of her headwear.

A dark-skinned man who had stepped from the boat looked across the harbour and waved in Dingo's direction. He presumed it must be Edmund, as he had no clear recollection of the man from the night of the accident. The fellow started walking from the dock to the narrow street by the waterfront. He slipped his cap from his head as he approached and offered his hand.

"How you doin', Mister Dingo?"

Dingo shook his hand. "G'day Edmund. You look familiar now

you're up close. I'm afraid my memory from that night ain't so clear, mate."

Edmund shuffled uncomfortably and his eyes wandered to the wheelchair, and more specifically the stump where Dingo's right leg used to be.

Dingo smiled. "It's alright, mate, just the way it goes sometimes."

Edmund seemed embarrassed to be caught looking, so Dingo carried on.

"Hey, I'd be fish food if it weren't for you and your boy. I owe you my life's how I see it. I want to thank you for what you did out there."

Edmund seemed to breathe a little more easily and stopped shuffling about. "Weren't nothing no one else wouldn't do, been in the same place. Healing up okay?"

"Toes itch," Dingo said. "Ain't that the darndest thing? Toes are in the dustbin, along with the rest of me leg, but it feels like they itch."

"Can't keep this one still for nothing," the nurse added. "He hop around the whole hospital, bothering all the nurses. I taken to hiding his crutches just to get him to rest."

"Don't surprise me," Edmund said. "I figure he ain't a man to sit still." The Caymanian shook his head, "I feel real bad about your plane though, it weren't out there no more I'm afraid."

Dingo nodded. "I guessed that blow a few days back might give us some trouble. Appreciate you getting out there to look."

Edmund waved his cap. "Oh, weren't me, was Mister Fairchild offered to take his boat out."

"'Cos you rallied the folks up to go," Dingo said, looking at the nurse. "I've had my ear to the ground."

Edmund grinned and put his cap back on his head. "Well, 'fraid it was for nothing, Mister Dingo, guess I didn't get that anchor hooked good enough."

"Did all you could do, and then some, I'm truly grateful. Like I said, just the way it goes sometimes," Dingo said, with his best effort at a smile.

He wasn't a religious man, but was starting to wonder if he ought to give it a try. Seemed like a judge and jury from somewhere acted pretty swiftly when he'd decided to transport guns for money. He had lost his precious aeroplane, his leg, and now a fortune to boot. Maybe it was a higher power intervening, he thought, or perhaps it was just the way it goes sometimes, when you buy petrol from a crooked liar in Mexico.

"What are your plans now?" Edmund asked. "This is not a bad place to spend some time to recover and all that, but I'm sure you have family somewhere. You must have a wife and a family someplace, don't you?"

"That's a good question, mate," Dingo replied, squinting against the bright sunshine, and he meant what he said. It was the question he had chewed on since the moment he awoke after the surgery to discover his life would never be the same. The next major factor had been whether his plane and its hidden contents would be recovered. He had that answer now, so he couldn't keep hiding from the answer to the question.

"I have, or had, a girlfriend in Acapulco." He expanded, "Margarita. If you saw the girl painted on the nose of Queenie, that's her."

Edmund raised his eyebrows. "Yeah, I saw that. My boy saw that too, he couldn't stop looking." He laughed. "That's a beautiful woman."

"Yeah, well, she won't have no use for a one-legged man, I reckon. Best let her find herself a new bloke. As you saw, she won't have no bother with that."

Edmund shuffled again, unsure what to say.

"Enough of that talk," the nurse scolded. "You ain't the self-pity type, and you ain't starting on my watch." She frowned at Dingo and he laughed.

"Fair enough, love. Anyway, I'm thinking of heading back to Oz as soon as my lovely nurse kicks me out the hospital."

He winked at the nurse and she shook her head, but couldn't help a smile creeping into the corners of her mouth.

"That'll be a long way to travel with..." Edmund nodded at his stump, "you know..."

"Fit in the seat better, mate," Dingo said and laughed.

Edmund smiled and stuck out his hand. "I hope I see you again before you go, Mister Dingo, and I'm sorry again about your beautiful aeroplane."

Dingo shook his hand firmly and looked the man in the eye. "Owe you my life, my friend, please pass on the same to your son."

Edmund turned to leave.

"Stop by anytime Edmund, you know which hotel I'm staying in."

Edmund shook his head and turned back. "I do at that."

The nurse pushed Dingo back along the dusty streets towards the hospital, and he mulled things over as they bumped along the road. He guessed Margarita would take him back gladly, but that wasn't his worry. She was young, ten years younger than him, and she was poor. She had been besotted with the glamorous pilot and his incredible aeroplane that flew celebrities around the skies over Acapulco. If he returned, without his plane, without an income, and without a limb, he would forever wonder if she had taken him back for pity, or for love. If he'd asked himself before he left if he loved her, he probably couldn't have answered the question. Sitting in a wheelchair, facing the thought of never seeing her again, the pain in his heart left him in no doubt. But what could he do to make a living? Maybe he could fly again. Douglas Bader flew in the war with two tin legs, but without a plane of his own, no one would hire a one-legged foreigner to fly for them in Acapulco. They had tried to ruin him when he was able bodied; they would laugh him off the airfield now. By the time they reached the doors to George Town's little hospital, Dingo had convinced himself that returning to Margarita would be purely selfish, no matter if they loved each other. She would be better off never knowing what had happened to him.

12

GRAND CAYMAN – JULY 28, 2020

AJ was still slightly unnerved by Whittaker's visit. Half of her uneasiness was the guilt from deceiving the man who she considered a friend, and the other part was Whittaker's annoying ability to give her the feeling he knew everything that was going on. She steered her fifteen-passenger van onto West Bay road and headed for the Yacht Club marina, two miles away. The sun was dipping towards the western horizon behind her and the roads were quiet, another result of the pandemic and the rules regarding essential driving. She was well aware she would probably have a hard time arguing her current errand was essential if she was pulled over. But she had adhered to the rules for months and after a couple of short drives they would be socially distancing by miles, so she figured it balanced out. A few minutes later, she stopped at the gate to the boat yard where her RIB was stored on a trailer while they weren't running dive trips. She got out of the van and punched in the code to unlock the gate, sliding it back after the lock released. She drove into the yard and pulled up behind Arthur's Odyssey, relieved to see the canvas cover was still snugly covering the boat, and everything appeared as she had left it several months before. She set to work releasing the multitude of straps she had used to secure the cover, until she could finally access the tank racks. She was disappointed to discover she only had four filled nitrox tanks on the boat; she was hoping for more, knowing she only had six on the Newton. She hauled the four tanks out of the boat and loaded them in the tank rack in the back of the van. After re-covering the RIB, she left the boat yard, secured the gate behind her and made the last few hundred yards into the marina. Once there she parked by the gate to the jetty housing most of the west side's dive boats.

Reg's old Land Rover was already parked and she saw Thomas striding towards her down the jetty.

"Hey boss, need a hand with your things?" he called out in his musical island accent.

She opened the back of the van and began pulling out the nitrox tanks.

"Yeah, that would be great, thanks. I brought you a sleeping bag as I guessed you didn't have one."

"Ah man, thank you. I never slept in a sleeping bag before, be like a real camping adventure," he said, picking up two of the heavy tanks and setting off towards the boat.

AJ slipped her mesh gear backpack on and grabbed the other two tanks, giving herself a load close to her own body weight. When she finally reached the Newton she plopped the two tanks down on the dock and dropped the gear bag from her back. Thomas grabbed the tanks and lifted them aboard to be racked with the others as Reg's dog, Coop, leapt from the boat to the jetty and wagged his tail so hard she thought he might fall over. She bent down and petted the Cayman brown hound mutt that Pearl had rescued earlier in the year. Reg appeared from the small cabin below deck.

"Hey there, want me to stow your gear?" he offered.

She had caught her breath but was happy to sling her bag over to the boat where Reg put it below with his. AJ and Thomas made one more trip to the van to retrieve the sleeping bags and several canvas shopping bags of food and a small gas camping stove. Once everything was aboard, the three sat down on the benches to compare notes on what they had brought along. Reg had a list in his hand and made a few notes as they went, with Coop sitting by his feet, eyeing the food bags.

"Let's start with the supplies and then we'll look at the dive gear," Reg said, and looked at the stuffed bags AJ had brought alongside several he had provided. "We may be provisioned for a week by the look of it."

"Yeah, I had a bunch of freeze-dried camping dinners, so I threw them all in," AJ replied. "I have the stove to cook them, so we could live on them alone I suspect."

"Alright, well as you can imagine, Pearl went overboard too, so we've got everything in there from crisps to rum cake, all packaged in Tupperware and labelled," Reg said, shaking his head. "I planned to catch some fish to eat, but according to my wife, man can't live on fish alone. I think it was more a comment on my fishing ability than the sustainability of humans eating fish for two days. I brought two five-gallon containers of water and some gallon jugs to fill from them that'll fit in the cooler. That cooler plugs into the 12-volt system. It won't keep anything ice cold during the hot day, but it'll stay cool enough."

AJ and Reg both looked at Thomas, who had a small bag at his feet. He grinned sheepishly. "I have some sodas, four energy bars and a couple of doughnuts me Papa will be mad are gone in the morning."

They all laughed. "I think we have enough to keep you fed." Reg added, "Plus our mystery guest, I suppose."

AJ almost said something, but stopped herself and just smiled at Reg. "We'll be fine with what we have. Oh, and I have plenty of coffee too – we can boil the water with my little stove. I actually remembered the igniter for it too."

"I'll bring the fishing gear in the morning," Thomas said. "I asked my Papa to set aside some deep sea rods and a tackle box so they should be at the house tonight."

"I'll bring the two I have so it'll look like we're geared up." Reg said, and looked at the tank ranks. "I brought all the tanks I had for going deep, in case we need to drop off the side of the bank. Fortunately, I filled all my personal tanks when the lockdown started in case I got called in by the marine police."

He looked down at the pad of paper in his hand, "We've got ten 21/35 trimix 80s, five 50% nitrox 40s and five pure oxygen 40s." He looked up at the racks and counted along a line of green-topped tanks. "I had ten regular 32% nitrox I pulled off my boats too. If we stay on top of the bank we'll burn through a bunch of them."

"Are the trimix the tanks with helium in them?" Thomas asked. He was trained as an instructor and guide for recreational diving but hadn't studied any courses on technical deep diving, unlike Reg and AJ.

"Yeah, these are 21/35 which means they have 21% oxygen, like your body is used to breathing regular air, then 35% helium, which apart from making you sound like Mickey Mouse and get a bit colder than normal, has no other effects. There's three gases, so they call it trimix, in this case the third gas in the mix is helium," Reg explained. "That reduces the nitrogen content to 44% instead of the normal 79% in air. It's the nitrogen that causes the problems, as you know. The body can't dissipate the gas fast enough through your tissues, and your brain can't handle it at depth either." He twirled his finger by his ear. "Sends you a bit goofy."

"Might not tell a difference with me," Thomas said, laughing. "But the oxygen is poisonous at depth too, right? So how come the 50% nitrox?"

Reg nodded. "Correct. Just adding oxygen, as with nitrox, to lessen the amount of nitrogen, doesn't work at depth because now the body can't handle that much oxygen passing through the system. But once we come shallower, the pressure around us lowers and we're breathing less gas with each inhalation, we're okay with more oxygen again. We'll switch to the 50% oxygen mix nitrox at around 70 feet and then pure oxygen at 15 feet to finish the dive."

Thomas shook his head. "That's way too complicated, man, how do you figure it all out?"

Reg laughed. "On my computer. I have a program that calculates it all. I brought my laptop in case we need to do any deep dives so we can figure it all out."

"What happens if the dive plan changes in the middle of the dive?" Thomas asked. "You know, like you have to go a bit deeper, or you stay longer? How do you calculate that when you're down there?"

"First rule of tech diving is the same as the first rule of recreational diving," AJ said, and paused, looking at Thomas.

"Plan your dive, dive your plan," he replied, beaming.

"Yup, just becomes even more critical on a tech dive," AJ added. "But your dive computer can help with some adjustments. But only some. If you don't have the right gas with you, or enough for the change in the plan, you're screwed."

"Huh," Thomas grunted. "One day I'll take some tech classes, but I don't think I'm in no hurry."

"It's a bunch of theory and maths, but it opens up a lot more ocean to dive," AJ said with a grin. "I have ten nitrox as well, so that gives us 20 total," she said, getting back to the inventory, as dusk settled and the light began to fade. "With three of us diving on top of the bank that's seven dives for two of us, and six for one. We could probably squeeze in three dives tomorrow after we arrive, leaving us four more for the next day."

Reg pondered a moment. "That bank is almost three quarters of a mile long and currents out there tend to be ripping. We'll likely have to drift dive, so it'll depend on the direction of the current whether we're going down the length of the bank or the width."

"I heard it's almost triangular shaped, so that makes it even harder to work a decent search pattern," AJ said. "But I have an idea how we can work around that."

"How's that then?" Reg asked, scratching his beard.

AJ grinned. "I'll save it for the trip out, give us something to talk about."

Reg laughed and looked at Thomas. "You know it's a harebrained scheme when she can't even bring herself to tell us about it."

Thomas laughed. "Crazy idea? The boss here? I can't imagine she'd be coming up with anything, what do you call it, hare brained? That don't sound like her to me."

AJ found a package of bagels in the top of the nearest grocery bag and flung it across the boat at Thomas, who caught them amid a fit of laughter.

"Bugger the pair of you, I'm going home," she said, standing and trying not to laugh as well. "And I may keep my incredibly clever idea to myself, so you'll never know how we could have scanned the whole bank in no time flat."

"Hear that, Thomas? She has one of them remote operated vehicles in her rucksack I reckon."

AJ gave Reg a two-finger salute and retrieved her bagels from Thomas. "See you two at 6am, bright and early, and you might think about bringing better attitudes towards your captain, or she may leave you out on Sixty Mile Bank."

"Aye, aye, your ladyship," Reg grinned and winked at her. "Oh, is this thing full of diesel?"

"Yeah, both tanks are brimmed full, so 360 gallons, plenty to get us out and back but not a lot of margin for trolling about," she replied, giving Coop an ear scratch before she left.

"I have some five-gallon cans, I'll fill them at the petrol station in the morning, give us a bit of extra run time," Reg offered.

"That would be good," she replied as she stepped to the dock and turned. "Not as good as my brilliant idea you may never know about, but useful at least."

13

CRONULLA, AUSTRALIA – MAY 1958

After five days of flights, hotels and more flights, Dingo finally cleared customs in Sydney. He insisted on using his crutches, rather than wait for a wheelchair, causing sweat to bead on his brow. His three-piece suit, purchased on Grand Cayman, looked worse for wear from the five days on airliners, where formal attire was expected. It reeked of cigarette smoke and a mixture of his own aftershave and the stewardesses' overabundance of perfume. He had enjoyed them all giving him a peck on the cheek as he deplaned, but now every inhalation smelled like a tobacconist's and a perfumery had collided. Everything he possessed was either on his body, or in the small travel bag slung over his shoulder. All other possessions had been lost with Queenie, or abandoned in Mexico, along with his former life.

It had been fourteen years since he had seen his mother and father, and the sight of them, aged and worried, surprised him. He saw the same look returned in their eyes. He had left as a seventeen-year-old boy, trying to forge his way into manhood, and hell bent on serving his country. He shaved his chin once a week, he'd only kissed one girl, but he was sure he could help win the war if they put him in the cockpit of a fighter. Fourteen years seemed like a lifetime. These days, he could get a start on a beard in a week, he had certainly kissed plenty of girls, and he was returning sure of very little.

His mother embraced him and cried into his chest, mumbling incoherently about her boy being home. His father extended his hand, and they shook firmly. His father's hand had a slight tremble, and Dingo could see his teeth were clenched.

"Welcome home, son," he said, his voice sharing the tremble.

"Good to see you both," Dingo replied.

His father took his bag and they made their way outside to where their car waited at the kerb. Thirty minutes later, and a thousand questions from his mother, they parked in the driveway of his family home in Cronulla. Once his mother had suitably fussed around, providing tea and biscuits, Dingo changed clothes into something more casual and joined his father in his study. The house felt like a distant part of a life he once lived, yet similar to setting eyes on his family again, although much had changed, underneath it was joyfully familiar. His childhood was indelibly connected to the place, with wonderful memories of simpler times, and a comfortable existence. Despite the years and events that had passed, there was still a warmth to the home, and he wondered if some day his own children might find the same sense of peace within those walls.

His father handed him a snifter with two fingers of neat whisky, as they sat in a pair of library chairs that Dingo remembered well. His father's study had been off limits to the young lad, so it was a proud moment when he had been asked to join him, as they did now, before he left for the war. That's when his father had given him the package.

Dingo set aside his crutches and raised his glass to the man who sat beside him.

"To family," he toasted.

"To family, and good health," his father added.

They sipped the whisky. The rich brown liquid burned down

Dingo's throat with a strong but smooth taste, the way a fine whisky assures you the second sip will be exquisite.

"You've lived quite a life for yourself, son. I believe you owe that sense of adventure to your mother," he nodded towards the kitchen where they could hear her humming a tune. "I'm afraid I've always been more of the regular-type fella. Meat and two veg, I suppose."

"You're the backbone Dad, look at all you've given us. Mum and I have been blessed," Dingo replied, sincerely. "I need to tell you something, Dad, and I'm ashamed quite honestly."

His father frowned and looked him over. "Don't know what you could possibly tell me I'd want you to feel ashamed about, mate, but best go ahead and just say it."

The weight of what he was about to say had rested on his shoulders since the morning he woke up in the hospital in Grand Cayman. When Edmund came back without Queenie, the burden felt like it had tripled. Every day from there, Dingo had blamed himself more and more, until he sat before his father with a crushing guilt.

"You entrusted me with something before I left, Dad, things of great value, with clear instructions. My intention was always to hand you back that gift, the day I returned."

His father's expression remained stoic so Dingo pressed on. "I broke one of the rules when I bought Queen of the Island Skies, but I truly thought I could make back all that money and more."

His father nodded his head slowly. "She was a beautiful aeroplane, son, we framed the picture you sent."

"Well, hidden inside her were the rest of what you gave me, and when she went down, they went down with her, Dad. I am so sorry."

Dingo's head sank with exhaustion from travel, his injury, and finally verbalising the failure he felt. There, he had said it. When he had left, his father was building his jewellery business, and while they lived an upper middle-class existence, he knew it was hard work and perseverance that had kept his shop open during the war.

What he had handed his son represented a large portion of his stock, certainly financially. It had not been something to simply lose with nothing to show for it.

His father smiled. "Son. When a parent watches their young man leave to fight a war, they pray with all their heart that child will return. But there's a part inside of you that prepares itself to never see the one you love again. What I did, wasn't for you. What I did was for me, and your mother. We couldn't protect you anymore, we sat here helpless. Proud, believe me we were awful proud of you, but helpless. I gave you the only thing I had in my power to give that might possibly help you. I never cared if it came back, all I wanted was for you to come back, son."

Dingo lifted his head with a lump in is throat. He never doubted the love of his family, but he also knew his father had hoped he would return home and take up his place in the business. Instead, Dingo had run around the Caribbean and Central America, flying and chasing dreams, and women.

"So, what's next son? You know you're welcome here for however long, but I also understand you have that adventurous spirit inside."

Dingo thought for a moment. It was the biggest question that had been eating away at him since the accident. Returning to Australia was half an answer. He could still pursue his own path, whether it was in Australia or leaving once again. Setting foot inside the family home had helped him decide. But his father's words, his patience, understanding, and willingness to let go again, was what made up his mind.

"I'm home, Dad. If there's a use for me in the business, I'd like to help. It's about the only way I can pay you back."

His father held up his glass. "There's no debt to be paid, son. I've had my sign-writer waiting fourteen years to add 'and son' to the front of the shop. Be the proudest day of my life, mate."

14

GRAND CAYMAN – JULY 29, 2020

AJ's mobile phone alarm, cranking out an old tune by The Jam, stirred her reluctantly into consciousness at 5:30am. She had hoped 'A Town Called Malice' would entice her to jump out of bed and dance around like the kid in the Billy Elliot film. It hadn't worked so far. For a moment she was puzzled why an alarm had gone off at all, she had gotten used to not setting one since she couldn't work each day. But then she recalled they were leaving for Sixty Mile Bank, and she only had thirty minutes to get to the marina. She also remembered she wasn't alone in her cottage, and wondered if Nora was awake. She leaned over and turned on her bedside lamp. Although she knew the young woman was there, it still startled her to see Nora's bright blue eyes staring back at her from the sofa where she had slept, squinting at the sudden illumination. She was already sitting up, dressed, with her rucksack next to her, ready to go.

"God morgen," she said, and smiled.

AJ groaned. "You're another one of those morning people, aren't you? You and Thomas will get along great."

AJ had given up trying to be the first one to the boat in the mornings when they were working. Thomas always beat her there, no matter what time she arrived. He seemed to have some weird sense of AJ's timing and would already have the boat on the way to the dock from the overnight mooring a hundred yards offshore. Plus he was always chipper, full of the joys of life at an hour AJ couldn't fathom anyone would want to witness, unless required.

She rolled out of bed and was relieved she had remembered to sleep in some cotton shorts and a tank top, instead of the nothing she preferred, and that the coffee maker was gurgling in the kitchen. She had owned the same coffee maker for as long as she could remember, and over the years it had taken on an interesting character as it boiled the water and brewed the coffee. The gurgling sounded more like a chicken quietly clucking, which she decided was perfect for the morning, and had become a reassuring part of her waking routine.

AJ stumbled to the bathroom, splashed some water over her face and avoided staring at herself in the mirror by cleaning her teeth while she sat on the loo. As much as she hated early mornings, her brain still kicked into gear and she always ran through her mental checklist for the day ahead. This morning seemed simple as best she could remember. Get to the boat and leave, with the hope Reg didn't get cold feet when her mystery guest, as he'd called her, turned out to be Nora. Reg and Nora had never actually met, but he had heard all about her from AJ and read plenty about the whole resort debacle in the newspaper. She had no reason to think he would be averse to helping the girl, but she was listed as a missing person and a suspect in the theft of the sailboat, two items she had failed to mention when he had asked if their venture was legal. As she dressed and gathered her rucksack and stainless-steel travel mug of coffee, it weighed on her mind that Reg may consider himself deceived. Short of telling him who it was behind this whole affair, she wasn't sure how she could have delivered the message differently, but that didn't stop it bothering her.

"Do you have everything?" she asked Nora as they stepped outside.

Nora grinned and shrugged her shoulders. "Always," she

replied, and AJ realised it was a stupid question. If the girl had her rucksack, she had every worldly possession she owned with her.

It was still dark outside but the Cayman night air was hot and packed with humidity that made their brows bead with sweat just walking to the van outside the garden gate. AJ had a sweatshirt tied around her waist as once they were on the water the breeze could be chilly until the sun came up. Nora wore a thin, dark blue, hooded rain jacket and a baseball cap, but they were more to hide her blonde hair in case they were seen on their way.

They pulled up to the gate in front of the dock at a few minutes before 6am, and parked next to Reg's Land Rover. The first hint of light was lifting the eastern sky from pitch black to a deep blue and the scattering of streetlights showed they were the only people around this early. As the two women walked down the jetty, AJ could see Reg and Thomas pause what they were doing on the boat and stare in their direction, trying to identify the mystery person behind the clandestine trip they had committed to. She saw Thomas nudge Reg and say something excitedly as they neared. When they stepped aboard Hazel's Odyssey the big man grinned and held out a beefy hand.

"I'm Reg, nice to meet you, Nora, I've heard a lot about you."

Nora smiled and AJ sensed a tension leave her. "Thank you. Thank you all for doing this."

She offered her hand to Thomas next, but he stepped in and threw his long arms around her. "It's good to see you. I hope you can meet with Hallie while you're here, she's been worried about you."

Nora squeezed Thomas in return and AJ thought she could see a glistening of moisture in her eyes, but she couldn't be sure in the dim light.

"Thank you, Thomas, I hope I can see her too," she said as she released his embrace. "It's a little difficult for me to be seen right now, but maybe after our trip we can work something out."

"Time's wasting," Reg said in low rumble. "Every thing's

aboard, so I reckon we should shove off. Be nice to clear the North Sound before the sun's up."

AJ nodded. "Grab the lines, I'll warm her up," she said, as she scurried up the ladder to the fly-bridge. At the top she turned and looked down at Nora. "You can stow your bag on the window shelf down there, then why don't you come up here. I want to show you how to pilot the boat on the way out. Never know, you may need to if we have to put all three of us in the water."

She stepped to the helm and fired up the twin diesel motors, letting them idle and gain some temperature. Nora soon joined her and AJ ran through the simple dash of gauges and switches, pointing out the kill switch and the emergency fuel shut-offs. Once the temperature gauge needles both moved off the stop, AJ called down for the lines to be cleared and she idled forward out of their berth. Once the stern was clear, she reversed the starboard motor with the port in forward and the Newton turned to starboard within its own length. Once parallel to the jetty, she engaged forward on the starboard motor and they eased along the row packed with boats on either side, and out into the channel leading to the main body of Governor's Creek.

The horizon was brightening by the minute as dawn eased its way across the island but the stillness and lack of any other activity on the water seemed eerie. The fishermen had undoubtedly left the harbour already and without the charter boats active during the pandemic restrictions, the waterways were quieter than usual. AJ turned to port and continued just above idle in the no-wake-zone of the channel leading to the sound. She sipped her coffee and slipped her hooded sweatshirt on in preparation for the open water. Once clear of the entrance marker pilings, she slid the throttles forward and the Newton accelerated up on plane in a few moments, as though she was ready for a run after several months of idleness. Cruising across the flat calm of the North Sound at a steady 16 knots with the wind cooling her face felt wonderful, and the stress and frustration of being isolated for so long seemed to blow out the back of the boat with the breeze.

"AJ! Trouble," Reg called from below.

AJ swung around and saw the red and blue lights catching them from behind.

"Go down, hide in the cabin below," she shouted to Nora who was already on the ladder.

AJ eased the throttles back and the Newton slipped off plane and settled in the water, slowing quickly. Within a minute the Marine Police boat was alongside, and with fenders thrown over to keep the two vessels separated, Reg and Thomas tied the lines they were thrown by the policemen.

"Hey there, Ben," AJ called over to the Marine Police boat, recognising the man at the helm.

A tall Caymanian man with skin the colour of milky chocolate and a smile as wide as his shoulders stepped from the wheelhouse.

"Well now, it's Miss AJ, how have you been?"

AJ leaned over the fly-bridge and looked down at the man she had met several times over the past few years – each time at one incident or another.

"I'm good, what are you up to at this hour?"

He laughed. "That's funny, 'cos I had exactly the same question for you."

"We're going fishing, Ben."

Reg pointed to the rods laying on the deck.

"Well, so you are," Ben said, still smiling, while the two other policeman eyed the Newton suspiciously. "Going fishing on a dive boat, huh?"

"Only got dive boats, Ben; if I'm going out on the water, that's what I'd have to be fishing from," AJ said with a grin, trying to sound casual while her heart thumped madly in her chest.

Ben chuckled and nodded. "Guess that would be the case now, wouldn't it, Miss AJ." He peered at Reg and tried to see if anyone else was behind the half-covered structure under the fly-bridge. Thomas stepped farther out on the deck so he could be seen and Ben nodded a greeting to him.

"Hey there, young Bodden," he said and looked back up at AJ.

"I hate to delay your trip any, but we're supposed to take a look around any suspicious boats, and seeing as we stopped you already, you mind if we see your fishing licence and have a quick look about? That way I can clear you on my report and you won't get bothered again."

AJ waved at him. "Of course Ben, whatever you need to do, Reg has the fishing licence. I'll come on down."

She made her way down the ladder as Ben stepped aboard, donning his face mask. AJ uncharacteristically gave Ben a big hug, her arms barely reaching around his neck as he towered over her. The other two policemen, still on their boat, grinned at each other and Ben looked a little embarrassed, although he didn't seem disappointed.

"It's good to see you without any bodies in the water, Ben," she said, hoping her charming act would hasten his search. AJ didn't play the female card too often but some situations require pulling out all the stops, she'd decided.

"Uh, you too," Ben babbled a reply. "Supposed to keep the social distance thing though."

AJ stepped back and gave him a big smile. "Oops, sorry about that."

Reg held out his fishing licence. Ben regained his composure and took a look.

"Thanks, Reg," he said, nodding appreciatively and looking like he might turn and leave. But then he paused and eyed the cabin door at the front of the covered deck, below the fly-bridge.

"I'd best stick my head in there and have a quick look," he said, and AJ stepped out of his way, nervously looking at Reg, who didn't appear concerned.

Ben pulled the concertinaed door back and peered down the steps into the open space towards the bow. On the port side was another door leading to the marine head and on the starboard side was an open space stuffed with rental dive gear, hanging on rails mounted to the ceiling. Their camping gear and food bags filled the remaining space. Ben's large frame filled the doorway and AJ could see he had turned on his torch to look around. He opened the door to the head and AJ held her breath. It was the only space Nora could really fit. Ben shone his torch around amongst the dive gear some more, before extricating himself from the narrow space and stretching back out to his full height. He slipped his torch back into its holster alongside the myriad of gadgets, tools and weapons Velcroed to his person, and walked over to the port side gunwale. He looked at the dive tanks behind the benches lining both sides of the deck.

"That's a lot of dive gear aboard for a fishing trip," he said, looking at AJ.

"It's where we store all our gear, Ben, it lives aboard the boat. When we're running trips we refill the tanks from lines run down from a compressor at the dock; the tanks never leave their racks, except to dive."

He nodded and a big smile crept across his face. He reached out and squeezed her shoulder. "Good to see you AJ, have fun fishing. Where did you say you were going?"

She figured the hand was to dissuade her from trying another hug, which she deemed unnecessary as he appeared to be leaving. "Offshore a ways, may even head for one of the banks. Planning on staying out overnight," she said.

"Alright, be safe now," he said as he stepped back aboard his boat. "Hope they bite for you."

"Cheers, Ben," AJ replied and her heart rate finally began settling back to normal.

Reg and Thomas cast the lines away with a wave to the policemen and they all watched the police boat motor away into the low light of dawn. AJ turned to Reg.

"Where is she?" she asked, looking at the cabin, amazed he hadn't found her in there.

"Let 'em get just a bit farther away," Reg muttered, watching the boat disappear into the distance before he and Thomas moved to the starboard side and looked into the water. AJ followed and looked down at Nora staring back up, hanging on a fender line they'd tossed over that side as well. The two men hauled Nora over the gunwale and back into the boat where she stood dripping water from her clothes.

"Well, we're off to a great start," Reg said, shaking his head.

AJ grabbed a towel from the cabin and handed it to Nora who appeared to be taking the incident in her stride, the same as she seemed to handle every trauma and challenge. AJ looked back at the boat that was now a dot in the distance, and couldn't help but wonder if Whittaker had something to do with them being stopped and searched.

15

ACAPULCO, MEXICO – MAY 2020

Ridley Hernandez nervously walked out into the arrivals area of General Juan N. Álvarez International Airport in Acapulco. There was none of the usual hustle and bustle expected of a busy tourist town, with the pandemic limiting the flights to a minimum, and keeping the holiday makers away. A handful of people stood waiting for friends and relatives coming through from the gates, and Ridley searched the crowd, hoping to see his mother. About half the people wore face masks and half didn't. Having only seen a handful of pictures of his mother since he was six years old, when his father took him across the world to live in Australia, he was worried he wouldn't recognise her, with or without a face covering. A tall, broad-shouldered man in slacks, a collared shirt and a sport coat held a sign with Ridley's name on it. The man had a severe-looking face and tattoos showed on his neck above his collar, and around his wrists beyond his sleeves. His mother had emailed that she would have him picked up and he wasn't sure what he expected, but this fella wasn't it. He walked over to the man and introduced himself in English.

"I'm Ridley. Did my mother, Zanita, send you?"

The man's expression didn't change. "Mister Trujillo sent me," he said flatly in Spanish, then turned and walked towards the exit doors.

He didn't need or expect help with his rucksack and small duffel bag, but he noted this guy wasn't going to offer. Ridley followed. He was disappointed, but not surprised it wasn't Zanita greeting him. His mother had remarried several years after he and his father had left, and Ridley knew very little about Aldo Trujillo. In her emails he received sporadically, she rarely mentioned the man. She had said he was a businessman, but never spoke of what business, and he had got the impression she didn't want Ridley to meet him all these years. She would talk about having him visit, but before anything could be arranged she would always postpone, for an array of different reasons, none of which were completely explained. By the time he was in his teens he had stopped asking, and she didn't offer anymore. It came as a surprise when she contacted him a few days back and asked him to come and see her.

A black Cadillac Escalade with tinted windows waited at the kerb and the tailgate rose as they approached. Tattoo looked all around the roadway and paths before nodding to the back.

"Put your bags in," he again said in Spanish, so Ridley decided the man either didn't speak English, or refused to speak English. That was fine, they were in Mexico and Ridley spoke Spanish fluently.

He opened the passenger side back door and nodded again. Ridley got inside and saw the driver was a similar-looking character to Tattoo, and after checking Ridley out in the mirror, ignored his presence. Tattoo closed Ridley's door and took a last look around before getting in the front passenger seat. As he did, his jacket fell open and Ridley saw a gun holstered against his side. 'Businessman', he thought to himself; he knew Acapulco had slipped further and further into poverty and crime, no longer a desirable holiday spot for international travellers, but he didn't expect your average business executive to require armed bodyguards. Besides, these two didn't look like any former military, professional protection; they were more like the type most people needed protection from.

They left the airport on the dual carriageway heading north, with the mountains to the east, and the ocean to the west. The view from the road did little to dissuade Ridley from all he had heard about the town of his birth. It certainly didn't appear as he remembered it. Of course, a six-year-old has a skewed view of their environment and he recalled sandy beaches, swimming pools with slides and ice cream shops with too many flavours to choose from. They soon came upon the hotels, condominiums and villas as they approached the south side of Acapulco Bay and the driver turned from the main road to wind through a more affluent neighbourhood as they approached the water. They arrived at a pair of huge wrought iron gates forming the only break in a tall stone wall that ran as far as Ridley could see around the corner. The gates slowly opened and they drove in past two guards with assault rifles slung over their shoulders. Ahead was a sprawling mansion with grand steps leading to an ornate wood and metal double front door. Ridley couldn't believe this was where his mother lived, and wondered if he'd been mistakenly picked up, or even kidnapped. The man had had his name on a sign and said he worked for Trujillo, so surely he was in the right place.

One side of the heavy front door swung open and a woman stepped outside. She looked thin and frail, but Ridley recognised her as his mother. She wore a long, loose, yellow dress with a brightly crocheted woollen shawl wrapped around her shoulders, despite the balmy heat. On her head was an embroidered head scarf with no signs of her long dark hair that Ridley remembered so well. She used to dance around the house with Latin music blasting from the CD player with her young son in her arms. Her beautiful hair would swish around her head as she wiggled her hips and sang along. The pale woman staring down clasped her hands together and smiled nervously as Tattoo opened the door and

Ridley walked around the SUV to see his mother in person for the first time in 17 years. He ran up the steps and threw his arms around her. She felt so thin and delicate in his arms and he felt her body shake as she cried into his shoulder.

"Mamá, you're not well," Ridley said softly. "Why didn't you tell me."

Zanita pulled away and held her boy's face. "Look at you, you're a man now."

She wiped her tears away and held his face again. Her hands felt cold against his cheek but his mother's touch brought back a flood of childhood memories, and an overwhelming sense of loss. The missing years without her, they could never get back.

"I didn't want to worry you. I'm fine now, it is in remission, thank the Lord," she explained, and crossed herself. "I had cancer, but they say it is gone now."

Ridley took her hands in his. She was 44 years old yet her skin seemed translucent, a delicately thin layer draped over her bones. She was still a beautiful woman, but she looked tired and much older than her years. He felt ashamed he hadn't turned up before; he shouldn't have waited for her to finally ask him, he should have come anyway. He heard his bags land heavily on the entranceway next to them, and turned to see Tattoo walking away down the steps.

"They're a chatty pair, huh?" he said, grinning.

She waved a hand in the air. "Pay no mind to them, they're Aldo's men. Acapulco isn't what it used to be I'm afraid, I'm lucky he has men like that to take care of us. They're not people I'd care to spend time with, but they keep us safe."

Ridley gathered up his bags and followed Zanita inside the house. Once through the entryway, flanked with marble stairs curving up to the second level, they walked through an archway into an expansive open living room with a breath-taking view of Acapulco Bay beyond a large patio with two swimming pools.

"This is a long way from that little house we lived in when I was a kid," Ridley said, staring around the huge room furnished with long, overstuffed leather sofas and lavish original oil paintings of sailfish and marlin.

"I've been fortunate," she replied as she carefully lowered herself into a chair by the floor-to-ceiling windows.

A nice-looking young maid hovered close by and Zanita turned to Ridley. "Are you hungry? Thirsty? Rosie, can you squeeze some fresh orange juice for us?"

The maid smiled and looked at Ridley. "Of course, madam. Some food sir?"

"No, no, please, I'm fine thank you, Rosie, don't trouble yourself over me."

Rosie bowed her head and quietly retreated.

"She's an angel," Zanita whispered. "I don't know what I'd do without that girl."

Ridley sat down across the small wooden table from his mother. "Will I meet your husband? Where does he work? Is his office in town?"

Zanita managed a smile as she appeared to gather her thoughts before replying. "You will meet him, I'm sure. He has an office in the house here, but he has an office at some of his businesses as well. Most of them are here in Acapulco, but he has some up the coast in Zihuatanejo. He travels a lot too, he has business associates all over Mexico, but I don't know all that he does. He has his own plane he uses, so he can go to a meeting somewhere and be back before dinner sometimes." She looked out across the gardens towards the bay. "He'll probably be home tonight. But sometimes he stays away longer."

"He should be here with you while you're not well, Mamá." Ridley said quietly.

"No, I'm fine." She looked back at her son, her eyes tired and sad, despite the smile on her lips. "He paid for the best doctors, he has taken great care of me. We had a nurse here at the house until a few days ago, but I don't need all that fuss. Once I get my strength back things will be back to normal."

She reached across the table and took his hand. "Enough of this cancer talk, I wanted to hear all about your life, my son. Tell me all about your life. You live in the Caribbean, yes? And a woman, you must have throngs of women chasing you all day, you're such a handsome man." She lowered her voice. "Just like your father."

Ridley blushed. "Not throngs, Mamá, but I have one girl who is very special."

16

CARIBBEAN SEA – JULY 29, 2020

As the island became a low, dark silhouette on the horizon, the sun steadily climbed and ramped up its intensity. All sweatshirts and wind jackets had been shed and the four of the them sought out shade, and the ocean breeze. The best place was up on the flybridge where Reg was taking his turn at the helm. Thomas climbed the ladder and cracked open a soda can as he settled against the railing. Reg turned and saw they were all gathered.

"How about we get the whole story now. We're on the open sea, and we're all here." He glanced over at Nora. "You ready to share what this is all about?"

Nora instinctively looked at AJ, who smiled and nodded.

"Probably a good time to clue us in, if you're ready," AJ said, knowing Reg's gruff manner could be intimidating.

"Okay," Nora said quietly, and thought for a moment before starting. "Some of this is hard for me to talk about, so forgive me if it takes me a little while." She looked around at the eager eyes upon her, and AJ could see she was nervous.

"Take your time, Nora, we've got another three hours until we get there," AJ encouraged her. "There's no rush."

Nora bit her lip, took a deep breath, and began her story. "I was in the British Virgin Islands a few months ago and I met a guy. He was teaching sailing from Road Harbour on Tortola, and from where I was moored in the bay, I would see him taking customers in and out each day. As you can imagine, I avoided contact with people as much as possible, but he stopped by the boat one day and introduced himself. He said he saw me every day as well, and wondered what I was doing on my own out there. He was nice, but I made some excuses and sent him away, because I can't risk these meetings." She looked at the deck sheepishly and AJ couldn't imagine how lonely her existence had to be.

"Anyway, he came back the next day and brought a picnic with him. There was something about him I felt a connection with, I don't know why. But I let him aboard and we ate the lunch and talked. He mainly told me about himself because I didn't offer much about me, and he seemed to sense I couldn't share much. He left again and I thought about pulling anchor and moving on. I really liked him, he didn't seem like the usual young guy looking for a good time. He was funny, and very easy to relax around, but that can be when I let my guard down, which would get me in trouble. I couldn't decide, so I did nothing, and before I know it he comes over some more and then we're going sailing together and then he's staying over... and you know."

Reg shuffled uncomfortably in the helm chair and AJ grinned. She loved to hear the young woman was having a proper relationship with someone after the dysfunctional trauma she had been through.

"This fella have a name?" she asked.

Nora looked up. "Oh, yes, his name is..." She trailed off and seemed to consider her wording, "His name is Ridley Hernandez."

"Ridley Hernandez?" Reg said. "That's an unusual name, where's this bloke from?"

"He was born in Mexico, but was raised in Australia since he was about six, I think. He had been in the Virgin Islands for a year when we met, but he learnt to sail in Australia."

"And what does he look like, this sailor who swept you off your feet?" AJ asked with a grin.

Nora smiled but the sadness was back in her eyes and AJ realised this story might not be heading for a happy ending.

"He's my height, twenty-three, and really nice looking. Not the magazine model type, just a normal, beach and ocean loving, surfer kinda guy. He has curly brown hair down to his shoulders..." Nora trailed off again and before she looked down AJ caught the tear escaping her eye.

"Nora, where is he now? What's happened?"

Nora sniffled and gritted her teeth as she wiped her eyes. When she looked up her steely reserve had returned. "I don't know. The last I heard from him was seven days ago. We communicate on a message site, using kind of a code, and it all went quiet. He was in Acapulco. He was supposed to be flying from there to Jamaica to meet me as I sailed by."

"Acapulco?" Reg asked, his voice less gruff than usual, "Why was he there? I thought you said you were in the Virgin Islands?"

Nora nodded. "Yeah, I'm getting there. I'm sorry, it's a long story."

"I'm sorry," Reg mumbled. "You go ahead, don't let us interrupt. Tell it as you need to."

"So, anyway, Ridley changed many things for me. We spent a lot of time together and he's the first person I have been able to really tell about some things that have happened in my life. He had a bit of a strange childhood, so he could relate to things not being so normal. He was born in Mexico, as I said, and his mother and father divorced when he was small. His father, Frisco, took him to Australia. Frisco had spent his whole life in Acapulco and hadn't known who his own father was until shortly before he left Mexico. Frisco's mother finally told him that his father was an Australian man called Dingo Doyle, who flew aeroplanes, and had just disappeared one day. He left for a job flying somewhere, she didn't know where, and never came back. She hadn't told this man yet, but she was pregnant with Frisco. She was a poor woman and never knew how to try and find him. This all happened in the late 50s, so there was no Internet and she didn't know what to do. When Frisco was older and his mother fell ill, he finally persuaded her to tell him the story and he started trying to figure out what happened. Frisco contacted the local airfield and asked around until he found someone that remembered his father. The old man recalled the plane he flew was named 'Queen of the Island Skies'.

"It took Frisco months of searching and writing letters, but he finally found records of the plane crash-landing into the Caribbean Sea, and the pilot being rescued by a fisherman. Reports said he recovered from his injuries in a hospital on Grand Cayman, and then there was no record of him from that point on. Frisco took a guess that his father had returned to Australia, and wrote to the Australian embassy in Mexico, giving them his full name, Rodney Doyle. He didn't hear a word for months, then a letter shows up saying the embassy had tracked him down and they gave Frisco an address outside Sydney. Frisco began writing to his father, who was surprised and happy he had a son. He explained he was injured in the crash and had gone home rather than burden his then girlfriend with a cripple for a husband."

"So that's what we're looking for? The downed plane from when, you say?" Thomas asked excitedly.

"1958 is when it crash-landed on the water. It was over Sixty Mile Bank," Nora replied.

"I hate to be the one to tell you this," Reg said, turning in the pilot seat. "There's not a lot of people been diving on the bank out there, but enough to have seen an aeroplane if there was one. Either it wasn't on the bank, or it's been blown off, and all around is deep, deep water – we're talking thousands of feet."

"We know it was on the bank when they left the plane," Nora said firmly.

"Wait, when they left it?" Reg asked. "You mean it was still floating?"

"Yes. It was not only floating, but it was anchored to the bank," Nora replied with a look of determination.

"Bloody hell," Reg mumbled and scratched his beard. "But obviously it sunk at some point, so likely it pulled the anchor in the next big blow and went into the deep."

Nora nodded. "That's very possible. Or maybe it's broken up and scattered on the top of the bank."

"Hang on though," AJ held up her hand. "Are we just trying to locate the old plane to say we found where it is? You talked about something of value?"

"We haven't got there yet," Nora said, blushing.

"Sorry, sorry," AJ apologised, and smacked Reg on the arm. "He keeps interrupting you."

Reg frowned and pointed at Thomas, but Nora ignored them both and started back into her story. "Okay, so as I was saying, Frisco and his father start writing back and forth and they're both excited to discover each other. By the time Frisco tracks down Dingo, his mother had passed away and apparently he's in trouble with some bad people in Acapulco. From what Ridley told me, Frisco had been quite the playboy until he finally married a girl a lot younger than him, Zanita, when he was in his late thirties. They had Ridley, and things were great for several years until out of the blue, Frisco told Zanita they had to leave. Ridley said he never really knew why until he saw his mother again, a few months back, for the first time since he was a kid. That's when she told him that Frisco had got into hot water with some bad people in Acapulco but she didn't want to leave the town and her family, so Frisco took Ridley one night and ran. He finally contacted her a year later to tell her they were safe with his own father in Australia.

"Dingo now has his son and his grandson nearby and they spend a lot of time together. Dingo is getting old and had always suffered from complications from the crash. When Ridley was twelve his grandfather became very ill and was confined to the hospital. He told me he would sit at his grandfather's bedside for hours on end, listening to him tell stories about the war, and flying planes around the Caribbean in the 50s."

AJ smiled and thought of her own grandfather, Arthur, and the wonderful stories he told when he was alive. It was his story that had led her and Reg to hunt for the U-boat she finally discovered off the west coast of Grand Cayman.

"One story Dingo told Ridley stuck with him more than any others. Dingo's family were jewellers, and when he left to join the RAF towards the end of World War II, his father gave him a small bag containing a dozen diamonds. He told him the stones were a currency that worked in any country, at any time. He should only use them in desperation, and never tell a soul or show them to anyone. Dingo never flew in combat and after the war he headed to the Caribbean and eventually ended up farther west, in Acapulco. He used a couple of the diamonds to buy his plane but the rest he always kept hidden and safe."

The three were even more intrigued in the story at the mention of the stones and Nora had their complete attention.

"Dingo hid the diamonds in the plane. He told Ridley he dare not ask the fishermen to get them after he crash-landed, as he was scared they would throw him over the side and keep them. He said by the time he'd recovered at the hospital and spent time around the man and his son that saved him, he realised he could have trusted them completely. They were simple, honest island people, but by then it was too late. A week or two after the crash a boat was sent out to retrieve the plane from where they'd left it anchored, but it was gone. A storm had rolled through, so they guessed it had taken on water and sunk."

"Or pulled the anchor and drifted to who knows where," Reg added.

"True," Nora said flatly.

"Has to be worth looking," Thomas said, beaming a big smile. "We got nothing better going on right now."

"That's true too," Reg admitted. "Worse thing we do is have some fun diving before we head home."

"But wait," AJ said. "What about Ridley? What has happened to him?"

Nora's expression turned stern and the sadness returned to

her eyes. "That's the last piece of this puzzle," she said. "Dingo never left the hospital; he died and Frisco inherited the family money from the jewellery business that Dingo had sold and retired from. Ridley grew up learning to sail, surf and dive, and after university asked his dad if he could travel for a while. His father didn't mind and Ridley set out for the Caribbean, taking a job over the Internet in the British Virgin Islands. He had kept in touch with his mother in Acapulco but had never visited her. He said he had wanted to but she always had a reason why he couldn't. She was remarried, although he'd never spoken to the new husband and she didn't say much about him. They had written and talked but he hadn't seen her since he was young. Earlier this year in May, she called and said she'd like to see him if he could make it to Mexico. She would buy his ticket. He got the first flight he could and stayed with her for a few days. Turns out she has been going through chemotherapy for breast cancer. He said she lived in this big house in the expensive part of Acapulco, but the city was nothing like how he remembered as a kid. It's one of the most dangerous cities in the world now, and Ridley got the impression the new husband, Aldo Trujillo, was probably involved in all kinds of illegal activities. He said he had armed guards all around the house, and with him at all times. His mother said he's just a businessman, but Ridley didn't believe her." Nora gritted her teeth and took a few breaths to keep her composure.

"He said his mother seemed to be doing okay; she had lost her hair and was very thin, but she told him she was in remission. This happened shortly after we had first met. He was so happy he'd spent some time with her..."

Nora broke off, her head dropped into her hands and she sobbed. AJ wrapped an arm around her and tried to console her, letting the tears flow for as long as she needed.

It took Nora another ten minutes to finish the story of Ridley and his mother. She struggled through, with more tears and several breaks while the others sat patiently listening, riveted and shocked by what they were hearing. When she finally made her way to the end of her tale, she looked up at AJ with moist, blurry eyes.

"I had no idea what to do, so I carried on with what we had planned. But I'm really scared what has happened to him."

AJ reached out and took Nora in her arms again. "Maybe he'll be there when we get back, or at least a message on your message site."

Nora buried her head in AJ's shoulder. "I don't think he will."

17

ACAPULCO, MEXICO – MAY 2020

Ridley and Zanita spent the rest of the afternoon catching up, and he enjoyed using the Spanish he had grown up speaking and rarely used these days. As the sun began to lower in the western sky, Zanita led him out into the grounds that stretched from the house to the rocks dropping down to the bay. They walked slowly down the winding pathway, with uniquely shaped swimming pools on either side and impeccably maintained flowers and shrubs adding splashes of colour to the garden. The path opened to a patio near the low, wrought iron fence before the rocks down to the water. They sat at a table under a bright blue umbrella and Ridley took in the magnificent view. High-rise hotels lined the inner shore of the bay to their right and to their left in the west they looked out to the Pacific Ocean past the island of La Roqueta. Native palm trees screened the sides of the garden but Ridley noticed the roofs of several buildings beyond. Garages for the vehicles, or living quarters for the many staff that seemed to be on the property, he figured. A sweet but slightly spicy aroma drifted across the garden and Zanita noticed her son taking in a deep breath through his nose.

"Mexican honeysuckle," she said with a smile.

"I remember that smell from when I was a child," Ridley replied, drawing in the fragrance and letting it rekindle his memories. "Our house had the same scent."

"It's my favourite, we had some shrubs in the tiny back yard. It used to fill the house with that lovely smell, carried on the breeze from the ocean," she said, closing her eyes and joining him back in time. "We had some great times in that house, didn't we?"

Ridley looked at his mother. "I am happy whenever I think of my life back then. I was too young to understand why it all changed and father has never really explained it. He just says people change sometimes – he's never really told me why we moved."

Zanita stared back across the water and breathed deeply. "I loved your father very much."

For a moment he thought that was all she was willing to share, but he gave her some time and she finally spoke again.

"I was very young. He was almost forty, and I was only twenty, twenty-one when I had you," she elaborated, looking back at him. "Your father was larger than life to me, he was worldly and he knew everybody. We would go to restaurants and get seated right away, people would always be coming by and saying hello. I grew up very poor and I felt like a princess on the arm of this shining light who attracted everyone to him like a movie star. That little house of ours in the hills was like a palace compared to where I'd grown up, with a dirt floor and never knowing when the next meal would come."

Zanita paused and looked away again. "But, like many things in life, it was a little too good to be true. Your father attracted many people. Many women. Many bad men. One day, he says we have to leave. I asked him why and all he would say was we were in danger and had to go now. I asked him where to. He said Australia. You know your father was raised by his mother here, and never knew who his own father was for many, many years. He had been working on tracking him down for a while and it was only a few months since he'd found him that all this happened. He told me he was in Australia."

She tipped her head back, looked up and closed her eyes again. "My father was not well, and my mother was struggling to look after my younger brothers and sisters. I had recently found out about your father's indiscretions, so I was broken hearted and angry. So I told him no, I couldn't leave."

Zanita looked over at Ridley, her eyes moist as she spoke. "I didn't know he'd take you. I woke up the next morning and you were both gone. I didn't think he would really leave, or maybe he'd go away for a while and come back. But I didn't expect him to run away with you. I was left alone with a note and some money. You changed the world for me, and then he took you away." A tear rolled down her cheek, "It was a year after that before he wrote me and told me where you both were. In Australia. He might as well have said you were on the moon."

Ridley didn't know what to say. He had deeply missed his mother, but he'd also had a wonderful childhood in Australia. He felt guilty that he had, hearing her story, but the truth was he loved his father and the life they had led together. He wasn't surprised his father had been unfaithful; there had been a trail of women through his life. Some had spent more time with Ridley than others, but they always seemed to leave in the end. There had been a void without his mother that his grandparents had tried to fill, but it was never quite the same.

"One thing Dad has always said to me, was that moving to Australia to live near his own father saved his life. He's never explained why, but he insists he wouldn't have survived if he'd stayed here."

Zanita wiped her tears away and nodded. "I expect that's true. I never knew what he was up to, I didn't care to be honest. I had him, I had you, and I had our lovely home. I didn't worry about how we came to live that way. But after he left, men came looking for him. At first they didn't believe me when I said he'd run off with you. They kept coming back, but of course they never found him. Finally, they took me instead, and I figured I was about to be another body dumped outside of town. They took me to their boss, and he asked me where your father had gone. I told him the same thing I'd been telling his men; the truth. I didn't know where, but my guess was Australia. He told me he believed me. I thought he'd have his men shoot me anyway to show an example or something, I just hoped it would be quick and I wouldn't be passed around like the horrible stories you hear. What I didn't expect was what he said next."

Ridley looked at her curiously and she shrugged her shoulders. "He asked if he could take me to dinner."

"Really?" He thought for a moment. "Wait, was the man...?"

"Aldo. It was Aldo, and he was a real gentleman. I explained I was devastated having just lost my husband and my son and he said no problem. He asked if he could call on me every once in a while, to make sure I was okay. What could I say? He was good to his word; he would stop by every few weeks and he always asked if there was anything he could do for me. He asked me for nothing, and he never mentioned your father. He would stay for half an hour, we'd drink coffee and just chat about life in Acapulco, how things have changed, news, the weather, all kinds of things. After six months of this he asked me one day if there was anything he could do for me, and I finally said yes, you can take me to dinner if the offer is still there. We were married one year later after my divorce was final from your father."

They sat in silence for a while, watching the sunset form on the horizon, lost in their own thoughts. Ridley was glad his mother had found another love, but it still felt strange to hear her talk of another man. All he had was his early memories of her, which were always with his father. It was easy to picture him without her, as that's what he'd grown up knowing, but his awareness of his mother was frozen at age six and had been spotted with occasional clips of her life ever since. Whatever he'd gleaned from a letter, an email or a photograph.

Rosie's voice startled him.

"Dinner is ready when you are, Madam."

Zanita turned and smiled. "Thank you Rosie, we'll be right in. Have you seen Mr. Trujillo?"

"No, Madam, not as yet."

Rosie left and Ridley helped his mother to her feet from the chair. He put his arms around her and squeezed her gently.

"We should never have let this go for so long, Mamá, I'm so sorry I didn't come before."

She held him like she would never let go. "It is entirely my fault my love, I wanted to see you so badly, but every time I arranged something…" She faltered and he could tell she was crying again. "Well, there's no excuses, I should have made it work and I didn't. I hope you can forgive me, Ridley."

She pulled back and held him at arm's length. "We can't change the past, but we have the time ahead. One thing this damn cancer has shown me is there's no time in life to put things off. Let's not wait again. I have the money, and I can fly you here whenever you want to come, just say the word."

He smiled and touched her face. "I promise I will."

18

CARIBBEAN SEA – JULY 29, 2020

The next few hours passed by slowly and relatively quietly. They all sensed Nora needed a break from their questions, so they trudged across the monotonous open sea at a steady 18 knots, making idle chatter about nothing in particular. Everyone took a turn at the helm, including Nora, who was an accomplished sailor, but had spent very little time on a motorboat. Winds were to their tail out of the south-east, and with gently rolling two to three-foot swells, they were making good time. The Newton had GPS and a good old-fashioned compass on the helm, but no auto pilot or guided steering, making piloting a full-time operation. As their target neared on the GPS screen, Reg, who was back at the wheel, called down from the fly-bridge.

"AJ. Come up here a minute."

AJ climbed the ladder with her travel mug full of water in one hand.

"What's up?" she asked, leaning against the roof frame next to Reg.

"What are the other two doing?" he asked.

She chuckled. "They're both asleep. You know Thomas, he can sleep anywhere, anytime. He's either going a million miles an hour, or asleep. I think Nora has learnt to grab sleep when she can."

"Alright, guess you'll just have to tell me, and they can all have a laugh later," Reg said, looking over at AJ with a big grin.

"Oh, so now you want to hear my plan, do you?" she replied, playfully punching his brawny arm. "I don't know that you're worthy of being brought into the know, not after taking the piss like that."

He shrugged his shoulders and turned back to the open ocean ahead. "Alright, never mind."

"You can't give in that easily, you pillock, you're supposed to beg me to know," AJ said, throwing her hands in the air.

Reg laughed in a low rumble. "Nah, that's okay."

"Ahhh," she groaned. "Well, you're gonna hear it whether you like it or not."

He shook his head, his whole body quaking as he continued to laugh. "Figured as much."

"So, what we do," she started, her expression turning serious, "is tie a couple of tow lines off the stern, then slowly troll the top of the bank in a search pattern, using the GPS and fish-finder sonar as a guide. Have a diver on each line at 50 feet, one scanning to port, other to starboard. From 50 feet we should be able to see the sea floor pretty well and on nitrox we can stay down a while and won't get too nitrogen loaded. This way we don't have to drift dive which would keep carrying us off the bank."

Reg waited a few moments, seemingly mulling it over, then he turned and looked at AJ. "That just might be..." He burst into a big grin. "...the dumbest bunch of balderdash I've ever heard."

She smacked him again as he rolled around the chair chuckling. "No it's not, it's a good idea. It would work."

He finally settled down. "Alright, alright, we can give it a try. But you and Thomas are first in; I'm not being your underwater kite-flying guinea pig."

AJ smiled. "No problem."

"How are you gonna signal if you see something?" Reg asked,

thoughtfully. "You'll be 50 feet down, you can't just pop up – you'll need to come up easy and do your three-minute safety stop on the way. The boat will have pulled you another half mile by then."

"I've thought of that," AJ said with a smug grin. "I'll tow a safety marker buoy with a weight, and 50 feet more line. I'll just drop it if we see something. When you see the buoy stop trailing, you just idle back around to that spot. It'll drop close enough to what we see for us to find it again."

"Hmmm," Reg nodded. "Okay then. Well, roust up sleeping beauty and get your gear ready, we're almost there," he said tapping the GPS screen which showed them less than three miles from Sixty Mile Bank.

Ten minutes later, Hazel's Odyssey bobbed on the water at idle and the four of them stared all around at the vast ocean. No land, no boats, no other signs of humanity as far as their eyes could see.

Thomas looked down at the water behind the Newton. "Hard to believe there's something just a hundred feet below us when all around is thousands of feet of emptiness."

"Yeah, kinda creepy isn't it," AJ said quietly.

"You telling me you two nancies dragged me all the way out here to chicken out?" Reg growled playfully.

"No!" Thomas and AJ said together.

"Pretty good surface current running," Reg said, looking at a tag line he had in the water stretching straight out behind the boat.

"From everything I've heard, the current will be bad down there too," AJ added as she sat down on the port side bench in front of her buoyancy control device, or BCD, that was strapped to a nitrox tank, ready to go. Thomas took a seat on the opposite bench where his gear waited. AJ slipped her fins on, then looped her arms through the shoulder straps of the BCD and fastened the buckles across her waist and chest. She checked her wrist computer was wirelessly reading her tank pressure and was set to the correct percentage of nitrox mix. The computer would give her all the vital information she needed during the dive; time underwater, depth, gas left in the tank, and the critical time she could stay at that depth without going into deco – the point where the nitrogen being introduced into the body's tissues reaches saturation and can no longer be dissolved safely. At 50' down that shouldn't be an issue, they would be low on breathing gas long before saturation using 32% nitrox.

She looked over at Thomas who nodded, indicating he was ready to go, and they both stood and waddled carefully in their fins to the swim step at the open transom.

"You'll have to go really slowly, Reg," AJ said, looking over at the big man.

"Crikey, how many times are you gonna tell me, girl? Get in before I throw you in," he said, grinning through his thick beard.

AJ looked over at Thomas. "You carrying plenty of weight?"

Thomas nodded again. "Yes, boss, I got an extra ten pounds – I'll be lucky not to head straight for the bottom."

AJ laughed. "You'll need it, just wait and see. When the boat's towing us it'll be trying to drag us up as much as along, especially when we're into the current. We'll need the weight to stay level at 50 feet."

Nora handed AJ a bundled-up length of line attached to a ten-pound dive weight and a deflated SMB, or surface marker buoy. AJ took them and crammed them in a drop-down pocket on her BCD. The tow lines were attached to the stern cleats on either side and they each took their line and attached it to their BCD using a carabiner tied to the end of the line. AJ pulled her mask down in place and put her regulator in her mouth. She felt a hand on her arm and turned to see a look of concern on Nora's face.

"Be careful. Both of you," she said, looking from AJ to Thomas.

AJ gave her a wink. "This will be fun, don't worry," she said, despite the butterflies fluttering around her stomach as she looked back at the vast ocean she was about to step into. Before she could think of more ways to get nervous, AJ took a giant stride off the swim step and dropped into the balmy water of the Caribbean Sea.

Once Thomas was in the water and they gathered the lines safely clear of the stern of the boat, they both released the air from their BCDs and descended. Once below, AJ could see nothing other than dark blue water around and below her. Although she knew they were over the bank it was still hard to register without being able to see it. She glanced up at the boat, which didn't appear to be moving away from them, telling her the current below matched that of the surface. They dropped quickly with the extra ballast they carried, and once they passed through 30 feet, the top of the bank appeared below them. Hazy and unclear at first, by the time AJ hit the fill valve and let air flow into the bladder of her BCD to slow her descent, the landscape had come into focus. She levelled off at 50 feet, as planned, and visibility was clear enough to see across a wide expanse of the bank to either side. With a stationary reference she could see they were moving along at a good clip in the current. She was surprised the sea floor was far more sparse than Twelve Mile Bank that she was more familiar with. There were very few coral heads, but large clumps of sponges and fans were dotted about the flat top of the underwater mountain peak. If there was an aeroplane there, no way were they going to miss it, she thought.

She looked over towards Thomas who appeared to have neutralised his buoyancy and gave her the okay sign. She returned the signal and pulled the SMB from her BCD pocket. The line was 120 feet long with a loop in the middle and a carabiner on the end. By hooking the carabiner through the loop and then a ring on her BCD she would have 60 feet of line to the SMB, which once inflated using her regulator would rise to the surface. She carefully blew a small amount of air into the SMB and let it go. The nylon tube accelerated towards the surface with the air inside expanding as the surrounding water pressure lessened the closer the SMB got to the surface.

The marker surfacing was Reg's cue to start towing them and she watched the twin props of the Newton start spinning as he must have seen the orange tube break the surface, and put the boat in gear. The slack in the tow lines quickly succumbed to the idling boat and AJ prepared herself for a sudden pull when it became taut. It was still more violent than she expected, yanking her forward and immediately upwards towards the surface. She quickly dumped all the air from her BCD and hoped she had enough ballast to hold her down against the line's goal of dragging her straight up behind the boat. She realised with the line pulling hard there was no way to release the carabiner in an emergency – such as her being dragged rapidly to the surface and risking the bends. She was about to grab her dive knife from its sheath to cut the tow line when she seemed to level out. She checked her depth and she was at 42 feet and slowly dropping. Now the boat had reached idle speed of a few knots and was no longer accelerating, everything calmed down and she felt in control again. She looked over at Thomas. His eyes looked a little startled through his mask but he too appeared to be in control and was setting his depth. He gave her the okay signal again, which she returned before tapping two fingers on her mask and then pointing them at the surface of Sixty Mile Bank, indicating they could start their search.

19

ACAPULCO, MEXICO – MAY 2020

Ridley woke and took a moment to remember where he was. The guest room was as luxurious as the rest of the house and while he had grown up in a nice home in Cronulla, an affluent town south of Sydney, it was not in the opulent style of Trujillo's fortress-like mansion. He slid from beneath the thick duvet on the king-sized bed and threw on a tee-shirt. He peaked through the curtains to see the sun was beginning to form a glow over the mountains. The bedside clock told him it was 6:43am. He wandered from the room down a long hallway with doors to more rooms than he had seen in many hotels. He found the kitchen, a sprawling array of restaurant-level cook tops and stainless-steel appliances faintly illuminated by the under-cabinet lighting. He opened the double-door refrigerator and found a pitcher of orange juice. After hunting through multiple cabinets he discovered one containing cups and mugs and chose a simple beaker. He poured himself some juice and returned the pitcher to the fridge.

"Good morning," a man's voice said in Spanish from the shadows of the living room.

Ridley jumped and almost spilt his glass he was about to sip from.

"Hello. I hope you don't mind, I was awake and thirsty. Time difference or something, I suspect."

"Help yourself to whatever you like," the voice replied.

Ridley didn't know quite what to do next; he didn't feel like venturing towards the dark room, but it felt awkward to leave and go back to his guest room. He supposed he was finally meeting Aldo but it appeared the man was happy to let him guess.

"Mr. Trujillo?" he enquired.

A light flicked on, revealing a man Ridley guessed to be around fifty, with a well-kept beard and wavy salt-and-pepper hair. He was dressed in jeans and an expensive-looking button-down shirt, but no shoes. He gave the impression he had thrown some clothes on, thoughtfully. He pointed to the other chair at the small table Ridley had occupied the day before with his mother. Ridley walked over and offered his hand. Aldo shook with a firm grip and Ridley sat down.

"It's nice to meet you, and thank you for your hospitality. Your home is beautiful."

Aldo looked around and shrugged his shoulders. "Thank you. I trust my men picked you up on time?"

Ridley thought about the two men that he wouldn't mind never seeing again. "Yes, thank you."

A slight movement in the shadows of the garden caught his eye until he realised it was a guard walking the perimeter. Aldo noticed him looking.

"Acapulco has become a dangerous town over the years, I'm afraid; these days it's pertinent to take precautions. It's not unheard of for people to be taken from their homes, if they're not careful."

Ridley looked at the man. He noticed he seemed incredibly calm as he talked about the possibility of being kidnapped and ransomed for money.

"I guess I'm glad my mother lives in a secure home, but it must be unnerving living where you're afraid to go to the shops without armed guards."

The man leaned back in the chair. "I am not afraid." He smiled.

"But tell me, have you been able to spend some time with your mother? She has been quite unwell as I'm sure you're aware. Fortunately, I believe it is behind us now."

Ridley was happy to move on; he got the impression Aldo was indeed not afraid. Although he might be the man that others were afraid of, he thought nervously.

"Yes, we talked a lot yesterday and we should get to spend the morning together. I wish I could stay longer, but it was difficult to figure out any flights at all with the travel restrictions. Hopefully I can come back again for a longer trip soon."

Aldo waved a hand in the air. "You're welcome anytime. If it makes my wife happy, I'll do everything in my power to make it happen. I wish I could fly you myself but the leeward islands are a little too far for my King Air."

"Do you fly yourself? You're a pilot?" Ridley asked.

"I am. I also have a pilot on staff, as many times I must work during the flight, or entertain guests, but I prefer it when I am able to fly."

Ridley smiled. "My grandfather was a pilot; he flew in the RAF at the very end of the war, but then had his own plane and a charter business. He was here in Acapulco, as I'm sure you know."

"Zanita mentioned that I believe. Acapulco was a wonderful city back then, a playground for the Hollywood crowd. Is your grandfather still with us?"

Ridley shook his head. "No, he died when I was twelve, but I was fortunate to spend some time around him before he passed. He was full of wonderful stories."

Dawn spread a beautiful glow across the bay, sparkling and glistening off the water as the soft waves rolled through.

Aldo looked at his watch. "I must be going, I have a breakfast meeting." He stood and extended a hand. Ridley followed suit and shook the man's hand.

"Thank you again for letting me stay, and taking care of the flights."

Aldo nodded. "I look forward to talking more on your next visit; as I say, you're welcome anytime."

The man strode away and Ridley sat back down and sipped the orange juice he had been ignoring while they talked. After a few minutes he heard his mother shuffling down the hall towards the kitchen. He got up and met her with a hug.

"How are you feeling today?" he asked. "What can I get you?"

Rosie appeared as if by magic, and Ridley wondered if she'd been present the whole time, hiding in the shadows somewhere.

"Morning my dear," his mother replied, and turned to the woman. "Hello Rosie. Coffee please, and I'll try some eggs I think. Would you like some eggs, Ridley?"

"Sure Mamá," he replied, smiling at Rosie. "Thank you."

Zanita made her way, wrapped snugly in her dressing gown, to a breakfast table next to the kitchen. A different embroidered scarf adorned her head and fluffy slippers kept her feet warm.

"Did you sleep well?" she asked.

"Wonderfully, that bed is a slice of heaven. I'm more used to makeshift beds and cramped berths on boats these days."

He sat across from her, and Rosie brought them both a coffee.

"I met your husband this morning," Ridley said, as he stirred in some sugar.

His mother looked up. "He was here?" She looked bemused, or embarrassed, he couldn't tell. "This house is so big, sometimes we go days without seeing each other. He has a bed in a room by his office. He sleeps there when he worries about disturbing me."

"He seems nice," Ridley offered, although he realised he was saying it just to say something. He wasn't sure how he felt about Aldo.

"This girl of yours, Ridley, tell me all about her. Is she pretty? I bet she's gorgeous."

He was more than happy to move the conversation on. "I think she is," he said, smiling. "She's from Norway, and if you picture what you'd think a blonde, Scandinavian girl should look like, that's her," he said, laughing.

"Oh my. I don't really know anything about Norway," she said, laughing with him. "Apart from the band in the eighties, what was their name? They were from Norway."

"A-ha?"

"That's them," she said excitedly. "I had a poster of the lead singer, he was dreamy looking. If she's as pretty as he was handsome then you're a lucky man."

He felt good seeing his mother laugh. He had the feeling her life had lacked humour for a while, cancer aside.

"She's only eighteen but she's travelled a lot and is an incredible sailor. I haven't asked her yet, we've only been seeing each other a short time, but I plan to sail to Grand Cayman in a few months and I hope she'll go with me."

He leaned over the table. "Grandfather told me about his plane crash; did Father ever tell you about this?"

Zanita nodded. "He said he had stopped flying after he crashed, but I didn't know, or at least I don't remember, much more than that. He was only in touch with him a short while before he left."

Ridley quickly continued, not wanting to linger on the leaving part. "Well, Granddad told me he had something hidden in the plane, something very valuable."

They both sat back while Rosie placed two breakfast plates on the table; his mother's consisted of scrambled eggs and a piece of toast, his was a feast of eggs, potatoes and vegetables. She topped off their coffees.

"Thank you, Rosie, this looks perfect," Zanita said, picking up her fork.

"I'm being spoilt," Ridley added. "Thank you Rosie."

Rosie lightly bowed. "Let me know if you need anything else, Madam."

Once she had retreated, Zanita looked at Ridley. "I thought for some reason he'd crashed in the ocean. I recall Frisco saying he'd found an old article in a paper about it."

"He did," Ridley said, between bites of the food. "But he knew where, and it might be possible to dive it."

"Really? That sounds awfully dangerous, Ridley."

He finished a long drink of coffee before replying. "I'm a certified diver, but this dive could be more technical than I'm trained for; I'll have to find someone to help me from the island. Nora mentioned she knows some people on Grand Cayman."

"What did he have on the plane that was so valuable? Surely whatever it is will have rotted away by now, all those years underwater," Zanita said, picking slowly at her breakfast.

"I shouldn't really be talking about it – we may be on a wild goose chase – but if we do find what he had aboard, they will not have rotted away. Or been crushed. Or anything else. They'll be as perfect as the day they went down. Just more valuable now. I'll be able to set up my own fleet of sailboats for charter, and then some. That's my dream, to have sailboat charters and live on the water. I'd be able to pay for my own flights to come see you as well."

Rosie leaned over and topped his coffee up again, surprising him as he hadn't seen her approaching. He thanked her again, and she smiled politely as she left.

Zanita crossed herself. "Please be careful, Ridley. I have just rediscovered you, I can't lose you to some crazy adventure, searching for lost treasure."

He grinned, "I promise, Mamá, I'll be careful."

That evening, Ridley left Acapulco with a full heart. He was excited to return to the girl he was falling in love with in Tortola, and he was equally excited to return with more time to spend with his mother. He had arrived the day before full of nervous anticipation and prepared to find a stranger with whom he felt no bond after their years apart. Instead, he found his mother, yearning to be reunited with her son as badly as he hoped she would. The burden of their time apart melted away, and while they brought each other up to date on the details of that time, their love was instantly uncovered. He felt an overwhelming excitement for the coming months, filled with love, adventure, and hopefully the key to his future.

20

CARIBBEAN SEA – JULY 29, 2020

Once the initial excitement of being towed underwater settled down, the searching became quite boring. The relatively featureless surface of the bank was easy to scan and with the boat having to pull them so slowly to be able to hold their depth, it was easy for their minds to wander. When they turned and headed into the current, things were a little more lively as the combined speed of the tow, plus the current running against them, made their masks flutter and it was harder to maintain their depth evenly at 50 feet. They could see a myriad of fish life near the few coral heads and they were passed by several schools of larger jacks. They had spotted a couple of nurse sharks settled on the sand and AJ thought she had caught a glimpse of a pair of eagle rays in the distance. What they hadn't seen was any sign of a plane, or man-made wreckage of any sort.

The bank appeared to be less than a mile long so each run along its length took about twenty minutes. Going with the current took slightly less time, and into the current slightly more, but after fifty minutes Reg was turning for another pass. AJ's dive computer showed she had 700psi of tank pressure remaining, it was time to finish this run. She waved a hand to Thomas, finally getting his attention, and signalled it was time to start ascending. She dug the weight and the rest of the SMB line from her pocket and thought about how the next step would work. The plan they had made on the boat was for them to unhook from the tow lines, deploy the SMB's extra line and weight, so it anchored to the bottom, and stay by the SMB while they did their safety stop at 15 feet. The boat would see the SMB had stopped moving, and circle back to pick them up. What they hadn't accounted for was the current. Somehow, AJ and Thomas needed to get within reach of each other or they risked being whisked away and separated. The plan also relied on the SMB being held firmly enough by the weight on the bottom that they could both hang on to the line to keep them in one place. The current would have something to say about that too, she realised.

Thomas was 10 feet to her right, so she angled herself in the water like a parachutist in free-fall and steered his way, surprising him as she bounced into him and clutched hold of the shoulder strap of his BCD. He quickly got the idea, and held her BCD to keep them together and free up her hands. She pulled another 10-pound dive weight from her BCD and after a good deal of fumbling managed to tie it to the end of the SMB line. Maybe it would stay put with the extra ballast, she decided optimistically. Thomas tapped her shoulder and offered one of his weights as well, which she gladly accepted and tied in place. Next, she took hold of her tow line and pulled herself forward against the strain of the boat. This put enough slack in Thomas's line for him to unclip his carabiner. He then reached forward and they both pulled harder on her tow line so she could unclip hers. The two tow lines and the boat began pulling away from them. Without the pull of the boat, they both immediately began to sink, so AJ quickly dropped the SMB weights, watching them plummet towards the sea floor. At the same time, with the loss of thirty pounds of ballast, they started to ascend faster than was safe and they quickly dumped air from their BCDs to control their rise. As they went, AJ unclipped the SMB carabiner from the loop on the line, and clipped it around the line itself, keeping it hooked to her BCD. They were now tethered to the SMB line, and the carabiner would slide up the rope with them as they ascended.

AJ was finally able to relax when they settled at 15 feet and the weights either held in the sand below, or had snagged on a rock. She hoped they hadn't bashed into any precious coral in the process, but they were back to being unable to see the top of the bank. Pretty soon they could hear the familiar drone of the Newton's diesels approaching, and before long they could see the hull cutting through the water approaching them. They hung in the water column, letting time tick by while their bodies dissipated more of the nitrogen through their tissues before they returned to atmospheric pressure at the surface. She checked her computer; they had less than a minute left on their safety stop. When she looked back up she noticed something at the edge of visibility, and slightly deeper than them. Before she knew it the faint image flashed towards them and for a second she thought it was charging them. A sailfish swooped by at an amazing speed, disappearing into the deep blue as quickly as it had arrived. The fish was a beautiful shade of blue with hints of silver and yellow along its body. She guessed it to be 8 feet from the tip of its long, pointed bill to the end of its forked tail. Its large dorsal fin, called a sail, ran the length of its back and made it look taller than it was. Its sleek, powerful body was able to propel the fish to speeds reaching in excess of 30mph. Thomas enthusiastically slapped AJ on the shoulder. Neither of them had ever seen such a sight in open water, and would be lucky to experience it ever again.

Back on the boat, after they'd excitedly relayed their sailfish sighting, shed their dive gear, and reeled in the SMB, they sat on the benches under the shade of the fly-bridge and debriefed.

"If it's there, we'll see it," AJ started. "The bank is barren compared to Twelve Mile, or from what I've heard about Pickle Bank off the sister islands. There's a few coral heads but they're low fingers rather than the tall stands of growth."

"We could see a decent distance too, I reckon you could move farther over between runs; we overlapped quite a bit I think," Thomas said as he stripped out of his wetsuit.

"I agree," AJ added, doing the same. "We can cover a strip 150 feet across each run, which still means we're doing 300 feet every fifty-minute session. It'll take nine more sessions to cover the whole thing if it's about 3,000 feet across, like we think."

Reg nodded. "Yeah. We don't have time for that."

"I don't think we gained much having two people in the water, we were only 10 or 12 feet apart so we're not covering much more ground. It would be easy to scan both sides yourself as it's not busy going this slowly," AJ said, as she draped her sodden wetsuit over the railing behind the tank racks to let it dry in the sun. "If we go one at a time we each get a 90 minute surface break and we'll use half the number of tanks."

"I don't know," Reg said, shaking his head. "We shouldn't be solo down there, in case something went wrong."

Thomas shrugged. "I think it's okay, Reg, it was harder dealing with the SMB with the two us than it would have been solo, and the emergency plan is the same whether there's one or two down there. Drop the weight, release the tow line and hang on to the SMB."

"S'pose," he grumbled. "Guess I'll find out as I'm up next."

AJ looked at her watch; it read a few minutes after midday. "Want to have some lunch first?" she asked.

"Nah," he replied. "I had a bite a bit ago, figuring we needed to get back in."

"I can try a go too," Nora said. "I have dived before, I'm just not officially certified."

"Appreciate the offer," Reg said, glancing at AJ before smiling at Nora, "but we shouldn't let you dive without your certification, especially on these dives. You'd need at least your advanced cert and nitrox class to do this. Besides, you need to show them how to pilot the boat; you were with me as we figured out the routine up here. Someone has to show these two plonkers how to do it."

AJ rolled her eyes. "Can't be difficult, you just did it," she retorted, grinning at Reg.

"This is still gonna take too long," Thomas said, looking out at the water. "Maybe we should change the search pattern." He turned back and looked at AJ. "If we think there's been enough divers on the bank to have seen a plane if it was there, the middle should be the last place to look."

"He's right, Reg," AJ said, thoughtfully. "We should go perimeter in. The bank is this odd, almost triangular shape, with the long side running about 310 to 320 degrees, which we just did. We're back near the south-west corner where we started, so let's head at 45 degrees to that corner which we think is pretty close, and then up the opposite side from our first run." She drew the shape of Sixty Mile Bank in the air. "Along the top to where we turned around this morning and then we'll work our way in."

"I agree," Reg said and looked at Nora. "I'm afraid it's far more likely your plane was swept off the bank a long time ago, if it ever sank on the top in the first place. The edges may show signs of it, perhaps a piece of wreckage."

Nora nodded and tried to smile. "I understand there's not much chance of it being here where we can find it, but I am really happy you're looking. Ridley would be really happy."

"Will be, Nora," AJ assured her. "Ridley will be happy. He's probably waiting in Jamaica right now, wondering where you are."

"You know he would have had a tough time getting a flight – there's still travel restrictions in place," Reg added. "He couldn't fly to the Cayman Islands, and if he did manage to get to Jamaica, he may have to quarantine for two weeks. I bet he's still trying to find a way to get over."

Nora did not look convinced, so AJ tried to move things along to at least keep her busy and her mind off her missing boyfriend.

"So, are you chicken now, Reg? Doing a lot of clucking and not much diving, aren't you?"

Reg shook his head. "You just worry about piloting the boat, you cheeky little wench – I'll show you how the diving's done." He stomped off down the steps to the cabin to get his wetsuit and AJ and Thomas both made clucking sounds.

"I'll use you both for bait on my hook later, you keep this up," he bellowed from below.

AJ started up the ladder to the fly-bridge and glancing back down, she was glad to see the friendly banter had Nora smiling.

21

ACAPULCO, MEXICO – JULY 19, 2020

Ridley and Zanita had decided he would fly back to Acapulco every three months to visit. Four times a year seemed like a workable schedule, and with their weekly Internet calls they were quickly becoming reacquainted. On their video chat the week before, they had talked about picking a date for August, as it would be three months since he first saw her again. He had commented how much better she looked. Her colour had returned to her cheeks and although she wouldn't take her head scarf off, she assured him her hair was growing back, albeit tinged by a few grey strands, to her annoyance. But it wasn't August, and he found himself flying back to Acapulco.

When he had answered his mobile the day before, he had recognised the Mexican number and happily greeted his mother. He was surprised when a man's voice spoke instead. Aldo went on to explain how he had found Zanita in her own bed that morning. The doctors were perplexed. If the cancer had returned it shouldn't have claimed her that quickly. If she had been exposed to the virus, she had showed no symptoms. They guessed she had suffered heart failure during the night. "Guessed?" he had asked. "You're guessing why my mother simply died in the middle of the night." Aldo had remained calm and explained that as Catholics they preferred not to perform an autopsy. It wouldn't change the fact that she was gone. He had moved on to suggesting flights Ridley could take to arrive for the funeral.

From the moment he had received the news, Ridley had been in a daze. He simply couldn't fathom how the woman he had spoken with, laughed with, and discussed how well she looked just a few days before, was now gone. There had been no accident, no catastrophic event, she had gone to bed well, and never woken up. It felt like a gift of a lifetime had been given to him just long enough to recognise its full value, before being cruelly wrenched away. He tried telling himself how lucky he had been to have that time with her. But his pain and anger would not let the passive sentiment used to placate the bereaved take hold. He envied people of faith who could channel the loss through their belief in God's will. It didn't remove the pain, but it took away the question of why. Or pretended to.

He once more walked through the arrivals to be greeted in the same disinterested manner by Tattoo. They managed to complete the journey without uttering a word from start to finish. That was fine with Ridley. What would they talk about? He was pretty sure the man didn't care if anyone lived or died, except perhaps his boss. Pay cheques stopped if he died. Ridley walked up the steps to the massive wooden entry doors and was surprised when Aldo stepped outside to greet him. The man held his arms open as though he was welcoming his own son back home. Ridley accepted the gesture but couldn't find it in himself to embrace Aldo in return. He didn't know this man; they had spoken for a few minutes in person and once on the phone. He felt a tinge of guilt that he wasn't more sympathetic; after all, Aldo had just lost his wife who he'd spent more time with than her own son had. He reached back and patted the man's shoulder.

"It killed me to make that call, Ridley – all I can do is tell you how sorry I am," Aldo said, releasing Ridley and stepping back.

"You know I would have done anything for your mother, if only we'd known something was wrong. It was so sudden."

He held out a hand offering Ridley entrance into the house and they walked through the grand entryway.

"The doctors really have no idea? Did they at least take a blood sample even if there's to be no autopsy?" Ridley asked, setting his bags by the hallway leading away from the living room.

"She had blood work every week; there was nothing out of place. As I'm sure you saw when you spoke to her, she was recovering well." Aldo walked across the living room and opened the door to the garden. "I have spoken to several doctors and they all think it was her heart. The chemotherapy puts a huge strain on the body. Her father had heart trouble, were you aware?"

Ridley shook his head. He realised he didn't even know his grandparent's names on his mother's side. They were Abuelo and Abuelita to him when he was six.

"No, I didn't know," he replied quietly.

They stepped into the back yard and walked down the same path he and his mother had strolled along just two months before. He was hit by the fragrant scent she had told him was Mexican honeysuckle. The evening sun across the bay was beginning to cast yellow hues as it prepared itself for another beautiful sunset. All he could think of was how much she would have enjoyed it. She often timed their calls shortly before dusk. My favourite person at my favourite time of day, she had told him.

"The services are tomorrow," Aldo said, leaning against the rail above the rocks down to the ocean. "We'll have a gathering here afterwards." He turned and looked at Ridley. "Do you wish to say anything tomorrow? The eulogy. I was to speak but I'm happy for you to, if you'd prefer."

A knot instantly formed in Ridley's stomach. He had never been much of a public speaker. His dad was an extrovert who could hold an audience, which he envied sometimes. Finding the perfect words was difficult, and he bumbled around in an effort to make his point and never quite landed on what he intended to say. Surely her husband would do a better job. He had been with her for the past 16 years, through the cancer. He would be the better one to capture her essence.

"No. Thank you for offering. I'm sure you'll do a much better speech than I could."

Aldo frowned and gazed over the water. "I don't know about that. I'm not sure anyone can do justice to a life in a handful of minutes. But I will try."

The man had the same aloof, slightly detached air about him that had made Ridley uneasy in their first meeting, but although he didn't appear to be breaking down over his wife's passing, there was a melancholy that had to be his way of displaying grief. No two people are alike, Ridley had learnt in his twenty-three years; whatever the emotion, each individual experienced, reacted to, and displayed their feelings differently.

Aldo turned back to the house and then paused. "María is working tonight, I believe. She will make you some dinner. Please use the same guest room as before and make yourself at home. She can help you with anything you might need – just ask."

Ridley nodded, and expected Aldo to leave, but he stood there looking at Ridley, thoughtfully.

"There's no hurry for you to leave after the services. With your mother gone, I understand there's little to keep you here, or bring you back here. But I would enjoy spending some time with you. Time we didn't have before."

He appeared to want to say something more, so Ridley waited, but after a hesitation he just nodded.

"I must attend to some business. I'm afraid the world doesn't stop on account of our personal tragedies. I will see you in the morning."

"Okay. And thank you," was all Ridley could muster as he watched Aldo walk away.

22

CARIBBEAN SEA – JULY 29, 2020

Using the GPS, but mainly the sonar on the basic fish-finder unit, they slowly ran along the edge of the underwater mountain top. The steeply sloping side of the bank was easy to see on the sonar screen, so fighting the current they were now running across was the biggest challenge. Guessing that Reg was also being dragged farther north-west by the current, AJ positioned the Newton close to the edge, hoping it put him 50 feet or so on top of the bank. Nora stood next to AJ and had been helpful showing her how they had used the instruments to make the first run earlier. Nora pointed to the top of the sonar screen.

"That looks like the corner already – this end is quite narrow."

AJ checked the screen and saw the edge of the bank turn ahead of them and veer in a more northerly direction.

"Yeah, see how it flares away from the opposite side? I was told it was more triangular shaped. The top side is much longer than the bottom here."

AJ started the turn and moved the boat farther away from the edge as they picked up the current to their stern. She also bumped the throttles back very slightly as they'd be carried faster. She looked between the speed the GPS showed and the boat's keel-mounted speedometer, and could see a 2 knot difference.

"They weren't wrong about the current out here either, it's ripping pretty good. It will take us a bit longer to get home than it did to come out – we'll be going straight into it," AJ said, absent-mindedly.

"That's why they sailed this way to go back to Europe," Nora replied. "The currents follow the winds and the winds sweep across the middle of the Caribbean then turn around Cuba and run along the Florida Straits, up the eastern coast of America, and finally across the Atlantic. I made good time heading west from the BVI."

AJ laughed. "So, that would be heading west on a sailboat then?"

Nora's expression turned serious. "Better I don't ever say the words. I don't want you to have to lie for me."

"Don't worry about it, I don't plan on saying anything," AJ reassured her. "But you're right, I'd prefer not to have to lie. An exclusion of all I know is not quite as bad as a lie."

AJ thought again about being stopped and searched that morning. Surely that was Whittaker's doing. She really liked the man and was sure he had no great desire to bust Nora. He had almost been amused when the sailboat had gone missing the same time Nora had disappeared. But he was a detective, and she knew he wouldn't turn a blind eye if he could prove the law had been broken. If Nora was right, and she had cleaned the sailboat well enough, then her only crime currently was not alerting the Immigration Department that she had returned to the island. That in itself was a pretty big deal during the pandemic lockdown. Of course, there was also the fact that she had disappeared in the first place, and the interest in her from the Norwegian authorities. None of those issues were criminal, as best AJ could tell, but they would certainly require some explaining.

"You don't have a husband," Nora said, surprising AJ. "Why not?"

AJ chuckled. She knew Scandinavians spoke more directly than the English, but she was still taken off guard. "Maybe I'm not desirable wife material."

Nora scoffed. "Are you crazy? You're beautiful, clever, funny, and you kick arse. Every man would want you."

AJ scoffed back, and blushed. "Oh, hush up," she said, waving a hand at Nora. "I don't think men quite see me that way. But I have a boyfriend, I just rarely get to see him."

"Who?" Nora asked.

"His name's Jackson, he works for Sea Sentry; you know, the environmental group?"

"Of course."

"Well, he's at sea most of the time, but fortunately they swing by Cayman on their way south and when they head back to their base on the east coast of America. He had retired from Sea Sentry after his last campaign, but then the pandemic hit. He was going to be stuck at home in California as he couldn't move to Cayman as planned, so he managed to get back aboard for another tour. Hopefully this COVID-19 business will be behind us soon, or at least under control, and he'll be able to move to the island." She smiled. "I can't wait."

"That's good you have someone, you deserve this. He's a good man? He treats you well?" Nora asked.

"Oh yes, he's super relaxed and easy going, unless it's about environmental stuff, then he gets really fired up," AJ replied, smiling. "But he makes me feel very special," she added quietly.

She heard footfalls on the ladder and Thomas joined them, carrying some fruit in a tin container.

"How long has he been down?" he asked, as he offered the women some of the sliced fresh fruit.

AJ looked at her watch. "About twenty-five minutes."

She looked behind the boat at the SMB bobbing along 200 feet behind them, and then back at the sonar screen.

"Looks like we're reaching the north corner, the edge is starting to curve west."

Looking at the GPS screen she pointed to a mark. "Ten or fifteen minutes and we'll be back to where we turned on the first run; we'll have done a lap of the perimeter."

Nora looked despondent and AJ quickly added, "Got this whole top edge to explore and then, who knows, maybe it's tucked away on the top where no one has actually dived yet. It's not like loads of people have been out here and dived the bank."

"Reg will be low on air soon," Thomas said, as AJ followed the edge of the bank around to face south-west and run down the final side they hadn't explored.

"Yeah, he's good on air for a big fella, but he'll still suck down a bit more than us. He's probably got another five minutes. I'll go in next. By the time we get him up I'll have been out of the water for over an hour," AJ said and looked at Nora. "I'll mark where we end his run on the GPS so you'll know where to start again when I get in, okay?"

Nora nodded.

"Hey!" Thomas said abruptly. "The SMB has stopped."

The women spun around and saw he was right, they were pulling away from the bright orange tube dancing on the surface. AJ shut the throttles down and took the boat out of gear.

"Check the tow line Thomas," she said, but he was already halfway down the ladder.

Once he reached the stern he began easily reeling in the line, indicating Reg had released it.

"He's off the line," Thomas called up.

"Let me know when it's clear," AJ shouted back down, not wanting to risk fouling the line in the props.

"Clear," Thomas called out.

AJ dropped the Newton in gear and began a wide circle back to where the SMB laid over at an angle as the current tried to drag it north-west. She checked her watch; he'd been down for over thirty minutes.

"He's low on gas I think, it's about the right dive time for him," she said to Nora. "Bigger people need more oxygen, same as a bigger car needs more petrol."

She let the boat drift and every thirty seconds or so engaged the transmissions and idled back towards the marker, adding the location to the GPS memory when she was close to the SMB before she forgot. After several more minutes, Reg broke through the surface and she carefully manoeuvred the Newton close to him and took it out of gear. Thomas flung a tag line off the stern, which Reg used to pull himself to the swim step where he climbed the ladder. AJ looked down from the top of the ladder as Reg took a seat and Thomas hauled in the SMB and its line.

"I'll do the next run, Reg, I can splash in a few minutes, we're nearly to the north-west corner again," she called down.

Reg looked up with water dripping from his hair and beard. "Did you mark the spot on the GPS?"

"Yup, I'll get ready and you can start me where you left off."

Reg slipped out of the shoulder straps of his BCD and nodded to Thomas. "Best take Thomas with you, I found something."

"What?" AJ said, scampering down the ladder. "I thought you were just done with your run."

Reg grinned. "I had about five minutes left."

"Well?" Nora said, joining them at the stern. "What did you find?"

Reg held up a hand, "Don't get too excited, it's no aeroplane, but it is the first man-made thing I've seen apart from fishing line and netting."

"What is it then?" AJ asked as they all huddled around Reg.

"I dunno," he replied. "It's a line of some sort. It's covered in growth but it runs straight so I know it's not natural, and it's too hefty to be any kind of fishing line, even a heavy rope to drag a net. It starts at a mound of rocks near the edge and goes over the side. The edge slopes away steeper than 45 degrees but not sheer like other parts, and I could see it run straight as a die as far as visibility would allow."

"Could it be a communications cable? You know, the kind they run across the ocean floor?" AJ asked.

Reg thought a moment. "I don't think so, I reckon they'd avoid going up and over something as shallow as the bank when they could easily go around it. Besides, they're on the chart I think. Didn't show any here."

"Could it be a chain?" Nora asked quietly.

Reg looked up at her and wrung sea water from his thick beard. "That would be my guess. Size is about right." He turned to AJ. "These two might be able to tell us if they'd get their arses into gear and go diving."

"Oh yeah, righty ho. Come on Thomas," AJ said as she collected her wetsuit from the railing. She began suiting up and thinking through what this dive would entail. They wouldn't be using tow lines, they'd just be diving, but the current would play havoc with them. Somehow, they had to leave the boat and reach the top of the bank at around 100 feet without getting swept off the top of the mountain out into the open sea.

"What's the floor like here, Reg?" she asked.

He finished struggling out of his wetsuit and sat back on the bench to catch his breath. "Mostly sand with this rim of exposed rock near the edge. It's not coral, at least it's not live coral, but there are some sponges and fans scattered about the place."

"Could we drop the hook?" AJ asked, zipping up the back of her suit.

"That's what I was thinking, but you may need to place it. I wouldn't want to drag it along – too easy to kill some live growth – but I reckon you could catch it on those rocks and it should hold against the current. That would work out nicely if we end up overnighting in this spot."

Thomas had switched both their rigs to new nitrox tanks while Reg was diving so AJ sat in front of her BCD and strapped in.

"How about you drop us 100 yards up current then drift back and lower the anchor over the sand. Try and put it 50 feet or so from the drop-off. Keep the boat idling into the current so it stays put and give me enough slack in the anchor line to move the anchor about. When I get it set I'll deploy the SMB as a signal. Then we can have a quick look around and see if it's worth exploring further. We'll use the anchor rope as an ascent line to do our safety stop."

Reg nodded. "Alright, that should work. If the SMB pops up beyond the drop-off I'll know you've been blown off the bank and I'll follow the marker until you surface. Just stay together if that happens, okay?"

"Yes sir," Thomas said. "If the boss gets blown away, I follow her."

"Hey," AJ held her hands up, "how come it's me that gets blown away? Could be you, then I'll have to allow myself to come after you."

Thomas beamed. "Nah, it'll be you, 'cos you'll be doing something crazy, and I'll just be hanging out laughing."

Reg laughed in his deep, raucous tone.

"Get the hell up there and pilot the boat, you don't need to be siding with him again," AJ said, pointing to the fly-bridge.

Nora smiled.

23

ACAPULCO, MEXICO – JULY 21, 2020

The drive to the church took only a few minutes, and Ridley was surprised when they pulled up in front of the non-denominational Capilla de la Paz on the hill overlooking the bay above Trujillo's mansion. He had wondered if the services would be held in the magnificent cathedral on the opposite side of the bay, the Sagrario Catedral Nuestra Señora de la Soledad. He certainly expected a Catholic church. He looked out the window of the Escalade at the relatively modest triangular shaped building with a strikingly large, white cross towering over it from the grounds alongside. He also noticed four armed men guarding both directions of the street, and at least six more around the front of the church. They openly displayed their assault rifles strung across their bodies. Tattoo exited the passenger seat and opened Aldo's door, standing to the rear, clearly shielding him. The man nodded his head to Ridley, indicating he should slide across the seat and follow. They walked briskly into the church entrance, where several guards closed in to remain outside the doors. The whole scene felt like something from a Scorsese movie. They were exciting to watch but Ridley quickly realised it was terrifying to be experiencing such a scene in real life.

The interior of the church had clean lines in the beams, benches and floor, using heavy, dark wood contrasted by white-painted walls angling up to the peak of the triangle. Rough-cut stone supported the wooden bench tops and covered the floor in an old-world, medieval feel. It was not a large church, yet only half the seats were filled. Ridley looked around at the attendees, wondering which ones were his mother's, and his, family members. The faces looking back didn't strike him as being poor, working-class people. The majority wore the fine cut suits of businessmen with wives on their arms in black, designer gowns. They all had several men seated either side who appeared to be personal protection. There were no children in the room, not one.

Ridley followed Aldo to a bench at the front, each row of attendees standing and bowing their heads as they passed. There, below the simple wooden pulpit, was the casket. A lump formed in Ridley's throat as he stared at the rectangular mahogany box containing his mother. A priest walked to the pulpit and began to speak, but Ridley didn't hear him. They all stood, they all sat, he followed along. He knew people would tell him he was lucky that his memories would be of her happy and laughing, enjoying their opportunity to be reunited. He had the wonderful memories of her from his childhood he could hang on to. They were right, to some degree. The two most vivid pictures he had in his mind at that moment were of the frail woman recovering from cancer treatment, and a wooden box. He was desperate to hold the image of her with long dark flowing hair as she danced with him in her arms. But he knew time was a vicious thief of memories, especially those from one's early years. His grasp was already slipping. The movies that played in his mind were becoming grainy, still pictures, replaced by the stronger, newer, high-resolution memory of a head scarf and a pale complexion. And now a beautifully carpentered wooden box.

The service was a blur. Before Ridley knew it they were walking out behind the crowd of who he suspected were nothing more than business associates of Aldo's. If the security outside was indeed necessary, he couldn't imagine anyone would want to attend the funeral unless they were made too.

"Were any of my mother's family here?" Ridley asked as they stood at the door waiting for Tattoo to clear them to leave.

Aldo slipped his sunglasses on and surveyed the road outside. "I didn't see any of them," he said in a detached tone.

"Did they know about the services?"

Aldo turned to him. "Of course, my secretary contacted them. But many of them are scattered about the country now," he replied, waving a hand. "She hardly ever saw them."

Tattoo nodded to his boss and they briskly walked to the car that was still by the kerb in front where they had left it. Ridley slid across the seat and started to put his seatbelt on.

"Don't put the belt on," Aldo said flatly as Tattoo closed the rear door and climbed in the front seat.

Ridley looked at him, puzzled. "No? Why don't you wear a seatbelt?"

Aldo appeared to be staring ahead but Ridley noticed his eyes were darting around, checking the area was clear. For a moment he thought he wasn't going to reply, but he finally spoke quietly.

"If you need to move quickly, it's one more thing to slow you down."

Ridley wondered why he might need to move quickly from what he guessed to be a fortified vehicle, with two armed guards up front, but then again he'd never been to a funeral, or any private event for that matter, that required armed guards. He left his seatbelt off.

It was a short drive back to the house, where it appeared the attendees had thinned out. They parked and walked inside where a spread of food was laid out on long catering tables near the kitchen. The expensive suits all nodded when Aldo was near, but Ridley noticed none of them spoke a word to him, unless he addressed them first. The whole event had a sterile, tense air, as though the crowd were unwilling players in a strange charade. Ridley saw Rosie in the kitchen. She was refilling a pitcher with juice and he realised how comforting it felt to see someone he knew. An employee he had barely interacted with felt at least like a connection to his mother who had seemed to like the girl. She glanced up and caught him looking her way. He smiled, but she quickly looked away.

"Let's take a walk."

Aldo's voice came from behind him. He turned and gladly followed him to the garden, anything to get away from the strange gathering that had nothing to do with his mother. Even if it was with the man who must have orchestrated the event.

"Cigar?" Aldo offered as they walked once more down the path between the pools.

"No, thank you," Ridley replied and watched Aldo light his cohiba.

Plumes of smoke emanated into the air as Aldo puffed on the cigar until an even burn glowed across the tip. Aldo held a hand out, indicating Ridley should sit at the table by the edge of the garden.

"I'm sorry today is not more..." Aldo started, then paused to collect his thoughts, "...personal, I suppose."

Ridley waited while the man took a long draw on his cigar before slowly exhaling as though he were pushing the stress from his body along with the smoke.

"My business situation is, well, as you have seen by the protection we have here, it can be... volatile. There are dangerous people who make a living preying on the wealthy in Mexico. As you can see, your mother and I live well..." He faltered again, clearly realising the present tense no longer applied to his wife. He pressed on. "My point being, we had to forgo certain things, such as eating out and socialising as most people enjoy, so our circle of friends became the business associates we could trust."

Ridley pointed to the house. "These people all work for you?"

"Most of them, yes. Some are men I do business with, but most manage my various concerns here in Acapulco."

"What business are you in?" Ridley asked, wondering how the man would reply.

"I have properties, a couple of restaurants, some nightclubs, many different investments," he replied nonchalantly. "I try to stay diversified. I would like it if you stuck around a few days, I could show you some of what we do here."

"Thank you, maybe I could visit again another time. I do need to fly back tomorrow," Ridley replied.

He expected the man to be glad to see the back of him; he felt like a loose end or a spare part in Trujillo's life, so his invitation surprised him.

"Why the hurry? You're here now, why not stay a little longer. I can have your flight changed. It would do us both good to spend some time together." He turned to Ridley, although he couldn't see his eyes behind the sunglasses. "Maybe we can help each other through this time. We will both grieve more than anyone over the loss of Zanita."

When his thoughts were drawn back to his mother they struck him like blows to his chin and emotions streaked through his brain like electric shocks. There was guilt, for his mind having left the thoughts of her, and the lump in his throat that threatened tears he wouldn't be able to control. He found Aldo incredibly hard to read, and with his own soul torn open and raw, he knew he wasn't in the best place for making decisions. But as much as he wanted to soak up anything keeping him close to his mother, the idea of staying in this place left him... What did it make him feel? He realised he didn't really know. Maybe it was the strange day, and the services, perhaps it was the pain of the moment, rather than the place. Whatever the feeling was, he wanted away from it, and more than that he needed the arms of his girlfriend around him. She was where he wanted to be; wherever that was, he could only guess.

"I'm afraid I do need to return, I've left my girlfriend taking a journey on her own, I must join her as soon as possible," he said, hoping he didn't sound ungrateful.

Aldo shrugged his shoulders, "I understand." His tone had brightened to Ridley's relief, and he didn't appear offended. "Your mother told me you were heading out on an adventure – I'm jealous, I must say. Tell me about it."

Ridley smiled. "Oh it's probably just a waste of time. An old tale my grandfather told me before he died; we're going to try and find his plane he had to ditch into the sea."

"My God, that sounds incredible. You are a diver?"

"I am, but I'll probably need some help if we do find the plane, from what I understand it's in tricky waters," Ridley said, glad to be talking about something he was excited about.

"I have access to boats and professional divers; if I can be of help in any way, please tell me. I don't wish to intrude on your adventure, but I would very much enjoy being involved if I can be of use."

"That's very kind of you, but as I say, there's every chance we'll find nothing," Ridley said, wondering whether he was being foolish turning down expert help.

"What do you hope to find in the plane?" Aldo asked enthusiastically.

Ridley looked down at the table. Outside of his immediate family, Nora was the only person he'd ever discussed this story with, so why he was opening up to this relative stranger, he didn't know. Maybe the emotions of the moment again, or maybe because his mother saw fit to marry the man, he couldn't decide. But something told him he had shared enough.

"Just to find the plane will be enough, no one else cares about it outside my family," Ridley answered carefully.

Aldo took a long draw on his cigar and fell silent for a while. They both gazed across the bay and fell into their own thoughts. Finally, Aldo rose from the table.

"Let me clear these people from the house, I would prefer a quiet evening. What do you think?"

Ridley nodded. "I'd prefer that too."

Aldo took a step towards the house and paused, looking back. "Please, consider staying just a day or two. I think it may benefit us both."

He continued on to the house, leaving Ridley wondering what these benefits might be.

24

CARIBBEAN SEA – JULY 29, 2020

AJ felt more comfortable descending without the extra ballast she had carried when they were being towed. She was back to her usual 4lbs, which meant she could control most of her buoyancy adjustments with her lungs, rather than by air in and out of her BCD. She could perform most dives without any ballast at all, but with a buoyant wetsuit, and an aluminium tank that lost 5lbs of mass between full and empty, it was wise to be safely weighted on the heavy side. The current took them immediately, but when she looked up, the boat was still overhead, carried by the same current on the surface. AJ turned head down and kicked her fins, speeding up her descent to make sure they didn't clear the bank before they reached the bottom. She kept an eye on Thomas who was close by but slightly above her. He kicked a little harder and pulled back level with her. The sea floor quickly appeared as they dropped, and AJ scanned ahead to try and locate the line of rocks Reg had described. A hard edge appeared at the far reaches of visibility at the same time they met the sea floor. Once they neutralised their buoyancy a few feet above the large expanse of sand and crushed coral, the effect of the current greatly lessened, and they were able to fin gently to stay in place.

From 100 feet down, she looked towards the surface and could make out the silhouette of the Newton backlit by the bright sunshine, still directly over them, but now turned into the direction of the current. She spotted a splash from ahead of the bow and watched the anchor fall towards them. It was pulled by the current as it dropped, so AJ and Thomas spun around and let the water float them towards where the anchor finally hit the sand. Thomas kicked ahead and grabbed the heavy Danforth-style anchor before it began to drag and bury its flukes into the soft grainy sand. He could shuffle the mass but without adding a lot of air to his BCD he couldn't float it. The danger would be with enough air in his BCD to float the 40lb anchor, he would shoot towards the surface if he dropped it. AJ looked ahead and could see the line of rocks less than 40 feet away. She checked on the boat and could tell Reg had Hazel's Odyssey holding steady above. He had also released plenty of slack in the anchor line as she could see it waving loosely in the water column. She joined Thomas, and with the two of them heaving and using their knees for leverage on the sea floor, they were able to manoeuvre the anchor towards the rocks. They dodged around several clumps of sea fans and one large orange tube sponge colony, both of which would have been in danger of getting scraped from the bottom if they had simply deployed the anchor and let it drag until it caught.

As they neared the rocks AJ could make out·the line that Reg had spotted. It was encrusted with years of coral growth, cloaking the identity of whatever was beneath. They finally reached the rocks and nosed the flukes into the base. They were both breathing hard and at 100 feet that meant they were consuming a lot of nitrox. As she let her breathing settle down, AJ pulled the trusty SMB from her BCD pocket and tied the end of the line to the anchor shackle. With a short burst of gas from her regulator, the SMB took off towards the surface. Now, as long as it doesn't go straight up into the boat's props we'll be fine, she thought. The current took care of sweeping the orange tube behind the idling boat and it surfaced well clear of the stern. AJ checked her computer; they had already been down there for fifteen minutes and she had used a third of her tank with the exertion. They needed to work fast. First thing, she decided, was to identify the line. She looked over the edge at the slope, which was steep but well short of vertical. The line ran straight down the side, seemingly cutting its way through coral growths, although, more likely, the coral had formed over the line. Thomas waved to get her attention and pointed to the rocks where the line appeared to start. Coral had not grown over most of the rocks, but had where the line landed. She moved closer and followed Thomas's finger as he traced the outline of something. An older hook-style anchor. Right at the top of the anchor's shank, she could make out a rusty ring connected to the first link of an equally rusted and pitted chain. From there, the growth covered it, making it appear like a heavy, colourful rope.

They both peered over the rocks at the line disappearing into the murkiness of the depths. Questions raced through her mind, but none could be answered without going deeper. The maximum safe depth on 32% nitrox was 111 feet; below that there was a risk of oxygen toxicity from the large volume of oxygen being inhaled at that depth. Meanwhile 132 feet was known as the contingency depth. The 111 number was based from averages, and 132 feet was the absolute maximum a diver should ever go on 32% nitrox. Oxygen toxicity would cause vision issues, muscle twitching and finally convulsions, making it almost impossible to breathe, generally resulting in a diver drowning. Not an outcome she desired, but as a female with good physical fitness and strong lungs, AJ knew she should fall well above the average those warnings were derived from. She had to look. Signalling for Thomas to stay by the rocks, she finned over the edge and began descending the slope, following the chain.

She kept a careful eye on her depth, while scanning below, hoping something would come into view. The chain most likely had nothing on the end, she thought, abandoned long ago by fishermen who couldn't free it from the rocks when they went to move on. But there was only one way to know. AJ heard the familiar echoing clang of metal on metal and turned to look back up the slope. Thomas was peering over the side, tapping his tank with a carabiner and pointing straight out into the deep blue. AJ looked out in the direction of his finger and took a sudden gulp of air. One of the biggest sharks she had ever seen was slowly cruising by less than 60 feet away. By the faint stripes along its body, and its impressive size, she could tell it was a mature female tiger shark. She knew she had a much better chance of being struck by lightning on the surface than to be attacked by the shark, but it still took her breath away. She was close enough to see the rows of jagged, flesh-ripping teeth in the mouth of the beast as it curiously passed her by and continued into the darkness out of view. She looked back up at Thomas. He had his hands spread apart, signalling he thought it was really big. No shit, she thought, and gave him an okay sign back.

She checked her computer. She was at 122 feet, and below there was no sign of the chain doing anything other than continuing into the depths. She finned down and carefully watched her computer. It showed 130 feet and only three more minutes at this depth before she would go into deco. Damn it, she cursed to herself, we'll have to use the trimix tomorrow to go any farther, and we still have no idea if this is a waste of time. If it was a goose chase, then they would lose valuable time and diving gas looking down here instead of elsewhere. She looked at her computer and let herself drop the final two feet and levelled at 132 feet below the surface. She stared down into the deep blue below her, and let her eyes adjust to the gloom. Surely she was imagining what began to take shape? She squinted, focused and stared intently at the end of the chain. No, she was sure there was something there. It could just be a clump of coral or a rock outcrop, she told herself, but it really looked like a uniform profile. She couldn't stay at this depth any longer; she knew she had to leave but she desperately wanted to go just a little farther. Whatever it was appeared to be quite big. All she could make out was a darker shadow in a background of darkness. There was no way to tell what it was and she could only guess at the depth based on the visibility they had already experienced. She was at 132 feet and could only just make out a shape which put the object at around 200 feet. She knew she had already pushed her luck on the safe diving scales. She turned and finned back up the slope towards Thomas, who anxiously watched her approach. They wasted no time. As soon as she reached him they both hooked an arm around the anchor line up to the Newton, and began their ascent.

Back aboard Hazel's Odyssey, AJ did her best to explain what she saw, or at least what she thought she saw.

"I've no idea what it is, but it's a decent size and the chain leads right to it."

"What shape is it?" Reg asked with one foot resting on the bench next to AJ.

"A block, sort of… I don't know, Reg, it was just a dark image, but not quite as dark as the deep water below it. I could barely make it out, but there's something there for sure."

He nodded. "But you couldn't see wings or nothing?"

AJ rolled her eyes. "Oh yeah, there were wings, I just forgot to mention that." She grinned at Reg.

"Cheeky little bugger. You deserve a bollocking for going down that deep, I've got a good mind to ban you from diving the rest of the trip."

AJ frowned. "It's my boat. I'm in charge on my boat, that's maritime law."

Thomas laughed, while Nora couldn't stop smiling as she listened to them banter and play with each other, as only great friends can do.

"What are you cackling at?" Reg growled, looking at Thomas. "You were her dive buddy, why did you let her go to 132 feet?"

Thomas held his hands up, "She's my boss, big boss, and to be fair now, I did say she would do something crazy."

AJ smacked Thomas on the arm and Reg shrugged his shoulders. "True enough, you did call it."

"What do we do now?" Nora asked.

"Nothing," Reg replied. "Next thing is to dive deeper to get a better look, and to do that we need the trimix gas. Can't get back in the water after the dives we made already today. Not for a decompression dive anyway. I guess I could, if we waited until the end of the day, as I only did one dive. But the safer thing to do is wait until the morning and the two of us can dive together." He looked sternly at AJ. "Hear that, Miss Wingnut; safer thing to do."

AJ stuck her tongue out at him.

"What about the sonar?" Nora asked, still smiling at them both. "Could we see what it is on the sonar?"

"Hmmm, maybe," Reg said. "Worth a look. Only thing is, unless it's pretty much below us we won't see it and we can't really move unless we pull the anchor. Which we're not doing."

They moved up to the fly-bridge and huddled around the fish-finder. AJ turned the power on and they waited for the screen to clear from a grainy image to a clearer profile of the sea floor below them. The current had the Newton out over the edge of the bank with the anchor line angling back to the rock ridge. Using the 3D view directly below the boat, the screen clearly showed the sloping side of the underwater mountain. AJ started the diesel engines. After letting them idle for a minute she put them both in gear and moved the boat ahead against the current, giving the sonar a better footprint to read. Once she was directly over the anchor line, she took the boat out of gear and let the current pull them back again. Before the line went tight, she engaged the transmissions once more, using them to slow their rearward movement in the current until the anchor line went tight again, making sure she didn't wrench on the anchor. With the extra passes over the terrain below, the sonar gave a more defined image of the slope. They all leaned in and peered at the odd-looking lump around the 200-foot mark. It didn't show a distinct shape, but clearly there was some form of structure there, protruding above the slope.

"Could be a pile of rocks." Reg said. "Or it could be a school bus."

The other three looked at him. "Or maybe it's an aeroplane," He added with a smirk under his beard.

"If it is the plane, which I say it is, where are these diamonds supposed to be hidden?" Thomas asked.

"Dingo told Ridley they were in a tobacco tin, behind the dashboard," Nora replied.

"That might have rusted through by now," Reg said thoughtfully. "Do you know how it was held there?"

"I don't, I'm sorry."

Something moved on the screen, coming from their port side.

"Looks like it's time to go fishing," Reg said, cheerfully.

Thomas and AJ looked at each other.

"Err, I don't think you want to catch that." AJ said as the fishfinder showed a large mass moving across the screen at around 80 feet down.

"That's a school of something," Reg said. "Might be tuna out here."

Thomas laughed. "Nah, that's the biggest tiger shark I ever seen, Reg, he dropped by and said hi when we were down there."

"Oh shit," Nora blurted out.

25

ACAPULCO, MEXICO – JULY 22, 2020

The evening had passed quietly. It was strange being in the large house with Aldo, and without Zanita. Ridley had hoped Rosie would be around; he wanted to talk to her about his mother, but she had disappeared after the gathering dispersed, and María had prepared their dinner. Ridley felt guilty picking around the plate of delicious food the woman had taken the effort to serve; he hated the waste, but he had no appetite. He knew it was her job to make it whether he ate it or not, but he hoped she didn't take it personally. Likely, she would give anything to have that food to feed her own family.

Aldo had made small talk, and brought up the search for his grandfather's plane a few more times, but Ridley had steered the conversation elsewhere. He had turned in early and sent Nora a note via the blog site they used to communicate. They kept everything in a coded form that wouldn't mean much to anyone else. Dates were offset, places were discussed by longitude and latitude, rather than name, with six degrees added to the figures. In the unlikely event that someone looking for Nora would find their blog, they would have more work to do to decipher anything left there. Ridley told her he would try and fly to Jamaica the following day. The island had opened its borders and with one flight change Ridley hoped he could meet her there as she sailed past.

His sleep had been fitful, but in the early hours exhaustion had overcome him, and the final few hours passed by. He quietly gathered his few things and walked through the house towards the front door. There was no sign of Aldo and he made a mental note to call him in a day or two and thank him for his hospitality, and his offers of help. Outside, it was still dark but the Escalade was running with Tattoo standing by the open tailgate. Ridley tossed his bags in the back and took a seat in the rear. He automatically began to put his belt on, then stopped himself. He almost laughed out loud. No one is interested in me, he thought, but there again, they may not know who was in the car. He left the belt off. They pulled out of the gate and Ridley tipped his head back, relaxed, and closed his eyes. He felt some of the tension drain away as they drove down the road and left Trujillo's mansion. Soon he would be with Nora and everything would be better. He really didn't care if they found his grandfather's plane or not; he hoped they did, but it was more about the time and the experience with her. He was young to be thinking about building memories, but his convoluted upbringing, and especially the emotional roller-coaster of the last few months with his mother, had proven how special these moments in time can be. He already knew these snapshots capturing the joy, the disappointment, the elation, and the pain of events that were shaping his life, were precious milestones.

The SUV screeched to a halt and Ridley lurched forward, slamming against the back of the front passenger seat. Voices shouted from inside and outside the car as his door was flung open and powerful hands wrenched him from the vehicle. He was being dragged across the pavement and he struggled to get his feet under him as he swung wildly at his assailants without landing a blow. He couldn't see their faces, and it all seemed a blur in the darkness. The sound of gunshots echoed loudly around him and he felt a second pair of hands flip him over face down against the pavement. A knee pinned him down, digging painfully into his back, scraping his cheek against the gritty surface. His shoulders screamed as his arms were pulled behind him and some kind of restraint cinched around his wrists, burying into his skin. He tried to kick but someone was sitting on his legs and his ankles were forced together by more restraints. He heard the sound of zip ties tightening as the shooting had appeared to stop. His head was yanked back by his hair and a bag pulled over his head. His heart pounded and the bag sucked in against his lips as he gasped for air. Lifted under each arm, he was dragged again, picked up and dropped heavily into what he assumed was the back of a vehicle.

"I'm not who you think!" he wheezed. "You have the wrong guy."

The boot, or the tailgate, slammed shut and he felt the vehicle rock as people got in and closed the doors. The engine was already running and the driver quickly moved away. Everything became strangely quiet. He expected squealing tyres and erratic driving, but all he could here was a soft purring of the motor above his own heartbeat and heavy breathing. He thought of trying to sense the turns they were making, but he didn't know where they were when they were ambushed, so he had no point of reference. He tried to breathe gently and calm himself. There was nothing he could do while tied up except try and get them to talk. Maybe he could learn who they were and more importantly convey who he was; a person of no interest to them. But what if he did convince them he was of no use? What would they do then? Clearly they weren't worried about pissing off Trujillo as they just ambushed his car. Once they figured out they had grabbed someone of no value they probably wouldn't take him back and say sorry. More likely they would shoot him and dump his body, he concluded despairingly. If they were out to execute Trujillo, they would have shot him at the scene. Why kidnap Aldo? You don't kidnap the person with the money, you kidnap the person that means something to the guy with the money. Damn, he thought, could they possibly think I'm of value to Aldo Trujillo. Surely not. Am I of value to him? His first thought was no, why would Aldo care. Ridley was technically his stepson, or was until his mother died, but they hardly knew each other at all. Although, Aldo had no children of his own, and he had repeatedly asked Ridley to stay and spend more time with him. But all that had transpired in the last twenty-four hours, how would anyone know? His thoughts were interrupted as the vehicle slowed, and by the bumps he guessed they were pulling into a driveway. They hadn't travelled that far, although at the early hour with little traffic it may have been farther than he thought. Scared and in pain, every minute felt like an eternity. They drove slowly for a little longer and he wondered if they had pulled inside a building. The engine noise hadn't changed so he decided they were still outside. The vehicle stopped and doors opened. His heart began to race again as he considered the possibility they had reached the spot they had chosen to execute him. The back of the vehicle opened and they dragged him out. It must be an SUV, he noticed, as they didn't lift him. Two men began dragging him again and he panted frantically wondering if he was about to be thrown from a cliff or dumped in the ocean. The ground beneath his feet felt different, smoother than the tarmac of the road, more like concrete he guessed as his trainers scraped and wore against the surface. He heard a door open, not a car door, but the door to a building, and the footsteps picked up an echo as they entered inside. An aroma followed them in, mixing with the smell of his own sweat as he was pushed down into the seat of a chair.

"Where am I? Who are you people?" he babbled, and realised he must sound like every TV show victim cliché.

Another restraint was looped through his wrist ties, and as his hands were pulled against the chair back, he sensed he was now strapped to the furniture.

"I need to use the head," he muttered.

"Go ahead," a gruff voice replied with a laugh.

Another voice grunted and he heard a slap, followed by angry, stifled whispers. Apparently their orders were not to speak. The door closed and the room fell silent. Ridley tried to settle his breathing once more, so he could hear any movement. Nothing.

Was he alone, or was someone still in the room, motionless. The blindness was terrifying, and his mind began a relentless assault of possibilities, feeding the fear. What, or whom, had they left him in the room with? If he tipped the chair over to try and break it apart, would he plummet off, or into something? He growled under his breath to regain control of his imagination. He needed to stay calm and keep his wits about him.

As he settled down, it came to him. Mexican honeysuckle. That was the fragrance. Mexican honeysuckle.

26

CARIBBEAN SEA – JULY 29, 2020

It was 3:30pm, with less than four hours until the sun would be setting. Reg and Thomas rummaged through the tackle box Thomas's father, Jeremiah, had provided. As they didn't have bait they would need to catch something smaller to use to entice a larger fish, unless they found a suitable lure in the box. The two women watched from the shade below the fly-bridge and occasionally threw helpful comments at the would-be fishermen. Thomas had grown up fishing on his father's boat so he had a good idea what he was doing, and Reg let him take the lead, especially with the audience adding their critique. Thomas held up a couple of jigs he deemed appropriate, and once they'd rigged their lines they cast off the stern. The current pulled their lures away over the deep water until they reeled them back in and repeated the process.

"Reckon we'd have better luck if we were over the bank itself. Out here we're likely to hit nothing, or hit bigger than we can handle," Reg said, after twenty minutes without a bite.

"True enough," Thomas said, leaning against the dive steps, appearing to enjoy the relaxing afternoon. "But we'd have to move the boat to get over the bank."

"Yeah, we're not doing that," Reg said, casting again.

AJ nudged Nora and whispered, "You'll get a laugh out of this."

"How's it going boys?" she called out loudly. "Getting any bites out there?"

Reg turned and scoffed at her. "Seen any fish on the boat yet?"

"No, not any I've noticed," AJ replied. "What do you think you gonna catch when you do get a bite?"

Reg shrugged his shoulders. "Snapper, maybe a tuna over the blue water here." He looked over at Thomas.

"There'll be some wahoo out here for sure," Thomas said, slowly reeling in his line, keeping the lure submerged.

"Oooh, that all sounds really tasty," AJ said, winking at Nora and trying not to laugh. "And when you guys land all these wahoo and tuna and snapper, how you gonna cook them?"

The two men looked over at each other and burst out laughing.

"Sushi?" Reg said, as they both brought their lines in. "Tell you what though, we better catch something when we head back in, or there'll be some explaining to do if they stop us again. And my guess is they will." Reg looked over at AJ who had finally stopped laughing. "Whittaker had something to do with us being stopped, don't you think?"

"Yeah, that's what I reckon," AJ replied. "He's smart, he knows Nora's back on the island. He made up his mind when the sailboat reappeared."

Nora shuffled nervously next to AJ. "There's no evidence on that sailboat, and if he finds a hair or something like he says, that doesn't prove who borrowed the boat, it just means that person was probably aboard at some point." Nora swung her feet in the air and looked at the deck. "If I've been on the island the whole time, I could have slept on the boat sometime. I'd be guilty of trespassing. For more than that the police must prove I've been somewhere else with the boat."

Reg walked over, sat on the bench in the shade and wiped the sweat from his brow. "For how long did you have a visa or stamp to be in the Cayman Islands?"

Nora looked up and frowned. "That is more of a problem. My

student visa the resort used to show we were legally on the island expired."

Reg nodded. "Yeah, figured as much. Unfortunately, that's what they could use on you. Either you stayed on the island and outstayed your visa, or you returned illegally to the island while our borders are closed. Both ways they can prosecute you."

"I thought they extended or waived some of the visa stuff for workers and what not that were stuck on the island when the lockdown started?" AJ said, hopefully.

"True," Reg replied. "But you were supposed to notify them and request an extension online, I think. But it still might be a loophole you could work with."

Nora bit her lip. "I disappeared before, I can disappear again," she said quietly.

AJ gave her a friendly nudge with her elbow. "Hopefully, it won't come to that, but we've got an aeroplane to find before you have to deal with it, so best we plan out our dive for the morning," she said, and jumped to her feet. "Grab your laptop, Reg, let's figure out how we'll pull this off."

Nora managed a smile as Reg stepped down into the cabin to retrieve his computer.

"How deep will you have to go?" Nora asked.

AJ laughed. "Well, that's the question we have to figure out. With tech diving you have to be really precise with the depth you plan for, as the gas you'll use for the dive and then the decompression stops changes dramatically with depth."

Reg reappeared with his laptop and sat next to AJ.

"I'm guessing from the sonar, and what I could see, that whatever it is at the end of the chain is around 200 feet down. What do you think, Reg?"

Reg hit the power button and thought a moment while it booted. "I think that's a reasonable guess. If we dive first thing tomorrow, shortly after sun-up, we'll be able to dive again later in the afternoon, or early evening. Means the first dive can be a quick look around. If it is the aeroplane, we can size up what we'll need for the second dive. If it's a school bus or a pile of rocks, we can resume our search pattern over the rest of the bank, with Thomas taking first shift."

Thomas had finished putting away the fishing gear and joined the group in the shade. "We won't be trolling no more. That's the plane down there. I feel sure it is." He beamed, and AJ chuckled at her friend's unflinching optimism.

"Let's plan around the first dive being 210 feet; if it's less, all the better," Reg said as he opened the tech diving software. "No point planning a lot deeper as it would mean we couldn't, or at least shouldn't, get back in later in the day. By 210 feet we'll know if it's a plane and, if it is, whether it's penetrable. That's all we need from the first dive. Second dive we'll adjust when we know what we're dealing with."

"Sounds good," AJ agreed. "What type of plane are we looking for again?" she asked, looking at Nora.

"What, in case it's not the plane we're looking for?" Reg interrupted with a laugh.

"No, you wally," she replied, rolling her eyes. "I want to know what access points it might have."

"I don't know much about planes, but Ridley showed me a picture on his computer. It was cool looking, all shiny like it was polished metal, and it had two engines," Nora said, clearly trying to recall the image.

"We should have done some Googling before we left, eh?" Reg said. "We don't have any mobile signal out here to get Internet. Be nice to have a picture."

"I didn't help you there, as I didn't tell you what we were diving before we left. Sorry," Nora replied. "I do know it has a door towards the tail on the left side. No doors by the pilot. But on the right side there was a hole in the body where the propeller went through."

"That helps though," Reg said. "So how big would you say it is? It's not the size of jetliner, right? More like a twin prop regional commuter?"

Nora thought for a second. "I guess it would have carried about 10 or 12 people, that size."

Reg nodded. "Alright, that's good to know. So if it is down there, it will be tight to get inside and we have to assume the door was closed, so the hole in the fuselage will be the only way in."

"Unless the windscreen is gone," Thomas said.

"Good point," Reg agreed, "but if the windows are still intact they'll be covered in growth. We need to take plenty of light with us."

"I brought two torches and some spare rechargeable batteries so we should be okay," AJ said. "I assume we'll be carrying four tanks?"

Reg had been making inputs into the dive software and with a final entry he angled the laptop towards AJ so she could see.

"Yeah, here's the profile. Fortunately, most of the deco will be on the anchor line. We'll use doubles of the trimix and carry one nitrox 50%, and an oxygen tank."

"You'll have all those tanks with you?" Nora asked. "How do you carry them all and still swim around?"

"We use a different style of BCD," AJ explained. "The ones you saw us use today, and what you would have used when you had a go at diving, are regular recreational BCDs. We'll use a harness and plate system that's designed to carry the extras. We'll have the two larger tanks on our backs and then one smaller tank slung on each side. It's quite balanced but a bit cumbersome."

"How will you fit inside the plane with all that on?" Nora asked.

"We might not," Reg said, raising his eyebrows. "If we can't safely penetrate the fuselage we'll have to figure out something else."

"What else can you do?" Nora asked. "Bring the plane up?"

Reg laughed. "No love, that's not an option, at least for us it's not. We might be able to cut our way in – you know, make a bigger hole – but we don't have any gear for that with us."

Nora bit her lip again. "Yeah, sorry, I should have told you more about it before we left, I just didn't know if I could…" She trailed off and looked away.

"Trust us?" Reg finished for her.

She shrugged her shoulders.

He leaned over and squeezed her shoulder. "That's alright dear, I don't blame you. No way to know until you spend some time around people. Hopefully you think we're okay now?"

She smiled. "Of course."

AJ stood up and put her hands on her hips. "Right then, I'm gonna put my gear together for the morning and write out the plan on my slate. Then, I'm going to bust out my camping stove and make a delicious meal of 'not fresh fish' for dinner."

27

ACAPULCO, MEXICO – JULY 26, 2020

Ridley had lost all sense of time. It felt like he had been held for weeks, but he guessed it was probably four days. They gave him water on what appeared to be a routine, three times on a shorter interval, and then a longer break. He presumed the longer break was overnight, hence this was the fourth day, as there had been three long intervals. On the first day he had shuffled around and checked the immediate vicinity with his feet. His hands were going numb and his whole body ached from being tied in the same position. He couldn't feel anything around him so he'd finally tipped the chair over and crashed to the ground. He hit hard, which hurt his shoulder, but the new position was a relief – for a while. When they came in they never said a word, picked him upright, shoved the water bottle in his mouth for a few seconds and left again. Since then, he had shuffled the chair farther afield, trying to figure out the layout of the room. From what he could tell it seemed to be square in shape and no bigger than 15 feet across. He had felt no framework along the walls suggesting a window, and there seemed to be one door. He couldn't remember now whether it felt like they dragged him through a hallway, or other room, before ending up in the one he was in.

His requests for a toilet had been ignored and he had finally succumbed to urinating on himself. The discomfort, smell and humiliation brought him close to tears, but his anger kept them at bay. Time became his worst enemy. Too much time to think, too much time to hurt, and too much time in fear. His hunger had steadily grown at the same pace that his strength withered away. It was easier to sleep lying on the floor, so more and more he tipped the chair over and tried to let the time pass while he slept. The pain from his restraints and the cramps he was beginning to get in his limbs usually woke him, and the best he could manage was short periods of unconsciousness. Over and over he kept asking himself, why? Why would they take him? If they were making demands of Aldo, apparently it wasn't working. When would they send him a finger or an ear? Wasn't that what these people did? That's what they did in the movies. At what point would they believe Aldo, when the man told them he didn't care what they did to his dead wife's son?

Nora was also a big problem. Clinging to thoughts of her was his lifeline, his hope, his determination to find a way out of this. The idea she would never know what happened to him was his worst nightmare. It destroyed him to think she might believe he had abandoned her; returned to Mexico and found another life to live, one that didn't include her. He dozed in and out of sleepy visions of her standing alone on the sailboat, searching the horizon for the man who had told her he loved her. More than anything in this world, he wanted to be with her. Saying the words 'I love you' was simply a gesture, a phrase used so commonly nowadays it had lost its true meaning. He needed the time. The time to show her how much he loved her. The time he was sure these men were robbing from him.

The door opening stirred Ridley awake, and he braced himself for the rough jolt of being pulled upright. He licked his lips and tried to moisten his dry mouth in preparation for the onslaught of water. He needed as much as they would give him but they squeezed a plastic bottle and it came out so quickly he tended to choke and splutter a lot of it away. He breathed heavily in anticipation. The stench was awful so he tried to breathe through his mouth, but then the hood sucked to his lips and made him feel claustrophobic, like someone was smothering him. The footsteps got louder, but something was different. It was usually two men, but there were more this time. He couldn't tell if there was a third person or ten more, he just knew the sound of footfalls had changed. He was quickly sat up, and the chair dragged a few feet across the room. He readied himself for the hood to be lifted enough for the water bottle to be shoved in his mouth but nothing happened. Silence. His panting breath was all he could hear, and his own sweat and piss was all he could smell. He tightly clenched his fingers, expecting the blade or the cutters to select a digit and the unimaginable pain that would follow. His weakened muscles tensed and shivered as his breaths turned unwillingly to grunts.

"Where were you going?" A man's voice he didn't recognise asked in Spanish.

Ridley was thrown off guard, and relieved at the same time. He tried to gather his thoughts, but his mind was slow to focus and it took him a moment.

"Huh? Where was I going? I was… I was going to the airport," he finally said.

"To fly where?"

"I was flying home," Ridley mumbled in confusion. Why did they care where he was going? Who the hell were these people? He was thoroughly bewildered. The question had no bearing on any scenarios he had conjured up over the past few days.

"Why would you lie to me?" the man asked flatly.

"Lie? I'm not lying," Ridley replied, further confused.

"You don't live in Jamaica," the man said firmly.

Ridley realised with a surge of fear, the man was right.

"I'm sorry, you're right, I changed my flight to go to Jamaica instead of Tortola."

"Why?"

Ridley felt like a boxer on the ropes, taking a barrage of body punches, yet the man had only asked him a simple question. He realised his exhaustion and fear had reduced him to a babbling fool. He needed to pull himself together.

"Could I have some water please?"

"Answer me, and you can have some water."

He needed more time to think clearly. The last thing he wanted to do was mention Nora, but how could he explain switching his travel? If he started intentionally lying he would be on a slippery slope from which he would unlikely be able to arrest his fall.

"I planned to meet a friend there."

He heard footsteps and the hood was loosened around his neck and pulled up. The water bottle cut his dried lip as it was shoved unsympathetically into his mouth, and he heard the crinkle of plastic a moment before the surge of water filled his mouth and throat. He choked, spluttered and gulped as much water as he could manage, which wasn't a lot. His shirt was soaked and the water washed down across his jeans igniting the foul stench of his own urine once more. The hood was once more cinched around his neck and he panted against the opaque fabric. He heard a few, light footfalls again, and he presumed the man had moved back in front of him. He guessed he had moved away in case Ridley had managed a peek from below the hood. That might be a good sign, if they don't want to be seen, he thought; if they planned to kill him regardless, they wouldn't worry about him seeing them. Or, maybe they thought it was more intimidating to remain unseen, leaving one more thing out of their captive's control.

"Who?" the man asked.

"A girl I met," he said, hanging onto a truth without saying her name.

There was a pause.

"Where were you going, the two of you?"

He was sure the man was going to pursue a name, so he was relieved he had moved on.

"We were going to sail around the Caribbean for a few weeks," Ridley said, telling the truth while avoiding any detail.

"Where first, after Jamaica?" the man continued, maintaining his flat, even tone.

"The Cayman Islands," Ridley replied, perplexed why any of this was of interest to his kidnappers.

"To do what?"

"What do you mean?"

"What did you plan to do in the Cayman Islands? Their borders are closed to visitors."

Ridley inhaled deeply and fought back the urge to panic. Somehow, the man seemed to already know his plans and movements and was testing whether he would tell the truth. For what reason he couldn't fathom. Then it struck him that maybe it's not about him, perhaps they're after Nora. But who would be looking for her? She had told him about running away from home but these men weren't Norwegian authorities; besides, she was a missing person not someone wanted by a government agency. The resort on Cayman that was busted? They were all in jail to his knowledge. None of this made sense in his sleep and nutrition starved mind.

"We were sailing around them to follow the trade winds north around Cuba, then circle back to the leeward islands. It's how you sail around the northern part of the Caribbean," he managed, impressed he came up with a plausible answer.

He heard the man sigh, then silence. With his hands strapped behind him, the blow that came to his unguarded abdomen knocked every ounce of breathe from his lungs, and the chair tumbled over backwards, crashing his head against the concrete floor. His world swirled and spun around in darkness; he vomited inside the hood, and passed out.

28

CARIBBEAN SEA – JULY 30, 2020

AJ stirred and opened her eyes to a faint glow from the east. She blinked the sleep away and noticed the silhouette of a figure in the helm chair.

"You're up early," she said groggily.

The chair swivelled towards her. "I like to see the sunrise." Nora replied quietly.

"I like to sleep," AJ mumbled, but hauled herself up into a seated position and leaned against the side of the fly-bridge.

The two girls had taken the fly-bridge and the men had slept on the main deck below. Reg's snoring had kept AJ awake for a while, but their long day and the rhythmic rocking of the boat had soon overcome any sounds and she had slept solidly.

"It is a beautiful time of day," AJ admitted, looking at the eastern horizon turning a lighter shade of blue. "I'm just not at my best first thing."

They sat in silence for several minutes watching the line between ocean and sky become more defined.

Nora finally spoke. "I like to start each day this way, when I can. Clear my head. Focus on what is important in my life each day."

AJ smiled to herself. At eighteen, this teenage woman had

her head screwed on tighter than most people twice her age, despite everything she had been through. Or maybe, she thought, because of everything she had been through. Either way, she was partly impressed, and partly sad for her young friend. It seemed her innocence and youth had ended at age 16; she had been forced to be an adult ever since, and there was no turning back.

"I always run through my to-do list and schedule at the start of my day, but I don't think I'm as meditative about it as you are," AJ laughed. "In fact, I'm more frantic and panicked about it until I have my coffee and get out on the water."

Nora smiled; the dim pre-dawn light began to illuminate her pretty face and long blonde hair.

"You have good friends," she said without a note of jealousy or resentment. "Reg is like a father you get along with."

"That's true. He and Pearl are just like a second set of parents to me. I'm lucky." She shifted uncomfortably on her sleeping bag, knowing Nora hadn't seen or spoken to her own parents in two years. "And Thomas is like family. He's more like a kid brother than an employee. He calls me 'boss' all the time. I used to tell him to stop, I was embarrassed to think of myself as someone's boss. We just work together in my mind. But he wouldn't. Said it was out of respect, so I've just gotten used to it. We'd do anything for each other, any of us."

"Like this trip," Nora whispered.

"Yeah, like this trip."

A hand reached over the edge of the fly-bridge from below, and placed a coffee mug down.

"Nora, want one?" came Reg's deep voice in an attempt at being quiet.

"Yes please," Nora replied.

AJ scooped up the coffee and took a sip.

"Would you do something for me, Nora?" she asked.

Nora looked over. "Of course. I owe you so much, I owe all of you for your help."

"You owe me nothing, there's no payback for what we're doing. But I would like a favour that would mean a lot to me."

Nora looked puzzled. "Okay, tell me what I can do."

"When we get back, would you use my computer and call your parents over the Internet?"

Nora sat quietly, staring back at the horizon where the first hint of an orange tone was beginning to take shape. Her lips parted as though to speak but no words came out. After a long pause, she finally turned back to AJ.

"I told myself I would call them, after I ran away. For several weeks it was impossible; I was stowing away on ships across the ocean. When I reached the Caribbean I told myself the first chance I had I would contact them, and several times I held someone's mobile in my hand but couldn't bring myself to dial the number. I didn't know where I was going, or what to tell them, and I knew they would have people start searching to find me. They would beg me to come home, and I wasn't ready to go home. Then I was recruited at the resort and I thought I had a plan. One year of my life and I would be set with money and a new identity. Instead of hiding and sneaking about from country to country and island to island, I could go where I chose. Even home to Norway. But you know what that turned out to be. I was left with a year of my life given to those pigs and still no money, no new identity, and more people who want to ask me questions I don't want to answer. But I have decided, whether we find the diamonds or not, and regardless of whatever has happened to Ridley, I need to face up to the questions. There is no new identity for me; I have to live with who I am, and what I've done. You make it sound like it's a favour for you, but we both know it's another favour you're trying to do for me." She smiled. "But yes, I will use your computer and call them."

Reg's hand reappeared with a second mug of coffee. AJ scooped it up and handed it to Nora. Then she sat up on her knees and wrapped her arms around Nora, squeezing her tightly.

Thirty minutes later, Thomas and Nora stood on either side of AJ with their hands under her arms as she staggered to the swim step. The four full dive tanks and all her gear added up to about the same weight as AJ herself, and her legs quivered under the strain. Once in the water, she would be weightless, but getting there to join Reg, already floating with a hand on the tag line, she was sweating profusely and trying not to trip in her fins. With an impressive splash, she joined Reg and took a minute to catch her breath.

"Blimey, Reg. Been a while since I went full on tech dive, forgot what a pain in the arse it is."

Reg laughed as they bobbed on the rolling swell. "Yeah, but in a few minutes we'll be a couple of hundred feet down looking at something no other man has ever seen."

"Or woman," AJ added.

He laughed again. "Right you are. Whatever is down there I'm sure we'll be the first humans to lay eyes on it, where it currently lies anyway."

"It's an aeroplane," Thomas shouted from the stern. "It's this fella Dingo's aeroplane, I'm telling you."

AJ looked at Nora smiling broadly, and realised how good Thomas was for her to be around, with his relentless optimism and beaming face. Everyone is better for being around Thomas, she thought. What a truly amazing thing to be able to say about someone she had the privilege to be around almost every day.

Reg pulled himself along the line they had strung from the stern, to the anchor line at the bow. He had to work hard to pull against the current, but at least it would be an easy ride back when they surfaced. They would use the anchor line as both a descent and ascent line, to avoid being blown off the bank by the current. When they came back up they would be spending most of their dive time in incremental deco stops along that line. They were both very aware if the anchor gave, the line broke, or they lost their hold on the line, they would have an uncomfortable time performing forty minutes of decompression stops while being carried across open water for miles, wondering if the guys on the boat knew. They both carried an SMB to deploy in such a catastrophe, so the boat had a chance to see them and they had agreed before the dive; if one of them lost the line, they would both release the line. There was no point one of them staying put and forcing the boat to stay on the anchor while the other diver drifted in the vast ocean. Of course, if the line broke or the anchor gave way, the boat would be untethered anyway, as would the divers. AJ caught up to Reg as he reached the bow and they both took a few moments to settle their breathing.

"You ready, girl?" Reg asked.

"Yup, let's go have a look, shall we?"

They both released the air from the U-shaped bladder attached to their dive plates and began their descent.

Methodically moving down hand over hand, they clutched the line as the current held them horizontally in the water column. Occasionally releasing one hand to pinch her nose through the silicone skirt of her mask to equalise her airways, AJ followed Reg until they reached the base of the line. She pointed out the encrusted anchor and the chain link she had identified. Reg nodded and they both finned over the rocks and began their free descent, hidden from the current in the lee of the bank. They quickly dropped past AJ's previous depth of 132 feet and the shadowy bulk below began to take shape against the deep blue water beyond. At 145 feet, the profile became clearer, but what exactly she was looking at was still unidentifiable. It looked large, even accounting for the lens effect underwater. Ten feet farther and the texture appeared to be coral encrustation and uniform lines gave the appearance of something unnatural. AJ tapped Reg's arm and pointed enthusiastically to the right side of the main mass. The distinctive shape of an aeroplane wing lay low against the slope, extending from the side of what she could now make out to be the fuselage.

They levelled off just above the wreck at 185 feet. The broad tail wing was draped with growth and debris that hung from the wing to the slope, making it almost indistinguishable until they were up close. The coral-encrusted chain disappeared into the heavy growth that grew plentiful facing the light from above. The plane appeared to be intact, with both wings attached and the rounded shape of the motors clear to the eye either side of the fuselage. No windows were visible, the growth having taken over every surface that sunlight could touch. AJ checked her dive computer, a large wrist-mounted unit, much bigger than her regular recreational dive watch. The bright LED screen displayed a myriad of information with even more available if she scrolled through the menu. They had started the dive using the trimix gas from the twin 80 cubic foot tanks on their backs. The plan called for a three-minute descent and then seventeen minutes at a maximum of 210 feet. The following forty-four minutes would be spent performing deco stops at ever shallower depths using the other gases they carried to safely meet their decompression commitments. She had been down for four minutes. They had sixteen minutes to explore.

AJ finned deeper. Her first priority was to establish an entry point. She carefully watched her depth and levelled off again at 205 feet over the right-side engine. Sunlight reached that depth through the relatively clear Caribbean water, hence the coral growth, but they were almost a third of the depth to where noticeable light can penetrate no farther. With the early morning sun still low in the sky, the landscape was dim and eerie. She switched on her torch and the mottled brown shades of the coral growth burst into bright reds and oranges wherever her beam fell. Along with the amount of light filtered at depth, the colour spectrum also faded – until the illumination from her torch revealed them again. She felt like she was turning a sepia tone painting into full colour with the stroke of her light brush.

Her beam revealed the hole Nora had mentioned in the side of the fuselage. A second stream of light flooded the area as Reg joined her and they could see the jagged opening wasn't wide enough for a person to wiggle through – with or without any dive gear. Their lights danced around the dark interior of the cockpit where no growth could form in the darkness. Everything was covered with a layer of silty debris, but the yokes and seats were clearly visible. AJ looked over at Reg and hand signalled that the hole was too narrow to fit through. He nodded and dropped a little deeper towards the nose. His light beam flashed around the inside of the cockpit, scattering a school of tiny silver fish, and for a moment AJ was confused. Then she realised the windscreen was facing down the slope and wouldn't have any growth. She was about to drop down and have a look when Reg finned forward and his hand appeared inside the cockpit and waved at her. The windscreen was missing.

Joining Reg above the nose they both stared through the opening and shone their lights around the interior. It looked really cramped inside and ominously dark and uninviting. Reg pointed at two spars running from the back of the nose to the roof which must have been windscreen supports. They would now be the only thing stopping them getting inside the plane. AJ checked her dive computer. They were right at 209 feet with eighteen minutes total dive time; they needed to leave. She finned to the opening and wrenched on the first spar. It flexed back and forth and quickly broke away from the roof, leaving it attached at the base. She bent and twisted the metal until it broke free from the back of the nose section, leaving a sharp-looking end where it broke away. Reg reached in and tried the same with the second spar. It too gave easily from the roof where it was heavily corroded but gamely hung on to its lower attachment. Reg wrenched and twisted but to no avail. AJ tapped his shoulder and thumbed towards the surface. He nodded. They both knew there was no margin at these depths; the turn-around time was a hard and fast number.

29

ACAPULCO, MEXICO – JULY 30, 2020

Ridley lay on his side against the cool concrete floor, still tied to the chair. His hands were trembling uncontrollably from being restrained in the same position for what he thought he had calculated to be eight days. That would be four days since the questioning and the beating began. But he wasn't sure – of anything. Each morning had been the same routine. They came into the room, stood up the chair and the same man asked him what he planned to do when he reached Grand Cayman. His answer had remained consistent: "I plan to sail around the islands and head for Cuba." Their reaction had remained the same with two exceptions. They now held the chair so it didn't topple over, and they hit him somewhere different each time. Holding the chair saved his head from being split open on the concrete, but it meant the full force of the blow was taken by his body. His attacker chose his chest on day two of the assaults, the side of his head next and, interestingly, his shoulder the last morning. The shoulder had hurt the least at the time but had throbbed and ached like a sore tooth ever since.

He lay on the floor in a stupor, waiting for the door to open and his morning questioning and subsequent beating. His stomach cramped and groaned from the lack of food and although he hadn't been hydrated enough to urinate in days, the smell still lingered and mixed with the foul odour of vomit, sweat and rank breath. He could no longer hold a thought in his head with any clarity. Images, random memories, dreams and notions floated through his consciousness like flames flickering around his skull. Any hope of survival had left him. His only remaining desire was to leave this world before he unwillingly told them anything more. He knew as control over his mind ebbed away, so went his ability to filter his words. He would gladly take his own life and suffer the karmic debt, but trussed up and desperately weak, he could conjure no options to end the pain. A clear vision of Nora now escaped him. In rare flashes of clarity he was glad, as perhaps he would forget her altogether and he couldn't give up something he couldn't recall. But mostly his mind yearned to capture a lucid picture of her pretty face, longed to summon the feeling of her arms around him, and her soft skin against his.

He was barely aware of the door opening, but he felt his head fall heavy as the chair was righted. His chin dropped against his chest. The hood was pulled back and the water striking his face brought Ridley back from delirium. He opened his mouth and instead of the usual surge, the water was tipped steadily down his throat. As the life-giving water surged into his system, he realised his mistake. He had just stepped further back from the precipice of death.

"What is your intention when you reach Grand Cayman?" The man's voice echoed the same words in the same, detached, even tone.

"Sail around the islands, head for Cuba," Ridley mumbled slowly and braced himself for the impending blow.

Instead of a punch from the henchman, he heard the man speak again.

"We've played this game long enough. I know about the plane, so let's move on."

He might as well have been punched in the gut, for all the breath left Ridley's body. This was about his grandfather's plane? It wasn't about Aldo, it wasn't about Nora, it was all about the lost plane. He would happily tell them anything about it, if it wasn't for one thing... Nora could already be there. He gasped for air and his mind raced. The water had brought him around, and adrenaline had forced his brain back to some functionality, albeit dull and slow moving.

"That's what you're interested in? My grandfather's plane? Why do you care about an old plane we'll likely never find?"

He immediately realised the answer to his own question. How did they know was the more pressing query.

"Come now, we're interested for the same reason you are," the man said, his voice finally hinting at a touch of impatience. "All I wish to know is where."

Ridley racked his brain for the list of people who knew about the diamonds. His own father, Nora, and his dead mother. His father had kept the secret for years, and had little interest in the story. He had inherited enough money from the family jewellery business to live very comfortably, and he knew it was Ridley's dream to search for the plane; he wouldn't have told anyone. Nora didn't have anyone to tell. Certainly no one that led back to Mexico. He couldn't conceive the idea that Zanita would have told a soul. He had asked her not to speak of it, although it appeared she had mentioned it to Aldo. But he only knew about looking for the plane, not about the diamonds. Could these guys be bugging Aldo's house? The thought seemed far fetched, like some outrageous plot from a Hollywood movie. But it was also the only idea that made sense. Somehow these people were listening in to Aldo's conversations, but happened to overhear him telling his mother about the plane, and the valuable cargo stashed away. If he ever got out of this mess he had to warn Aldo his house was bugged. He thought back through his conversation with his mother, trying to recall the details of what he'd said. He was sure he hadn't mentioned the diamonds, he had only talked about something of value. His sluggish mind hunted and searched his foggy memory. He remembered pausing while the maid brought their food, and then again when she brought coffee. Surely, it couldn't be? He groaned aloud as it hit him. No wonder Rosie wouldn't look him in the eye after the services; she's the bug.

"Let me explain something to you," the man said, snapping Ridley's attention back. "You can tell me now where to look for the plane, or, we're going to cause you a lot of pain, and then you're going to tell me. I don't mind either way, but you'll regret the second way, I assure you."

Ridley desperately tried not to vomit again, or dry heave, as he had long since emptied his stomach of any contents to bring up. Every man likes to think they would be tough, brave and everything society perceives as macho, but very few ever face true evil and brutality. Ridley had never felt so helpless and terrified in all his life. He cursed himself for accepting the water that had cleared his mind enough to understand what was happening. He gritted his teeth and tried to relax his body to accept what was to come. The perfectly placed blow landed at the base of his ribs and brought a searing pain and a grotesque snapping sound. His head spun and the more he tried to draw in breath, the more the pain resonated and he seemed to lose his hold on consciousness. He wanted to pass out but his body's instincts hunted for oxygen and wouldn't let him go.

"Where is the plane?" came the flat, even voice, like a droning, emotionless machine.

"I don't know," Ridley spluttered.

A rough thumb pressed against the fractured rib with the precision of a surgeon and pushed him back against the chair. The pain shot through his whole body like lightning striking every nerve. He tried to scream but his voice was empty.

"Where is the plane?"

Ridley whimpered and delirium returned amongst a churning

sea of agony. The thumb moved slightly up and down, starting a new avalanche of nerve endings desperately firing.

"Where is the plane?"

Ridley felt like he was stepping away from his own body as confusion overwhelmed him, and the world seemed to fall into slow motion. The last thing he heard sounded like his own voice, saying something incoherent from across the room.

30

CARIBBEAN SEA – JULY 30, 2020

The four relaxed in the shade, chatting, nodding off to sleep, and watching time slowly pass by until Reg and AJ could get back in the water. Usually, a diver wouldn't perform two deep dives of this nature on the same day, giving their body as much time to recover as possible. But as they had perfect conditions and were so far from home in the middle of the ocean, they decided an eight-hour break between dives was acceptable. They had surfaced around 8am after eleven stages of decompression stops on their ascent, most lasting a minute, except the final two on pure oxygen that were eight and thirteen minutes. After they shared the excitement of finding Dingo's plane with Nora and Thomas, AJ had made some sketches of the wreck while it was fresh in her mind. They discussed the tools they should take down to remove the second spar and clean up the broken parts to safely access the fuselage. With the bulky tanks and dive gear, AJ suggested she try reversing into the windscreen opening, so she would be facing the dashboard once inside. Their next problem would be locating the tobacco tin that could be anywhere after the crash, sinking and over 60 years in the salt water. The best place to start was the location they last knew it to be, and that was behind the dash, so the plan for the second dive was check there and see what they could find. Their seventeen minutes at the wreck would pass quickly, but with the tanks they had left on the boat, they would only have enough gas for one of them to make a third dive. If there was any way to retrieve the stones on the next dive, they would try their best to do so.

Finally, four o'clock rolled around, they geared up and were glad to get back in the water. Armed with a hacksaw and a pair of channel lock pliers, they started their descent down the anchor line with a wave to Thomas and Nora, eagerly watching from the boat. The current had not relented, and if anything felt stronger than it had that morning. They both carefully pulled themselves down the rope and were relieved to reach the rocks and drop over the edge into the sheltered lee of the bank. With the confidence of knowing what lay beneath them, they swiftly descended the slope and levelled off over the nose of Queen of the Island Skies. Reg began work with the hacksaw on the brace that wouldn't break away, while AJ used the pliers to bend the jagged pieces out of harm's way. Maintaining their buoyancy at 210 feet, with over 100lbs of tanks and gear hanging from them, while they performed manual tasks was challenging. The trick was to hang on to the wreck with one hand, while working the tool with the other. Still, they bumped and banged around into the nose of the Beechcraft, and each other.

It took over six minutes to get the opening clear and ready to try moving inside. AJ took another minute to drop her breathing back down to a normal level after the exertion. Their dive plan was based on their normal breathing rates and if they spent too long at elevated levels, breathing more gas, they would need to shorten the dive time to compensate. She gave Reg the okay sign and turned around, facing down towards the tip of the nose. Reg took her by the shoulders and steered her backwards up into the windscreen opening, like he was reversing a trailer. The gap was barely tall enough for her to fit through and the trimix tanks on her back scraped the ceiling, while the other two tanks hanging at her sides bounced and banged on the bottom of the windshield bed. Only once had AJ been subjected to an MRI, but being slowly reversed into the dark and confined space of the cockpit gave her an eerie recollection of the uncomfortable experience. Her knees grazed against something she decided was the top of the seats, and a stream of silvery bait fish flashed past her mask on her left, temporarily expelled from their home. Darkness seemed to envelop her as her head moved inside the fuselage and she reached down to clutch a yoke in each hand to steady herself. Reg released his grip, letting AJ manoeuvre herself from there, and he backed away, allowing a little more light into the fuselage. A brown cloud wafted around her from the sediment coating everything inside the plane, and she paused, staying as still as she could to let the fog settle.

AJ looked out the front of the plane, which pointed down the slope into the abyss. If the chain had been longer, and the plane had made it another 40 or 50 feet, it would have reached the point where the slope became a wall and fell vertically away. Between her and that edge was a handful of sponges and one rock that protruded a few feet from the sand and crushed coral. Reg had moved to the side and as the brown mess cleared, he caught her eye. He pointed to himself, then his mask and then his dive computer. He was signalling that he would watch their time while she got to work, which was also a nudge for her to stop gazing off into the distance, and get on with it. Every movement she made inside the cockpit sent more of the sediment into a willowy cloud that seemed to take forever to dissipate. She moved her hands from the yokes to the two seats and lowered herself down onto her forearms until her eyes were level with the underside of the dashboard. Her heels wedged against the ceiling and once the dust settled again she carefully shone her torch around. She could barely make out the foot pedals protruding through a pile of debris and silt ahead of her, and looking straight down between the seats, she saw something sticking up out of the floor. She wondered what it could be, but knew there was no time to investigate.

AJ shifted her weight to her right arm while holding the torch in that hand, and reached under the dashboard with her left hand. The metal panel had a small return that added strength, and feeling beyond that she touched several bundles of wires. More silt and debris rained down reducing her visibility to zero, but she continued fumbling her hands along in search of any clues. She felt something solid and round but realised it was the body of one of the gauges, touching several more as she stretched towards the starboard side. If there was a tin up there, it must be buried in a tiny space somewhere, she decided, as the whole area seemed to be filled with wires, cables and gauges. Surely if Dingo had hidden it under the dash it had to be reachable without doing what she was doing, she thought. There was no room to kneel on the floor between the seats and the dashboard, as the yokes were in the way, so he would have had to access his hiding place from one of the seats. That meant it would be in the lower three or four inches behind the panel, as that's all you could reach with a hand underneath. Maybe it's at one of the ends against the side of the fuselage on the outside of the yokes, she thought, as she waited for more sediment to calm down. The right side was where the propeller blade had made a gaping hole and she could see the edge of the dash was torn back slightly on that side. She reached down to balance herself and pushed on the object she had noticed below her. It felt sharp and misshapen under her weight, and she realised it was the twisted sheet metal of the floor where the blade must have penetrated. That had to mean he was seated on the left side, surely, or he would have been cut in half. If he flew from the left side, then more likely he would stash his tin that side too.

Reg tapped on the fuselage and held up three fingers. She only had three minutes left before they had to ascend. She quickly heaved herself up on her hands with her body still balanced across the seat back and shuffled herself to the left side. The yokes were strange affairs that ran vertically up the sides of the cockpit then angled towards the centre of each seat where the controls were mounted in front of the pilots. AJ tried to fit under the angled part of the yoke as close to the side of the cockpit as she could get. Her side tank hit the sheet metal and the seat, arresting her movement as her left hand slipped in the silt. She dropped amongst a huge cloud of brown muck and glanced her head off the yoke as she did so. The control knocked her mask askew, allowing a rush of filthy water to flood her eyes as her face came to a halt on the front of the seat and her heels smacked against the ceiling.

"Bugger," she blurted into her regulator as she gathered her wits back up. She was now blind in every sense with one arm against the floor and the other caught around the right side of the yoke assembly. She couldn't reach her face to reset her mask but knew she wouldn't be able to see anything in the mess she had stirred up anyway. Sod it, she thought, I might as well have a grope around before I try and extricate myself. She managed to slide her left hand up the port side of the fuselage feeling odd bits of debris or material flaking away as she went. Her hand found the underside of the dash and she leveraged against her face on the seat to stretch her fingers up behind the panel. This side felt different to the touch. The return didn't have an edge; it was more like the panel was three quarters of an inch thick. She slid her fingers towards the centre of the plane and it became an edge again after four or five inches. She stretched with all her might and felt her mask slipping farther up her face. As much as she couldn't risk losing her mask, she desperately wanted to feel what was above the part she was touching. Sure enough, it was a lip back to the panel. What she was feeling was a rectangular container fixed to the back of the panel. In the middle she felt a small lump of some kind, which she guessed was a bolt holding it in place. Her mask finally slid the rest of the way up her head and she felt the pressure of the strap go away as it fell aside. Without a mask she would be blind and she wouldn't be able to recover the mask if she couldn't see. A rapping resounded through the fuselage which had to be Reg signalling time was up. She quickly pulled her left hand back from the dash and reached up as her mask dropped away, luckily hooking the strap with her thumb. Clutching the strap tightly, she pushed off the seat with both hands and after smacking the back of her head on the yoke, she wriggled herself around the control, and shoved upwards. Her tanks clanked loudly against the metal ceiling and she felt two big hands grab the shoulder straps of her harness. She relaxed and let Reg pull her forward through the windscreen opening.

Once clear of the plane she refitted her mask and purged the water. She blinked a few times but it felt like someone had poured sand in her eyes. Hoping she was in clean water and away from the sediment she removed the mask and carefully rubbed her eyes in the sea water. When she put the mask on again her eyes were sore and irritated, but she could at least see. And what she saw was Reg urgently pointing both thumbs upwards towards the surface. They needed to leave in a hurry.

31

ACAPULCO, MEXICO – JULY 30, 2020

Ridley faded in and out of consciousness, with dreamlike glimpses of his surroundings. He was being carried somewhere, he was in a vehicle at some point, and then carried again and placed into a seat. It was all hazy and camouflaged by the pain in his ribs, every time he breathed. The seat was small but felt padded and comfortable compared to the wooden chair he'd spent over a week tied to. His hands were still bound, but they were in front of him now. He had no recollection of when that changed. His hood was pulled back far enough to have some water administered and then he tasted a gooey substance that reminded him of the energy gels he sometimes took when he went for a long run. His body eagerly accepted the nourishment while his mind was still incapable of deciphering what was happening, or deciding whether he should. The combination brought him back to some lucidity and he was given water several more times. It felt like the same hands holding the hood up against his forehead, but the fluid was poured gently and steadily into his mouth. The hood was never pulled back enough for him to see around him, but looking down he caught a glimpse of his hands tied together in his lap and noticed wherever he was appeared to be well lit. His jeans had been changed for grey tracksuit trousers and he realised he didn't stink anymore. Heat on his right shoulder suggested sunlight through a window and he remembered he had kept track of the days, back in the room, but now he couldn't recall how, or the amount of time. He heard voices, men's voices, but he couldn't make them out clearly, or tell what they were saying. Wherever he was seemed to rock very slightly as the men moved about. Not the bobbing sway of a boat, but it didn't feel like the vehicle he had been in either. The thoughts and small observations continued to ebb and flow through his mind like packages on a conveyor belt. They held clarity for a fleeting moment as they passed right in front of him, before fading into obscurity as the next sound or memory shoved its way down the belt.

Every inhalation felt like a dagger to his ribs, but the pain, combined with the water and the gel, was slowly steering his mind back into focus. He remembered the man with the monotone voice asking him over and over about his grandfather's plane. He had refused to tell him where it was, he recalled that much. So why did they stop? It didn't make sense in his mind why they chose to move him. They had made him more comfortable and even given him water and sustenance; why would they do that if they wanted to continue questioning him, he wondered. He thought of Nora and felt a warm rush of life flood through him as her image came clearly to him. She was at the helm of the sailboat, smiling, with the boat keeled over, making a tack. He wished he could piece together his timing, then maybe he could figure out where she might be.

Maybe it was simply the fact that he was still alive, or perhaps that he had been cleaned up and made more comfortable, but despite his continued pain and captivity, he wanted to live. Hope had found a way to wriggle back into his psyche. His kidnappers had pushed him to the brink of death, and yet here he sat, beaten, dazed, but alive. He must still have value to them.

He heard movement near him and the hood was pulled up

again. He accepted the water and another packet of gel that was squeezed onto his tongue. The hood was dropped again and cinched at his neck. He reflexively lifted his hands towards the hood but a tether stopped his reach and he felt the pull on his ankle ties. His hands might be in front of him but he was still fully restrained. Ridley made an effort to keep his breathing soft to minimise the sharp pain from the broken rib, and relax and let the nutrition find its way into his bloodstream. Part of him wanted to sleep to hide from the constant agony, but the part of his brain that was gaining clarity knew he should stay awake and aware.

The room, or whatever it was he was being held in, rocked as footsteps thumped like someone rushing upstairs, and he heard the person approach him. The hood was loosened and pulled from his head. Ridley blinked and squinted against the brightness and struggled to focus his eyes.

"Are you okay?" came a familiar voice.

As his vision cleared, he realised it was Aldo, warmly smiling at him. A surge of elation poured through him and the memory of his epiphany back in the room where his kidnappers held him came back with a jolt.

"Aldo, thank God it's you. It was Rosie! I figured it out, Rosie is working for the men that took me. She's spying on your house, Aldo."

The man reached up and laid a warm hand against Ridley's cheek.

"It's okay Ridley, I know," he replied softly as he took his hand away.

Ridley held up his bound hands so he could be cut free and looked around. He was inside an aeroplane. Aldo was sitting on a seat facing him, and beyond him was a bulkhead, and then the cockpit. In script letters on the bulkhead wall were the words 'King Air 90', which meant nothing to Ridley. The aisle between the seats was narrow and the seats themselves plushly upholstered in beige leather. He felt the plane rock again and turned to see Tattoo entering through the doorway on the port side behind his row of seats, crouching to fit inside the low cabin. He turned his huge frame and pulled the door closed behind him. Ridley looked back at his hands held up against the tether and then at Aldo. He hadn't made a move to untie him.

Aldo smiled. "Thank you for the location of your grandfather's plane. My men didn't think you would break. But I told them, everyone does eventually."

He rose from the seat, staying low in the cramped cabin. "Now, sit back and enjoy the flight while we go and take a look."

Ridley's jaw hung open. He couldn't believe he had revealed the location. He had no memory of saying anything. He slumped back in the seat and his hands fell back to his lap. Aldo's betrayal hit him harder than any of the blows he now figured came from Tattoo. He had let his family down, and more importantly he had put Nora in danger. His only hope was that she had been delayed in travelling to Grand Cayman, or unable to secure help when she got there. How had his mother ended up with this man, he wondered despondently. His heart sank even further.

"My mother?" Ridley gasped, and Aldo halted his retreat to the cockpit. "You killed my mother, didn't you?"

Aldo shrugged his shoulders. "Everyone has their time; she was no longer the beautiful woman I married. Cancer does that to a person," he said, nonchalantly. "When she refused to tell me anything more about this valuable treasure of yours, well..." He waved a hand as though fate had intervened. "It was her time."

"She didn't know anything more than Rosie must have overheard," Ridley groaned through gritted teeth.

"No matter, you told us what we need to know." Aldo shook his head. "As I tried to tell you at the house, I enjoy a good treasure hunt, and I offered to help, but you didn't want to make it easy."

Within a few minutes the plane was climbing out of Acapulco airport with the deep blue Pacific Ocean beneath them. Aldo banked the King Air to the south, making a long, sweeping turn to head back over the Yucatan peninsula on their way towards the Sixty Mile Bank, north-west of Grand Cayman. Ridley looked out of the window at the blur of the starboard propeller, crushing the air alongside the nose and cockpit, ahead of where he sat, and thought of his grandfather. He would gladly sacrifice his own life to see that propeller come through the side of Aldo Trujillo's plane.

32

CARIBBEAN SEA – JULY 30, 2020

Both Reg and AJ triple counted the tanks on the boat. Everything matched the inventory they had made before they left, and Thomas had diligently marked every used tank with the remaining pressure written on a piece of masking tape. There were only enough tanks for one of them to dive again. Reg stared off into the distance where the late afternoon sun was beginning to lose its intensity.

"I'll go," he said, and turned to face AJ. "No point going back home in the dark, so before we leave in the morning, I'll have a quick look and see if I can reach it."

AJ smiled; she knew he would insist on going if either of them did another dive, alone. Not because he wanted to go, but he didn't want her to take the risk.

"Reg, there isn't enough room in there. You won't fit."

"Then we'll just have to come back out," he said firmly.

"How will we get the tanks filled?" AJ pointed out. "We can't fill them, and Island Air are closed during the lockdown."

Reg shrugged his shoulders. "Then we'll have to wait until after the lockdown. I'm sorry, but there's only so much risk we should take."

"I don't want you to do something too dangerous. If it's that risky, Reg is right, we should go back and try again whenever we can," Nora said, putting a hand on AJ's arm.

"I suppose," AJ replied reluctantly. "But what are you going to do when we get back to the island? We can't hide you away for months. It could be that long before we can come out here again."

Nora took a moment and shuffled anxiously as she thought. "I don't really know. I need to find Ridley. Or find out what has happened to him," she added quietly.

A distant drone could be heard above the sound of the ocean slapping against the hull, and all four of them looked around, trying to locate the source. Nora scanned across the water, but Reg looked up.

"That's a plane not a boat."

Thomas pointed towards the western sky where the sun made them squint and shade their eyes.

"There, I saw something. Now I've lost it again against the sun."

They all struggled to make out anything with the bright light making their eyes water, as the sound of the engines grew louder. Finally, lower in the sky than they expected, the plane became clearer.

"He's bloody low," Reg muttered.

"Probably wondering what we're doing out here." AJ said, as the plane continued to approach, and descend.

The twin-engine King Air 90 flew past them a few hundred yards to their port side, less than 500 feet off the water, and banked hard in a turn to circle back.

"What the bloody hell are they up to?" Reg said.

"Shit," Nora blurted.

"What?" AJ asked, turning to her in surprise.

"Look at the tail number," Nora replied.

"X... B... I can't make out the numbers now," AJ said, staring at the plane as it approached even lower off their starboard side.

"Mexico. That's a private plane out of Mexico. They have XB tail numbers, right?" Reg said, watching the plane flash by.

"Yeah," Nora replied, her expression riddled with concern.

The plane circled twice more and they strained to make out the people inside. Thomas grabbed the binoculars they kept on the boat, but between the glinting of the low sun and the speed the plane flew by, they couldn't pick anything out. As the King Air receded into the distance, returning to the west and climbing, AJ turned back to Nora.

"That was weird. Could that have anything to do with Ridley and his mother?"

Nora opened her mouth to reply but didn't speak, lost in thought.

"Why would a plane come all the way out here from Mexico, drop down to check us out, then turn around and head back the way it came?" Thomas said, verbalising the thoughts going through each of their minds.

"Don't seem like a coincidence, does it?" Reg said. "It's gotta be over 300 miles to the Yucatan peninsula from here. A lot farther to the mainland. Don't know why anyone would fly all this way just to stare at an empty ocean for hundreds of miles."

"It's Trujillo, it has to be," Nora said.

"Ridley's stepfather?" AJ asked. "How would he know we're here, or even where here is. There's only four people who know we came out to the bank, and we're all standing on this boat."

Nora shook her head. "One other person knew we would be coming."

"Who?" Reg asked.

"Ridley," Nora said quietly, and a tear escaped her eye.

AJ put an arm around her. "He wouldn't have told them anything about this though, would he?"

Nora turned her face into AJ's shoulder. "Not unless they made him."

AJ hugged her and after a few sniffles she felt Nora tense and compose herself.

"But why would his stepfather force him to talk about the plane? How would he even know?" AJ asked.

Nora wiped her cheeks. "Ridley said he'd told his mother he

was going to look for it. He didn't tell her about the diamonds, but he told her there was something very valuable aboard." She sighed. "I don't know, it's all guessing. I just know Ridley was worried about Trujillo. He told me he was a dangerous man, and everything about his mother's death was suspicious. Maybe I'm crazy, but it all scares me."

AJ let her go and looked at Reg. "How quickly could they get a boat out here?"

Reg thought for a moment. "I dunno. Does this Trujillo guy have serious money, Nora?"

She nodded. "I think so, from what Ridley said he does. He told me he has fancy cars and boats, I don't know about a plane."

"But he's in Acapulco, right?"

Nora nodded again.

"The plane he may have flown from there, but a boat he'd most likely bring from Cancun. Acapulco's on the west coast, you can't get from there to here by boat, short of going through the Panama Canal." Reg paused while he did some more maths in his head. "But, if it is him, and he wanted to come back out here, that plane could drop him in Cancun where he could rent a boat. From there, he could be back out here tomorrow sometime, if they left tonight."

"Ridley was pretty sure Trujillo was part of a cartel. He said he seemed like the boss in Acapulco, but he heard him on his mobile one time, talking to someone that he clearly was taking orders from. He could have connections all over the country, so it might not be hard for him to arrange a boat."

"If it's one those crazy offshore, go-fast boats the drug dealers all seem to have, he could be here pretty fast," AJ added.

"I don't think Hazel's Odyssey will be a match for any boat that gets them here before we leave," Thomas noted. "We can't even go wide open, or we'll run out of diesel getting back."

"Hey, look," Reg said calmly, "we're making a lot of assumptions. That could have been anyone in that plane. A bloke out for a test flight, or logging hours for some reason. Might have been planning on turning at Grand Cayman but saw us and said sod it, might as well turn here and not deal with air traffic control on the island."

"That's a point. The airport's closed, they'd probably get uppity with him if he entered Cayman airspace," AJ mused.

"See? Any number of reasons that plane was out this way," Reg concluded.

AJ looked at Nora. She didn't look convinced. If it was Trujillo, AJ thought, he still has to fly back, organise a boat of some sort, gather provisions, fuel, people, all during the evening when it would be more difficult, and then make the run out to Sixty Mile Bank. She had a hard time seeing how they could do all that by 8 o'clock in the morning, which was the time they could be on their way home, if she dived at sun-up.

"Okay. Here's what we'll do," AJ started assertively. "I'm going back down at first light tomorrow."

Reg began to protest but AJ held up a hand. "Hear me out." Reg relented and she continued, "I know where to look, and we'll work out a plan to undo, or more likely break off, what I think is an old rusty bolt. I don't think I'll need to get all the way inside again, I reckon I can do it through the window opening. If what I felt was the tin, great; if it turns out it's not, then we know we did all we could. Anyway, we put Thomas in the water with me. He can stay at the bottom of the anchor line on regular nitrox as a safety diver. If there's anything I need between 130 feet and the surface, he can help. When I get to 70 feet and switch to nitrox 50, we'll float the SMB so you know where we are. I can be in the water before 7am and we'll be heading home before 8. This way there's no coming back out here, we don't have to figure out how to get tanks filled or any of that. Nora will be able to focus on reaching Ridley."

Reg groaned. "I don't know. I don't like it."

"We've been down there twice, Reg. I know the layout, I know exactly where I need to look. If it's not the tin then I'll knock it on the head, and we'll be home for lunch."

"You're gonna give me a bloody ulcer, my girl," Reg

complained, shaking his head. "Fine. But you gotta promise me, any trouble and you forget the tin and come up."

AJ crossed her heart. "Scout's honour."

"You weren't in the bloody scouts," Reg growled.

"Brownies honour then."

"Were you in the brownies?" he asked.

"Well… No."

"I was," Nora said.

"There you go, Reg, I swear on Nora's brownie troop honour. Happy?"

Reg threw his hands up. "No I am not. I'm many things, but happy is not one of them."

AJ and Nora grinned at each other.

33

PLAYA DEL CARMEN, MEXICO – JULY 30, 2020

The King Air had landed at a much smaller airport, and sooner than Ridley had expected after they had circled the boat on which he had seen Nora. They had left his hood off, which he determined was undoubtedly a bad sign for his future, and released his ankle bindings. When they deplaned, Tattoo led him by the arm as he hobbled and stumbled on weak legs to another black, tinted-windowed SUV. He had caught a quick glance at a sign over an unimpressive brick building that read 'Aeropuerto Nacional de Playa del Carmen'. Ridley had never been to this part of Mexico before, but he knew the geography well enough to know they were on the east coast of the Yucatan peninsula, south of Cancun on the mainland facing the island of Cozumel. From the airfield, they drove farther south for twenty minutes on the main highway, before winding their way back towards the coast through a country club with a sprawling golf course, upmarket condos and finally large homes on several fingers of a marina. Tattoo pulled the SUV into the driveway of a large home where a man in slacks and a golf shirt swung the tall iron gates closed behind them. Ridley noted the handgun tucked in the back of the guard's trousers.

It was late afternoon according to the clock in the vehicle, so Ridley guessed they were spending the night at the house. He was surprised when he was led around the side to a large patio surrounding a swimming pool, fronting the marina. A 44-foot Contender centre console with triple 425hp outboard motors sat idling against the sea wall. A fat, older man with thinning hair, wearing cargo shorts and a brightly decorated Guy Harvey fishing shirt, stepped to the patio, took the cigar from his mouth and spread his arms wide. Aldo laughed and embraced the man. They made no effort to hide their conversation from him.

"Pablo, it's been too long my friend," Aldo said, slapping the man on the back.

"You dog, Aldo, all I hear is your name on everyone's lips. I'm told you're practically running the whole east coast, all the way up to Mazatlán."

Aldo released the man who was at least a foot shorter than he was. "Someone had to bring those fools together. Too much infighting and bullshit. But forget about business, I'm here for some fun." He looked past his friend at the sleek boat with its engines ticking over with a guttural throb. "This is a beauty, my friend."

Pablo turned and smiled broadly. "Yes, yes, she'll go over 100 kilometres an hour, but I'm afraid you'll run out of gas not far past Cozumel at that speed," he said, bursting out laughing.

Aldo walked to the edge of the sea wall and admired the boat. "You have extra tanks though, yes?"

Pablo shrugged his shoulders. "Of course. Franko is going to get all three filled now; it comes with a 600-gallon tank and I added two more 200 gallon tanks in the hull. At 50 kilometres an hour you have a range of around 900 miles." Pablo waved a hand at the man behind the helm who nodded and idled the boat away down the channel.

"Where are you going, anyway?" Pablo asked, and looked back at Ridley standing forlornly near the pool with Tattoo still holding his arm. "Who's the kid?"

"That's my stepson," Aldo said with a straight face. The two men burst out laughing and Pablo started towards a palapa-style outdoor bar next to the pool.

"Let's have a drink, it's hot out here," Pablo said, stepping behind the bar that sported shelves lined with a large array of liquor bottles.

For the first time, Ridley noticed a woman sunbathing next to the pool, near the house. He assumed it was Pablo's daughter, as she looked closer to his own age. She was slim and tanned with a bright red two-piece bikini that he guessed cost a fortune, as it utilised barely any material. He'd never figured out why the skimpiest bikinis cost the most money, but there again, he bought his board shorts at the thrift store most of the time. She had a mobile phone lying next to her, wireless earbuds in her ears, dark sunglasses and a book she was pretending to read. From where he stood, Ridley could see behind the glasses and her eyes were directed at him. He wondered how he must appear to her. Exhausted, bruised, sweating in the hot, sticky air, and bound at the wrists. Maybe she was used to seeing house guests this way, he pondered.

"Clara!" Pablo snapped, and her head turned slightly towards the man. "Tell Juanita we have guests for dinner."

Pablo pointed towards Ridley. "You feeding the kid?"

Aldo shrugged his shoulders. "Sure, he can have a last meal."

Pablo belly laughed again and waved at Clara. "Five, dinner for five."

Without a word, Clara picked up her mobile, stood, and strutted provocatively to the sliding door into the house. All four men watched her in silence until the door slid closed again.

"How about that?" Pablo said with a grin.

"Bravo, my friend, bravo," Aldo replied, and took the glass of liquor he was offered. He glanced at his watch. "We can't stay too long, Pablo, I want to be there by first light."

"Where is there?" Pablo asked again.

"This side of Grand Cayman. From what you're telling me about your boat I believe it'll take us eleven hours to get there." Aldo replied.

"Grand Cayman? Jesus brother, that's a long way. Go five miles offshore and ditch the kid, the currents will have him in the gulf by the morning." Pablo lifted his own glass. "Well, we chum them up so the sharks take them long before then. Haven't had a body show up yet." He tapped his hand on the bar top, then crossed himself. "Touch wood and God willing."

"I might need him yet," Aldo said, barely loud enough for Ridley to hear. "Or maybe I'm just sentimental as he's the son of my dead wife."

"I heard about your wife, my friend, my condolences," Pablo said and held up his glass once more.

Aldo clinked his own against it and took a sip before responding. "Thank you. But I killed her, so I can't mourn too much."

The two men laughed loudly some more and Pablo's face turned red as he slapped the counter with his hand.

"You're something else, Aldo," he bellowed.

It was cooler outside by the time they were aboard Pablo's Contender, ready to leave, the sun having set several hours before. Aldo had tried for ages to break away from the man, but the drunker Pablo got, the more insistent he was that they stay a little longer. Clara had watched the evening in silence, as had Tattoo. The food had been good, although Ridley's stomach ached and groaned at the reintroduction of solid food. Tattoo had fed him, as he was never untied, a chore he clearly didn't care for. The triple engines rumbled as they idled through the marina towards the open sea and Aldo turned on the electronics to familiarise himself with the controls. Ridley had been set down on a bow seat over the cabin and he noticed Tattoo was keeping a careful eye on him. He was curious about the large duffel bag Tattoo had brought aboard that lay on the bow deck, but between his restraints and his vigilant guard he had no way to investigate. He thought about rolling over the side to cause them a delay, but decided to keep that trick for when he thought it might cause them more disruption. He guessed in the marina they'd quickly fish him out of the water, beat him and restrain him more securely. It didn't feel like a worthwhile trade.

Once they had left the marina, Aldo opened up the throttles and the big boat easily carved through the long, gently rolling swells. Ridley wondered how the seas would be once they cleared the lee of Cozumel island. From the plane the ocean had looked relatively calm, but it was hard to tell from thousands of feet above. When they had swooped down low to look at the dive boat he had been more concerned with looking for Nora than judging the swells. After a few minutes, Aldo had Tattoo take the helm and walked to the bow.

"Come below, you can rest while we ride out there, it's going to be a long night."

Ridley looked at the man. "What's the point? I'm not going to survive this trip, am I?"

Aldo thought for a moment. "I don't know, I haven't made up my mind to be honest. Believe it or not, I like you, you seem like a good kid. I would have considered having you work in the business, but you're not cut out for what we do."

"What makes you say that?" Ridley asked, knowing the man was right. He would never work for Aldo, or anyone in the kind of business he was sure the man was involved in. But, if Aldo thought there might be a chance things could work out, he figured it may keep him alive long enough to help Nora.

"Because your mother didn't have the stomach for it, and I see a lot of her in you. She was a good woman, she cared about people. Caring is a weakness I cannot afford."

Ridley stood, still shaky on his feet as the boat rose up and down with the ocean. Aldo took his arm to help steady him as they walked to the steps leading below from the port side of the helm station.

"Why are you going to so much trouble for something that is

most probably a lost cause? You understand no one has seen this plane since 1958, and it may be at thousands of feet, where it can't be reached without a submersible," Ridley said, as he carefully stepped down into the cramped but well-appointed cabin.

Aldo followed him and guided him towards the bed in the front of the cabin. "Here, lie down. I'm going to tie your ankles again as I don't know what Pablo has hidden away down here. Can't have you causing trouble or I will have to throw you to Pablo's sharks."

Ridley obliged and laid on the bed while Aldo used industrial-sized zip ties to secure his ankles. He also strung a couple together to loop from his wrists to the ankle restraints to stop him raising his hands.

"To answer your question," he said, after Ridley had figured he wasn't going to respond, "in my line of work we rarely get to use our imagination. Most of the time I am watching my back for the next guy that wants to take my place. I know to do this, because it's the same way I got to be in the position I'm in. The alpha dog is on top, until the next alpha dog comes along." Aldo sat on the edge of the bed and looked thoughtful. "I will not grow to be an old man. People like me do not have long lives. One day, someone will take my place, it's the nature of the game, and they'll remove me to do it. So, when an opportunity arises to escape from that world for a few moments, to have some adventure, to use some imagination, it feels very good to do so."

He stood again and started to leave but paused when Ridley spoke.

"If you'd explained that to me, maybe we could have done this all differently."

Aldo smiled, sadly. "Perhaps. But would you have overlooked the fact I took your mother from you?"

"Why did you have to do that? Just divorce her for Christ's sake. You didn't have to kill her."

Aldo shook his head. "If Zanita had left my home she would have suffered a great deal of pain before she died. My enemies would see to that. She did not know much, but they're not aware of that. The wolves would have been at the door the moment she set foot outside. Believe me, what I did was much kinder."

He turned and left, switching off the cabin light on his way, leaving Ridley to seethe, alone in the dark.

34

CARIBBEAN SEA – JULY 31, 2020

AJ had slept well again. Diving put a strain on the body's systems, especially deep diving, that made most people feel incredibly hungry and extremely worn out. She had devoured her dinner from a freeze-dried pouch and then snacked her way through more goodies until she went to bed at 9pm. As she slowly awoke, shortly before dawn, she felt a flutter of butterflies in her stomach at the thought of her upcoming dive. Deep dives were technically challenging in the best of conditions. Throw in the isolation of the open ocean, the difficulty of working inside the wreck, and the fact she would be doing it alone and she knew she would be foolish not to be nervous. Those tickles in her stomach, tightness in her chest and slight dryness in her mouth were all there to remind her she needed to be well prepared, and very careful. She propped herself up on her elbows and let her eyes become accustomed to the dark.

"Morning," Nora whispered, sitting up against the opposite side of the fly-bridge.

"Hey," AJ replied softly, "What time is it?"

"Almost 6am."

AJ pushed her sleeping bag away and the inflatable sleeping pad creaked as she stood and stretched.

"I'm going to run through my gear one more time," she said as she stepped to the ladder.

"Want me to make some coffee?" Nora asked.

AJ grinned although she doubted Nora could make out her expression in the dark. "Too right, just try not to wake Reg up for a bit, he'll just be clucking and fussing around like an old mother hen."

She heard Nora chuckle before she replied. "I'm not sure what all of that means, but I'll make coffee and leave Reg alone."

"Too late, you schemin' women," Reg growled from below.

Half an hour later, with the sun barely climbing above the horizon, and the seas glassy calm, AJ stepped off the stern of Hazel's Odyssey into the Caribbean Sea. The dawn light cast eerie shadows through the water as AJ pulled herself down the anchor line. The current had subsided a little but she still hung from the line like a flag in the breeze as she descended to the rocks. Thomas followed her down the rope and they exchanged 'okay' signs before she continued over the edge towards the Beechcraft, leaving Thomas to watch her disappear into the darkness below.

AJ felt very alone as she approached the ghostly image of the old plane in the dim, early morning light. She knew Thomas was less than 100 feet away, but she also knew he could do nothing for her down here. She had suggested his safety diver role to help appease Reg, but they all knew it was little more than a gesture. On nitrox, Thomas couldn't descend to her depth, but more than that, he couldn't see her. If something untoward happened at 200 feet, her friends might never know what happened, she would simply never return. Visibility would increase as the sun rose, but for now she could see no more than 40 feet around her, and she sensed more than spotted some big fish close by. Shadowy movement filled her peripheral vision, and while she knew there was nothing in the water that should be threatening, she remained tense as she arrived at the tail of the plane.

On the prior two dives Reg had been carefully watching the dive time; while she investigated the wreck now, alone, AJ needed to carefully monitor her depth and time to stay on the critical dive plan. She levelled off above the nose and shone her torch beam inside the cockpit, which was now quite familiar to her. The small silver bait fish flashed and glimmered in the light as they scattered and receded into the darkness at the back of the fuselage. She pulled the channel lock pliers from a utility pocket she had strapped around her thigh and finned gently into the window opening. Her plan was to try and stay outside of the cockpit, instead of backing inside, and reach down and under the dash. She softly rested against the nose and the top of the dash, bending at the waist to drop her upper body down between the yoke and the instrument panel. It felt like she was sticking her head into the jaws of the lion. The yoke hit the back of her head and her chin was scraping down instrument bezels and switches as she rubbed the sediment free in a billowing brown cloud. She reached down and felt the floor, then bent her right arm and tried touching the backside of the panel to find the block she'd discovered the day before. Everything was upside down and backwards. She needed joints that hinged the opposite way, and the best she could do was feel the end of what she hoped was the bolt securing the block. The block she further hoped was a tobacco tin.

There was no way she could use her right hand at the awkward angle it was in, but she thought she might be able to have better reach with her left. Still working blind as the cloud of debris swamped all vision, she switched hands and dipped her left shoulder farther into the cockpit. The two side tanks scraped and scratched across the old sheet metal as she teeter-tottered with her legs hanging in mid water and her head against the yoke holding her in place. Her neck muscles were throbbing and her shoulders ached, but she was sure she didn't need long if she could only get the pliers on the old bolt. She stretched and fumbled around with her left hand and finally felt the block and the lump sticking through. She retrieved the pliers from her right hand and banged them around behind the dash until she felt the lump again. Holding the channel lock pliers was one thing, but having the dexterity to open the jaws and clamp it on the rusty nub was another. She brushed the jaws of the pliers back and forth but couldn't feel them drop over the end of the bolt. She shuffled her body to try for a better position and her neck screamed in pain. She reached with her right hand and grabbed the base of the yoke to take some of the effort away from her head and neck, setting off another cloud of sediment. Her position was incredibly disorientating, and as she reached again with the pliers her shoulder dipped farther into the cockpit and she clung to the yoke to stop from sliding sideways as everything seemed to shift. Bloody hell, she thought, I almost slipped off the side of the nose. Once she felt secure again she knew she needed to get to work, time was racing by and she was determined to get that block off the dash. If it wasn't the tin containing the diamonds, so be it, but she was hell-bent on finding out.

She felt the head of the pliers knock against the nub and, moving very slowly, she opened the jaws and slid the pliers over it, pinning them back against the block. Wiggling her fingers to the back of the handles she closed the jaws shut and finally felt them bite on the nub. Her whole plan rested on seventy years of immersion in salt water having rotted the metal to the point of crumbling, or at least easily breaking away. She prayed Dingo had used a cheap bolt. She pinched the handles tightly together and carefully rocked the pliers, testing the resistance. It felt like chalk and seemed to give way almost immediately. She wrenched harder and the pliers fell away. Reaching to the floor, she placed the channel locks down and put her hand back up to feel the block. It moved under her touch and she excitedly felt for the edges and rocked it around. She laughed into her regulator in delight as the rectangular shaped object came away in her hand, just as she felt herself sliding again. She clung to the base of the yoke with her right hand and with her newly claimed prize held tightly in her left hand, she reached to the floor and braced herself. It was then she realised it wasn't her that was moving in the aeroplane. It was the whole plane that was moving.

Queen of the Island Skies juddered and rocked as the nose dipped and the build-up of debris and sand in front of the plane gave way. Her weight on the nose must have disturbed the plane's delicate balance on the slope enough to free it from the sand, and the rusty chain undoubtedly snapped like a carrot. AJ looked to her left, and through the gouge in the side of the fuselage could see the slope which she, along with the plane, was now slowly slipping down. Grinding, creaking and groaning sounds echoed through the water as metal bent and ground against rock and other metal. If the plane made the steep drop she had seen 40 feet below, it would plummet to the depths, with her along for the ride. She considered pushing herself off the side of the nose but with most of the air out of her rig to keep her planted on the nose, she would drop and be hit by the wing or the large motor. Desperately hanging on with both hands, there was no way to reach her inflation control to lift her up and swim above the wreck as it ground its way deeper. Wrapped over the dashboard with her head still buried behind the yoke she couldn't see anything outside the plane except the sliver through the hole in the fuselage, which was mostly blocked by the starboard motor. She knew if she continued this slow-motion ride down the side of the mountain she couldn't survive the eventual drop to the abyss, but she felt paralysed in her precarious position and less than nimble with four unwieldy dive tanks strapped to her. She decided her only hope was to push herself away from the nose and hope she could get enough air quickly into her dive wing to not be steamrollered by the plane. She searched with her finned feet against the top of the nose to find any kind of purchase to push off from, but found nothing. She let herself slide backwards, releasing her grip on the yoke and grabbing the edge of the instrument panel with both hands to stop herself. Her feet were now clear of the nose and flailed in open water as she dug her fingers into the top corner of the dash with her right hand, in order to free her left and reach her inflation button. The tiny muscles in her fingers strained and screamed at her to let go but she locked her fingers at ninety degrees like a hook, and grimly hung on. She fumbled for the inflation button as the plane shuddered violently, bouncing her whole body against the nose. She squeezed hard on the button and heard the rush of gas hiss into her rig just as her fingers could hang on no longer. The starboard wing ploughed into a mound of sand, pivoting the whole plane as the bottom of the nose hit the rock protrusion she had noticed on the slope. AJ was thrown off the nose ahead of the plane, but was quickly halted with something pulling violently from her left side.

A huge cloud of sand and sediment washed over her as the old Beechcraft groaned to a halt, leaving her blinded in a fog with sand particles pelting her face around her mask. The debris field in front of her cleared with a gush of bubbles revealing her nitrox tank regulator, which had been carefully stowed against the tank under an elastic band, caught on the window surround which now tethered her back to the wreck. AJ reached back to the window opening amongst a storm of air bubbles and sediment as the mouthpiece free flowed. The cloud of debris blocked most of the light and the bubbles spewing from the reg made swirling psychedelic patterns in the fog, as her precious deco gas was dumped into the ocean at an alarming rate. Still without enough air in her dive plate bladder, she banged against the nose of the plane as her hand swiped for the trapped regulator. Her fingers dragged over the reg but she was sliding backwards again and couldn't break it free. Hanging onto the regulator as it sprayed a constant fire hose of bubbles, she kicked her fins and finally wrenched the reg clear. She poked inside the mouthpiece with her finger which immediately stopped the free flow, and pushed herself away from the Beechcraft in case it began to move once more. She closed the valve on the nitrox tank so the free flow wouldn't happen again and cursed herself for having left it on after her final checks on the boat.

In a dense cloud, she couldn't tell up from down or if she was still descending or shooting dangerously towards the surface, risking the bends. She gathered the regulator hose back up and secured it once again under the band while she decided what to do. She had dropped against the nose of the plane so she guessed she was most likely dropping ever deeper. She kicked hard with her fins, hoping she was orientated facing up after pushing herself clear of the wreck above her. With a few more kicks she cleared the cloud and found herself in deep blue open water. She looked at her dive computer. She was at 258 feet, 48 feet below her planned depth and four minutes over her maximum time at depth. She needed to get shallower in a hurry. She also needed to settle her heart rate that was understandably spiking and causing her to use her trimix at an alarming rate. She had managed to avoid certain death over the drop-off, but now she faced a physiological threat that could be just as potent. She finned towards the brighter water she could now tell was above her, and angled back in the direction of the slope before the current could whisk her away. As she swam, she looked at her left hand, where pinned between her thumb and palm was the tobacco tin she had managed to hang on to.

35

CARIBBEAN SEA – JULY 31, 2020

Sleeping on a moving boat was something Ridley had become very accustomed to over his years of sailing. Combined with the exhaustion from his brutal captivity, he slept like a log, only waking briefly when Aldo and Tattoo rotated down in shifts during the night to get some sleep. He found the constant drone of the powerful engines and the sound of water against the hull comforting somehow. Perhaps because they represented a time in which Nora and her friends were safe. When the engines slowed, things would get far more dangerous. He still clung to the hope that the dive boat had left Sixty Mile Bank and headed home overnight, curtailing Aldo's pursuit in an empty ocean. With the Cayman Islands closed to visitors, they were not about to sneak a 44-foot Contender ashore without being spotted, so he would be forced to turn around. It would also mean the end of the road for Ridley, he was certain, but that was okay in his mind. As long as Nora was safe.

He lifted his hands to rub the sleep from his eyes but they snapped to a halt with a tug on his ankles. The faint light of dawn cast a soft, warm hue across the cabin floor below the hatch, and Ridley thought he could hear the two men talking at the helm. He wriggled to the edge of the bed and carefully swung his feet to the floor. He stood and was relieved to find some life had returned to his sore limbs. He shuffled closer to the open hatch at the top of the stairs.

"Here, widen the range," he heard Aldo say. "Go to the maximum, should be 72 nautical miles."

Ridley stood still and listened intently, realising they were using the boat's powerful radar array mounted high above the centre console's roof.

"There," he heard Tattoo say. "Is that something? It barely registers."

"I believe it is," Aldo replied, with a hint of excitement in his voice. "We won't see a boat that size clearly unless we're within about 10 nautical miles, but the radar is hitting something there. It must be them. We'll keep watching and see if they're moving or just sitting still. If they're stationary we'll say good morning in just over two hours."

"Why don't we go faster and get there quicker? If they move we might lose them. This thing can go twice this speed."

"Because I'd like to make it back home again. We run faster and we'll use a lot more petrol; we have some margin, but not enough to get careless. That dive boat can't even go at our cruising speed, so we'll catch them regardless. We'll save our petrol for when we get closer."

The Contender jarred and rolled to starboard as it crashed through a slightly bigger wave and Ridley stumbled against the wall of the cabin. He immediately heard Aldo from above.

"What's he doing down there?"

Ridley opened the door to the head and shuffled inside as footsteps started down the steps.

"What are you doing?" Tattoo growled through the door.

"What do you think I'm doing? I'm in a bathroom, I'm trying to take a piss."

"Well hurry up."

"Why? You need to go? It's not easy taking a piss when you're trussed up like this. Want to come in and give me a hand?" Ridley answered, and cringed as he waited for Aldo's henchman to react.

"I'll give you a hand, you little shit," Tattoo hissed quietly. "I'll put my hands around your throat and snap your puny neck if you give me any more lip."

Ridley decided he'd baited the man enough, and surprised himself when he managed to produce a stream, adding authenticity to his quick-witted escape. He heard Tattoo's heavy footfalls back up the stairs to the helm and him mumble something to Aldo. As Ridley finished in the head, he tried to figure out a plan. Disabling the boat would be the best option, but tied up the way he was he had almost no ability to use his hands. He also didn't know where anything vital was on the boat that he could interfere with. Jumping overboard would only cause a delay if Aldo came back for him. He had no idea whether he would or not. On one hand the man had told him he hadn't decided his fate as yet. Of course, he thought, that could be a tactic to keep him from doing something desperate; but assuming it wasn't, jumping overboard may make his mind up. Bobbing in the water watching Aldo and Tattoo speed away, to do who knew what with Nora and her friends, would be devastating and ultimately pointless. As much as he feared the thought of being present when Aldo caught up to them, at least he would have some chance to help them. What he could do, he had no clue, but being absent guaranteed his ability to be of no help. It all hinged on whether Aldo would turn the boat around.

Ridley shuffled from the head and nudged the door closed with his elbow.

"They're not moving," he heard Aldo's voice from above. "They might still be diving today. That will make it easy, they can't leave with someone in the water."

Ridley made it back to the bed and sat down. He kept chewing over the limited options he faced until he heard footsteps again and looked up to see Aldo going into the head. He waited for him to finish and when he came out and looked over, Ridley spoke.

"Could you release these ankle ties? I can sit up top if you want to keep an eye on me, it's just really hard to stand up or move about."

Aldo laughed. "That's the point."

Ridley smiled at him, "I get that, but seriously, where am I going? What am I gonna do, run across the water?"

"If you do, he'll think you're Jesus himself returned," Aldo said, nodding towards the helm. "Me? I'll take a video and sell it for a million dollars."

"I thought you were a Catholic; you don't believe in God?" Ridley asked.

"I'm Mexican, we're all Catholic. But if you believe in God, you're supposed to believe in hell, and if I believed in hell, I wouldn't do what I do, because I would certainly spend the afterlife in damnation."

Aldo crossed himself and laughed. "But still I must pretend." He walked towards Ridley and pulled a switchblade knife from his pocket. "Sure, I'll free your feet."

36

CARIBBEAN SEA – JULY 31, 2020

AJ's dive computer recalculated the dive plan based on her actual time and depth, and the display instructed her to ascend to 120 feet. The rocks along the edge of the bank quickly came into view and she could see Thomas's face peering over and him frantically waving to her with one hand, while his other held up the okay signal. It was a question rather than a statement, and without the ability to explain the dramatic events in sign language, she signalled okay back. She levelled off at 120 feet, where her computer instructed her to stay for one minute, and then move up to 110 feet. It would be a long process, allowing the excess gas molecules to dissipate through her tissues while still under the pressure of depth. If she ascended to the surface without these steps, the gas bubbles would expand as the surrounding pressure reduced, and course through her bloodstream, likely causing an embolism. She finally calmed her breathing back to a normal level by the time she joined Thomas at 100 feet. His eyes were wide inside his mask and she wanted to hug him and tell him everything that had happened, but dive gear wasn't conducive to hugs, and communication was reduced to sign language and her dive slate. She took her slate and drew a crude outline of a plane, then an arrow and redrew the plane below the arrow. His eyes got even wider.

After AJ settled Thomas back down, she held up the tobacco tin. The rectangular container was in remarkably good condition. The thin, tin-coated steel was heavily tarnished but hadn't rusted. A hole ran through the middle of the base and the lid, with rust rings and marks around its edges from the old bolt. The lid appeared to be firmly stuck but AJ dared not try and remove it for fear of losing the contents – if indeed there were contents. She rocked the tin back and forth but couldn't tell if anything was moving inside, dampened by the water. She handed the tin to Thomas and pointed to his BCD pocket. He would need to surface long before her on his single 32% nitrox tank, so it made more sense to get the tin to the boat than remain down here with her.

After a minute, they moved over to the anchor line extending up to Hazel's Odyssey and ascended to 90 feet, where her computer instructed her to remain for two minutes. She needed to take stock of her situation and see what obstacles lay between her and joining her friends on the safety of the boat. The boat she could easily see, silhouetted above her through the now brightly lit ocean. It seemed so close and yet she knew the distance between her and the surface was as deadly as a minefield. She closed her eyes and breathed smoothly, calming herself and bringing her focus back to the things she could control. Thomas. She took his arm and looked at his dive computer on his wrist. He had been at depth for over thirty minutes and on 32% nitrox; his no-deco time was down to eight minutes, although he still had just under 1,000psi left. He needed to ascend. She pointed to him and then towards the surface with her thumb, signalling he needed to go. He nodded but didn't move. She frowned at him through her mask and pointed again towards the surface. He reached over and squeezed her arm, his eyes clearly telling her he didn't want to leave her alone. She winked at him and gave him the okay sign, trying her best to appear unconcerned, a feeling she didn't currently possess. He reluctantly began his steady ascent up the line to his own safety stop at 15 feet. Watching him leave, with safe passage through her minefield, she felt alone once again.

She needed to stay focused and get back to taking stock. She scrolled through the screens on the dive computer to see the stages of decompression stops the algorithms had calculated. The times at each shallower depth got longer and at 70 feet she would switch to the 50% nitrox tank.

"Bugger," she squealed into her regulator; the nitrox tank. She remembered the free flow and, reaching down, released the dedicated pressure gauge held under the elastic strap. The gauge read 1600psi. It should read 3,000psi. She had lost almost half the 40 cubic foot capacity. Going back to her dive computer she checked for the total volume of nitrox gas it estimated she would use. The display read 31.5 cubic feet. The screen flipped back and instructed her to move to 80 feet for three minutes and she shuffled up the line another 10 feet. Scrolling back through the menu, she checked the volume of trimix predicted for the modified dive; it read 164.6 cubic feet. She had two 80s on her back, meaning 160 cubic feet, and she had been breathing like an Olympic sprinter using more gas than the algorithm knew. She looked up at Thomas now hanging far above on his safety stop and wished she'd thought of this before she had sent him away. She checked her trimix pressure and sure enough it was down to 200psi. She still had over two minutes until she would move to the next stage and switch to her nitrox. There was no way to signal Thomas and get more trimix lowered down in time, plus it would mean having Thomas blow off his safety stop, which she wouldn't do.

AJ pulled the SMB from her pocket and unclipped her dive slate, attaching it to the inflatable tube end. She quickly scribbled on the slate and, using her fourth tank, the one with pure oxygen that she had plenty of, she blasted some gas into the tube and let the line run through her hands. Thomas looked down from above in surprise, as the bright orange SMB rose up towards him. He quickly saw the slate hanging and read the note. He peered down at AJ and she could tell he was trying to figure out what more he could do for her. Just follow the instruction, Thomas, she willed to him through 65 feet of ocean water. Please don't try and come back down or shorten your safety stop. He read the note again and, to her relief, signalled okay. AJ went back to focusing on gentle breaths, preparing herself for the moment she knew was coming. She hung to the line with the current gently floating her, and stared down at the bank below. A large shadow moved across the sand flats, and for a moment she wondered if it was a cloud. But clouds move slowly. A boat? She pulled herself more upright and searched the water above. The friendly neighbourhood tiger shark was back. The beautiful, powerful creature took a long circle around her and she watched it move effortlessly through the water, unaffected by the current that tugged and dragged her body around. For many, the sight would be terrifying, but for AJ, who understood he held no threat to her, she found the vision relaxing. As the shark disappeared into the deep blue, she felt ready.

With just over a minute left at 80 feet, her regulator became harder to breathe through for two final inhales before she felt and heard the clunk of the valve as the gas supply ran out. AJ enjoyed free-diving and had practised with Jackson when he had been on the island. He was much better than her and had taught her how to relax and realise the oxygen in your lungs will last much longer than your brain thinks; it's the carbon dioxide that triggers the panic. She let the current pull her, holding securely to the line with her eyes closed and tried to think of anything relaxing that came to mind. She pictured Jackson's face, lying next to her in the early hours of dawn with a trickle of light sneaking through the window. He was smiling and brushing a gentle finger across her forehead and through her hair. He leaned slowly over and kissed her softly. For a moment she was lost in the memory, lost in the precious reflection, but the tightness in her lungs made the vision dance in and out of focus. She tried to bring his face back into her mind but her fingers tightened on the line and her chest felt like a clamp. She opened her eyes and looked at her dive computer – she had ten more seconds until she could move. She fought to calm herself and stay focused. She didn't need a breath, she kept telling herself; she wanted a breath, but she didn't need one yet. She reached down with her free hand and released the nitrox regulator from the band in readiness. It felt like an hour waiting for the final few seconds to tick away, but finally the arrow on the screen pointed up and the direction told her to switch gases. She spat the dead regulator from her mouth and eagerly stuffed the nitrox mouthpiece in, exhaling the last of the spent air in her lungs to purge the regulator. She drew in a big breath. But she didn't breathe in anything; the reg felt empty like the one she had just taken out.

"Idiot," she screamed inside her head and twisted the valve on the tank to the open position. Beautiful, precious, dry gas surged through the mouthpiece and she gulped it down, filling her lungs. Once she had recovered, she looked up in time to watch Thomas climb the ladder onto the boat. She checked the nitrox pressure gauge, which now read 1500psi. According to her computer's plan she had twenty-one minutes across four more stages to make half the tank last. Unless they could help from above.

Thomas climbed aboard and removed his regulator from his mouth. He handed AJ's slate that he had brought up with him to a nervous-looking Reg.

"Bloody hell, what happened?" Reg growled as he read.

"I think the plane slid down while she was inside. She ended up a lot deeper than planned. I guess she needs the extra nitrox because she was down deeper?" Thomas asked as he ditched his BCD and tank in a rack.

"Nah," Reg mumbled, scratching his head. "She ought to have plenty of nitrox, it would be the trimix she'd be short of." He put the slate down and looked around at the tank racks, "Well, it don't matter what we think, she has the dive computer that knows what's going on, so if she wants nitrox, that's what she's getting."

He chose AJ's used nitrox tank from their first dive, as it had the most gas in it, and they were out of full tanks.

"What depth was she at when you left her?" Reg asked as he fitted a harness strap around the tank.

"I watched her move up as I surfaced, so she'd be at 70 feet now."

"Did she seem okay?" Nora asked, helplessly watching the two men prepare the tank.

"She seemed a little shaken at first, but yeah, she was okay," Thomas reassured her. "Oh, here," he said, remembering what AJ had given him. He dug through his BCD pocket and produced the tobacco tin. He handed it to Nora and they all stared at it for a moment.

"Oh, wow," Nora whispered.

"Come on Thomas," Reg said, returning his attention to the nitrox tank. "Get me some line to lower this with."

Thomas disappeared into the cabin below the bow and returned quickly with a length of line. Reg swiftly tied the end of the line to the tank harness and made sure the regulator and pressure gauge were well secured under the elastic band.

"Get your mask and fins, Thomas," Reg barked, and he made his way around the cabin structure to the bow.

Thomas slipped his fins on his feet and with his mask in hand he jumped from the swim step and began to swim around the boat as he secured his mask in place. Looking down he could just see AJ in the deep blue water, hanging on the anchor line. Reg lowered the tank into the water and began playing out line as Thomas held onto the anchor line where it met the ocean surface.

"The current is pulling it away from the line, Reg," Thomas shouted, looking up at the big man on the boat.

"Damn it," Reg muttered and stopped lowering the line.

"I'll try swimming against the current and pulling the line back towards the bank," Thomas yelled, and he floated back towards the bow to grab the rope to the tank. He hooked the line over his shoulder and tried swimming but the line slipped off as soon as his arm swept back. He retrieved the line and kept it in his hand as he tried swimming again. Reg could play out plenty of slack from the boat but the line underwater had the drag of the heavy tank being pulled by the current, making progress incredibly hard. Thomas made it a few feet forward until he came to throwing his arm forward with the rope in his hand, which then pulled his whole body back.

"I'll get my rig and take the tank down, Thomas," Reg yelled and was about to tie the tank line off to a cleat when Thomas flipped over on his back.

"Wait! Let me try this, now," Thomas spluttered from the water.

Once on his back he could use both legs and one arm to swim and kept a tight hold on the line with his other hand. He slowly started making progress into the current, and swam beyond the anchor line. Reg kept feeding more line and occasionally Thomas would flip over and check to see if he was above AJ yet.

AJ was now at 50 feet and four minutes into her five-minute stage at that depth. The pressure gauge on the nitrox tank read 450psi. The shallower she got, the longer the gas lasted as the surrounding pressure of the ocean reduced, but she was about to start her final stage of nine minutes at 30 feet. Below 20 feet, pure oxygen could cause convulsions so unless they reached her with another nitrox tank she'd be forced to skip some vital time at 30 feet and go up shallower. The whole system was evolved around safety margins but having used a lot more trimix than the plan had called for with the exertion in the plane, all her margins were used up. One good-sized gas bubble in her bloodstream from ascending too soon could easily make its way to her brain and render her unconscious. If helped to the surface, the situation would only become worse. She still had over thirty minutes on pure oxygen until she was safe to return to atmospheric pressure. Stay unconscious below, and she would drown. Her minefield was now condensed to the final 40 feet.

The nitrox tank dangled well above her but still angled backwards behind Thomas, who she could see swimming overhead. He was making slow progress in the surface current but she could tell he was trying to swim far enough out that they could lower the tank to meet her on the line. Her computer urged her to move up to 30 feet and she gladly obliged. She had nine minutes of decompression obligation at this depth, and glancing at her pressure gauge told her she had much less than that in gas remaining.

Thomas felt like his lungs were ready to burst as he kicked and pulled and stroked his way painfully slowly through the water. He was sure he was towing the whole boat behind him, rather than just the dangling tank. He rolled again and saw AJ had moved up closer. That had to mean good and bad news. The good being she was closer to the surface, so he had less distance to get the angled tank line to her. The bad was she must be getting closer to emptying the tank she was breathing from. What could he do if she ran out of gas before he got the tank to her? Could he free-dive down, he wondered. But the tank was at the end of a rope stretched behind him; he would never gather it up in time. He kicked harder and ignored the pain from his muscles and the searing in his overworked lungs as he sucked in all the air he could. Because he could, and AJ couldn't. If she ran out of gas he knew she was trapped below the surface. He reached even farther with his one arm and kicked with all his might. He took a big gasp of air and spun around again to look down. The tank hung in mid water, over halfway to AJ, and looked like it would meet her if he lowered it. He pulled more slack in the line and let the tank drop through the water towards her. The surface current instantly swooped Thomas up, now he wasn't swimming, and dragged him back towards the bow of the boat. If the tank missed her on the line, he would be starting all over again. He was certain she didn't have that time.

AJ watched the tank drop closer, as Thomas played out the line from the surface. It was no more than 10 feet above her but was already nearly directly overhead. It was going to miss her. The reg breathed heavy. She felt her heart rate pick up, as she watched the tank drop and pass beyond her, as her reg started breathing hard. On the next inhale she felt the awful clunk as this tank too ran dry. The life-saving bail-out tank they were trying to lower was passing over a mere five feet above her and would soon sweep away out beyond any reach. With it would go any hope of surviving this dive. AJ did the only thing left she could do. She released the anchor line and the current whisked her away. She met the descending tank and looped her arm around the line to secure herself while wrenching the reg from its band and shoving it in her mouth, as she spat the old one out. Before she tried to inhale, she cranked the valve and opened the supply. She sucked down the nitrox and looked up to see Thomas being dragged back to the boat by her pull on the line. He lurched for the line they had strung from the swim step to the anchor line off the bow and jerked to a stop. The rope down to her wrenched tight a moment later, and she quickly checked her dive computer. It showed 35 feet but with the line now tight she was beginning to ascend. She reached back and dumped the air from her wing, which slowed and finally stopped her ascent. Looking up, she could just make out a figure above the water animatedly doing something on the bow, and then Thomas let go of her line. She floated for a few feet until the line went taut again, now safely tied to a cleat.

37

CARIBBEAN SEA – JULY 31, 2020

After a long forty minutes hanging on a flailing rope focusing on maintaining an even depth in the current and swells, an exhausted AJ clambered aboard the Newton with the help of her friends. They fussed around her and helped dismantle the five tanks now hanging from her body. Once free of her harness she hugged each one of them in turn before she pulled her wetsuit down and peeled her way out of the neoprene. Reg handed her a travel mug of steaming coffee which she gladly accepted. Over ninety minutes underwater, much of it breathing trimix which stole heat from the body, she was chilled despite the balmy Caribbean morning.

"What on earth happened down there?" Reg finally asked, standing over her like a papa bear with his cub.

"I was upside down with my head stuffed in the cockpit, and the bloody plane tried to fly again," she said, rolling her head and stretching her sore neck. "It slid, with me in it, and I thought it was going over the drop when a wing dug in and caught it."

"Blimey," Reg said, holding his forehead as though the very thought gave him a headache. "How deep did you end up?"

AJ looked up and squinted against the bright sun now well above the horizon. "258 feet."

Thomas whistled.

"Strewth, girl," Reg muttered. "How come you ran out of nitrox? I figured you'd use all the trimix if you went deeper."

"I did," AJ replied. "I ran out of trimix over a minute before I could go up to 70 feet and start on nitrox."

"What did you do?" Thomas asked.

"Nothing," AJ said with a grin.

"What do you mean?"

"I mean I did nothing. I stayed at 80 feet and didn't breathe for a minute. Then I went up to 70 and breathed again," she explained flatly.

"Boss, you crazy. See Reg, I told you she'd find a way to do something crazy."

AJ laughed. "Creative in unfortunate situations would be a kinder description. But the trimix wasn't the problem. Well, it was for a minute, but the bigger problem was the nitrox. The reg got caught in the wreck and free-flowed half the gas away – that's why I needed the other tank."

"Jeez," Reg said, blowing out a long breath. "How about we call this good and head home?"

"Wait," AJ blurted. "What about the tin? Is it the right tin?"

"We couldn't open it until you were back, it didn't seem right," Nora explained. "But I agree with Reg, we should leave as fast as we can. I'm really nervous sitting out here after that plane came over. I've put all of you in enough danger already. Let's get going then we'll try opening the tin once we're under way."

They all agreed and with a bustle of activity they had their gear secured, the motors warmed up and the extra lines pulled aboard. Idling slowly forward against the current, Reg eased the tension on the anchor and they were able to drag it clear from the back of the rock pile. Thomas hauled it up and stowed it before joining the group on the fly-bridge, as Reg eased into the throttles and aimed Hazel's Odyssey towards Grand Cayman island.

Nora held the tin and they all looked at it carefully. It was rectangular, with curved corners and a lid that hinged at the back.

Rust-coloured sea water dripped from the hole through the centre and as Nora turned the tin around they could hear things sliding around inside. She tried pulling the lid open but it wouldn't budge. She handed it to Reg who tried with the same result.

"Too much crud and maybe some rust under the edges, I'd say," Reg said, handing the tin to Thomas. "Why don't you grab the toolkit from down below and we'll see what we can use."

"I hope you don't need channel lock pliers," AJ said sheepishly. "I'm afraid they didn't make it back."

Reg grinned at her. "You can pay me back for them when we get home."

She thumped him on the arm. "They were mine, you pillock; remember this is my boat."

He laughed. "Oh yeah, I forgot we're not on one of mine."

Thomas was quickly back with a wooden tote full of assorted tools and small parts, which he placed on the deck and began to rummage through. He set aside the hacksaw Reg had used the day before, and took out a can of brake cleaner spray.

"We could use this to clean stuff up," Thomas said, setting the can down.

Nora picked the can back up. "This stuff is tough on the hands; my dad used to use it in his shed for cleaning parts." She grinned. "I used to get in trouble 'cos I thought it was fun to set light to the spray."

AJ laughed. "You're as big a tomboy as me."

Thomas found a set of wire-cutting pliers and laid them next to the tote.

"We don't have any proper snips or cutters really, I reckon we'll have to saw at it some," he said, picking up the hacksaw.

Reg looked down at the three others huddled on the deck. "Watch yourselves, it'll be hard to hold that little tin while you cut it."

Nora pinned the tin to the deck with her weight over it, while Thomas lined up the saw at one end of the lid. He slowly drew back the blade, which immediately slipped off the side of the tin as the boat jolted over the long rolling swells of the open ocean. He put the saw down and dug a screwdriver and hammer out of the tool tote. He lined the screwdriver blade up on the edge of the tin lid and gave it a solid tap with the hammer. The screwdriver put a channel-shaped dent in the lid as he had hoped, and he switched back to the saw. Laying the saw blade in the channel he drew back before thrusting the blade forward, throwing small shavings and swarf from the cut. With three more strokes back and forth the lid was cut through and the blade hung up on the side of the tin. Thomas wiggled the blade free and set the saw aside.

"Okay Nora, let's have a look," he said, and picked up the tin once she had taken her hands away.

He pushed the screwdriver blade into the cut he had made, and easily pried the thin metal up on one side. He shook the tin until the contents fell against the opening he had created and held his hand underneath to catch what came out. Nothing came out and he peeked inside.

"Wow. Whatever is in there is pretty big."

AJ handed him the wire cutters. "See if you can snip a bigger hole."

Thomas took the pliers and slid the cutters inside the open gap. He squeezed the handles together as hard as he could and tugged up and down until the sheet metal finally gave way and opened another cut. Peeling back a corner opened a large hole, and once again he shook the contents of the tin until they finally spilt from the tin into his hand.

"Bloody hell," AJ blurted as they all stared at the large grubby looking lumps that sat in Thomas's hand.

AJ grabbed a rag from the tool tote, and picking up one of the dirty lumps, rubbed the grime away. She held up the result; a very large, glistening diamond.

"Shit," Nora breathed.

"Blimey," Reg said, nearly falling out of the helm chair. "I've never seen a diamond that bloody big in my life."

"And there's more in there," Thomas said, wiggling the tin, causing several more to drop into his hand.

AJ looked at Nora. "Does Ridley have any idea what these are worth?"

Nora shook her head and stared at the stone in AJ's hand. "Not really, he said he thought they were very valuable. It only took his grandfather two of them to buy his aeroplane."

"No wonder this Trujillo bloke is interested," Reg said. "Must be over a million dollars' worth there."

"Hey guys," Thomas said, standing at the railing by the ladder. They looked his way.

"What's that?" he said, pointing at the horizon behind them.

"Oh no," Nora said quietly.

Reg turned back to the front and pushed the throttles forward. "We better get a move on."

The Newton picked up speed, its broad hull shoving its way through the water as the diesels strained to reach its maximum speed of 26mph.

38

CARIBBEAN SEA – JULY 31, 2020

Ridley sat on the bench seat behind the helm chairs that were folded up for Aldo and Tattoo to lean against. The Contender continued to carve through the ocean in a smooth, steady, effortless rhythm, its sleek hull sitting high in the water, up on plane.

"See them?" Aldo said, grinning at Tattoo.

"Yeah," he replied, looking down and tapping the radar screen, "but they're moving now."

Aldo reached over and zoomed in the range of the radar for a more detailed look.

"They're less than five miles away from us – even if they go full speed we'll catch them in an hour or so."

Tattoo looked from the dot they could just make out on the horizon to his boss standing next to him.

"Let's go faster. Then when we catch them, we'll take their petrol so we have plenty for the trip back."

Aldo laughed, and Tattoo snapped around as Ridley chuckled as well.

"We won't get far if we put diesel in our petrol tanks," Aldo said, and Tattoo glared at Ridley.

They continued in pursuit and Ridley kept an eye over their

shoulders on the radar and GPS screens, as well as the boat growing slowly larger in the distance. After less than ten minutes they passed over the Sixty Mile Bank and the live depth measurement showing on the screen quickly changed from over 1,000 metres to 34 metres. Aldo turned to Ridley.

"What do you think they found?"

The man seemed truly excited, and Ridley wondered what his intentions were once they caught the dive boat. He appeared deceptively innocent, like an angler with a bite on the line or a yachtsman with a sail full of wind. But Ridley knew better. Aldo's line between acceptable and out of bounds was so off kilter he was likely to do anything.

"Probably nothing," he answered.

"Why would they leave, if they found nothing?" Aldo said, looking curiously at Ridley.

"Maybe they saw you coming."

Aldo shook his head. "No, we were too far away when they first started moving. It's possible it's a coincidence and they planned to leave this morning. But I prefer to think that they were successful, and whatever secret of value your grandfather had on his plane is now on that boat." He beamed like a child, "So what is it anyway? What are we all chasing here?"

Ridley shook his head. "Hate to tell you, but it's just some worthless family heirlooms, trinkets. They're of great value to my family, but financially worthless."

Aldo's smiled faltered ever so slightly, but then he laughed. "That's good, I told you I like you."

He turned back to face the front.

"Aldo," Ridley said, and both men looked around.

"What would you do if you were me?"

Aldo looked confused. "How do you mean?"

Ridley repeated. "What would you do, if you were in my situation?"

Aldo frowned, thinking about the question and the moment his expression changed to one of realisation, Ridley slid off the seat, took a step towards the port gunwale and dived over the side.

At over 30 miles per hour the water was like hitting concrete and Ridley bounced off the surface, skipping twice more before his velocity slowed enough to dig into the water and wrench him to a halt. All the wind was knocked from his lungs and pain flashed from his broken rib throughout his body. He couldn't tell which way was up, and his vision was blurred by the salt water and the force of the impact that felt as though his face had been spun around on his skull. He spluttered, choked and kicked like crazy, desperate to reach air, although he didn't know which way it was. He rolled over and felt his leg thrash above the surface, finally getting his head to follow and gasp in a breath. His eyes slowly cleared as he winced in pain and trod water. All he could see was three outboards heading straight away from him, and the backs of Aldo's and Tattoo's heads.

He really thought his question would be enough to get Aldo to come back for him. Aldo would not sit idly by and allow himself to be taken without a fight. Of course, Aldo had grown up with blood on his hands, so he would probably have chosen to attempt a violent solution, but no way would he be passive. Ridley had no chance against these men in a fight, and all three of them had to know that. He had done the only thing left at his disposal to delay them reaching the woman he loved. Aldo had to respect that. He'd kept him alive and brought him along for a reason, so Ridley had gambled that his willingness to sacrifice himself, plus whatever that reason was, added up to Aldo turning around. He watched the Contender continue towards Nora and cursed himself for being so stupid. He looked around at the open ocean rising and falling as far as he could see. His heart sank as he realised he faced a long, slow demise, with plenty of time to fret over his mistake.

The note from the engines growing fainter in the distance changed. Ridley swung back around to see the boat making a wide arc as it turned to come back towards him.

"Ha!" he yelled, causing his ribs to hurt like crazy.

39

CARIBBEAN SEA – JULY 31, 2020

AJ and Nora helped Thomas drag the fuel containers across the deck. Running at this pace they would run out of diesel before they made it back, even with the extra they had brought. But Reg had asked for every drop they had to be in the main tanks so they tried not to spill any as the Newton bounced across the ocean at her top speed.

"AJ, bring your binoculars up here," Reg shouted down.

AJ retrieved the glasses from the cabin and scampered up the ladder. Guessing what he wanted to see she steadied herself against the railing and trained the lens on the boat that appeared to be chasing them.

"He's turned around, Reg," AJ exclaimed. "He must be turning back."

Reg turned and squinted over his sunglasses from the pilot's seat, staring into the distance as he thought about it.

"I thought he'd stopped gaining on us. Don't make no sense, does it," he said, shaking his head. "If he's come all the way from the Mexican coast, why would he give up now and turn back?"

AJ shrugged. "Maybe he's low on fuel. If he only had enough to make the bank, perhaps he had to."

"It takes all sorts, but any sailor worth his salt ain't gonna run it that close."

"We are," AJ said and winced, hoping Reg wouldn't be insulted.

He laughed. "True, but we were fine until this bugger decided to chase us. We had plenty of margin to run at our cruising speed." He eased the throttles back and the boat sank a little lower in the water as it slowed back to their comfortable pace.

"Could be he wasn't chasing us after all, of course; we could be running from a fisherman who just turned for another run over the bank," AJ said, taking another look through the binoculars. "He's still heading away."

"That what you reckon?" Reg asked with a smirk.

AJ took the glasses down and looked at Nora, who was holding the funnel while Thomas poured the last of the extra diesel into the port side tank. She glanced up with a questioning look.

"They turned around," AJ shouted down.

Nora looked back at the funnel, making sure she held it steady, but AJ guessed she was deep in thought.

"I don't know what to think, Reg," AJ said, looking over at him. "It's easy to feel like we're being paranoid, but if Nora's right and this Trujillo bloke is coming after us, I'd rather be running as far away as possible."

Reg nodded and they looked at each other a moment, both chewing it over. Nora had finished helping with the fuelling and came up the ladder.

"Did they make a big turn or whip around and go back?" she asked.

"Not sure, one minute they was coming straight behind us and next they looked like they were getting smaller again," Reg replied.

"Still straight behind us?" Nora asked.

"Suppose, yes, best I could tell."

"If you were running about, fishing, or even cruising around on the water, would you turn around in a long easy turn, or would you slow down, cut it hard, and go again?" Nora asked.

AJ didn't let Reg answer. "If you had to go back for something in the water, the fastest way is to slow down, turn in a tight circle and head straight back, cover a lot less distance. That where you're heading with this?"

"Wait though," Reg said. "Book says make a wide arc so you can keep a man overboard in your sights the whole time."

"Not if speed is your priority," Nora retorted. "If they turn again in a minute and come after us I promise you it's Trujillo, or someone he's sent."

"What would they have gone back for?" Reg asked. "From what you're saying this bloke ain't the sort to go back 'cos his hat blew off."

"Ridley," Nora said firmly. "Ridley was aboard. He would do anything to stop them, I know he would. Including throw himself over."

"If that's true, it's good news on two counts," AJ replied, putting a hand on Nora's shoulder. "It means he's alive, and it means they went back for him, so they want him alive."

"If you think he's on that boat, let's turn around ourselves and go get him," Reg offered.

Nora shook her head, "Do you have guns with you?"

Reg looked surprised. "Of course not."

"Then you don't want to go up against these men," Nora said and tried to smile. "But, thank you."

AJ threw her hands up. "Look, I try and figure things out by upside versus downside, right? If you're comparing two scenarios, what's the best result and the worst thing that can happen for each outcome."

Thomas climbed the ladder and joined them. They all looked at AJ to carry on.

"So, if we run as hard as we can, we might get away from the bad guy that might be chasing us. That's our best scenario. Worst case is he still catches us, but we gave him the best run we could, yeah?" They all nodded. "If we cruise along and it is this Trujillo fellow, he'll catch us way out from the island and we'll be completely screwed. Bad, bad, downside."

"I hear you, but if we carry on wide open I don't think we'll make Grand Cayman. We will run out of diesel," Reg said.

"We don't have to make the island," Thomas said. "We just gotta make it to about 20 miles off the coast; we can reach the coastguard's tall aerial on the VHF from there. We'll call in some help. They got guns."

Reg smiled. "Yeah, that's true, they got big guns."

AJ lifted the binoculars once more and found the boat in the distance.

"Wait, I think he just turned or maybe stopped. The white water off his stern just went away."

"Keep watching, I'm telling you it's them," Nora said, her voice cracking. "I can feel it, I know it was Ridley."

"Hang on tight," Reg said, and pushed the throttles back to the stops.

40

CARIBBEAN SEA – JULY 31, 2020

The Contender swung around and coasted alongside Ridley, who floated in the water, watching them carefully. Tattoo stood by the gunwale with a vicious-looking gaff in his hand. Aldo took the motors out of gear and joined him. He laughed.

"You were right, of course, I would do something too." He held his hands up in a gesture as though to say 'you got me'. In his right hand was a pistol. "Now, you have proven you will do what you can, so I salute you, but I cannot have any more delays. I can shoot you and leave you here, sparing you a long and horrible death in the water. For your mother's sake, you understand. We can gaff you and drag you back aboard, which will be as it sounds, most uncomfortable for you, and messy on my friend's boat. Or, you can come around to the ladder and get back on the boat. All three take about the same time, so it's no matter to me, it's up to you."

Ridley quickly figured option three was preferable; he had caused a delay, and he was going to be given the chance to fight another day. He kicked and wriggled as best he could to the back of the boat, Tattoo tracking him all the way, and by the look on his face he was dying to use the gaff. He reached the ladder and tried to pull himself up with his bound hands on one side of the frame but he swung awkwardly and fell back in the water. He saw the gaff swinging in the air at the same time he heard Aldo's voice.

"No! Help him up."

Tattoo growled in displeasure but threw the gaff to the deck and leaned over. Ridley got his feet back on the ladder as Tattoo's huge paw grabbed him under the arm and roughly dragged him into the boat, sprawling across the wet deck.

"Get after them again, cruising speed," Aldo barked and Tattoo returned to the helm.

Ridley started to pick himself up but a blow to the side of his head sent him crashing back to the floor. His ribs hurt like crazy and now his head was spinning. He pulled his knees up and lifted his hands to cover his head before he turned to look up. Aldo stood over him.

"Do not mistake me for a weak man, Ridley. My patience will only go so far."

He tried to kick Ridley in the ribs but Ridley's legs deflected the shot so he swung down hard and punched him again, this time in the face. Ridley groaned and blood spilt from his nose, mixing with the sea water washing around the deck. Aldo grabbed him by the zip ties around his wrists and dragged him over next to the helm station, on the port side near the steps down to the cabin. He released him to fall against the deck, moaning and wiping the blood from his face. Ridley looked up and saw the smile on Tattoo's face. Made sense, he thought; Aldo had to show his man he wasn't going soft. But he hadn't left him behind, he hadn't shot him, and he wouldn't let his thug beat him any more. Ridley was convinced there was a chink in the armour of his captor; he just hoped he had another opportunity to exploit it.

He lay on the deck and stayed quiet for over half an hour while the Contender continued across the Caribbean Sea. Aldo and Tattoo said very little except for the occasional comment on their estimation of the dive boat's speed, and how quickly they were gaining. Ridley finally sat up, with his back against the gunwale. Aldo glanced down but didn't say anything. They both knew it was hopeless to try and go overboard again; Aldo wouldn't turn around a second time. The blood had clotted in his nose but his face was sore and he could feel his cheek swelling to go with the knot on the side of his head. His ribs still hurt with each breath or movement, but the sharp pain had dulled somewhat, the nerve endings having worn themselves out, he guessed.

"Another forty-five minutes and we'll catch them," Aldo told Tattoo.

Ridley let his chin rest on his chest as though he was nodding off to sleep, hoping they would spout more information if they thought he wasn't listening. They stayed quiet for a while but finally started talking.

"That boat must be at its maximum speed. I'm surprised their tanks hold enough diesel to run that hard," Aldo said quietly.

"Do you think they know we're chasing them?" Tattoo asked.

"It sure seems like they do. Don't know why they'd run that boat this hard if they didn't."

"Must have something on board they're worried about someone taking," Tattoo said, and chuckled.

"They're paranoid for some reason, I'm betting you're right. Another thirty minutes and we'll find out."

"Maybe they'll run out of diesel. That'll make things easy," Tattoo commented.

"Yeah, still, why would they risk that?" Aldo mused. "Shit, turn the VHF up, make sure it's on channel 16."

Tattoo reached over and made sure the radio was set, which it already was. "It's on, what are you thinking?"

"I'm thinking we need to reach them before they reach VHF radio range to the island, that's what they're charging for. They don't care if they don't have enough diesel to get home, they just need to call in the cavalry. Son of a bitch."

Aldo took the throttles and eased them slightly forward. The powerful four-stroke motors surged the big boat ahead.

"Hell yeah, now you're talking," Tattoo said with a broad smile.

41

CARIBBEAN SEA – JULY 31, 2020

AJ stood at the back of the fly-bridge and looked through the binoculars.

"It's them, Reg, they're coming again."

Reg nodded and kept his eyes ahead. The Newton didn't have radar so they had no way to see the other boat until it was visible on the horizon. It was hard to tell distance across water with the curvature of the earth and the waves conspiring to limit the view, but AJ guessed they were less than five miles back.

"What if we offer to trade the diamonds for Ridley? Nora is sure he's aboard, they had to bring him along for a reason. Maybe it's to trade him?" AJ said, putting the glasses down on the console next to Reg.

"Possibly, but I doubt they have him to trade with us. More likely a hostage in case they run into the authorities." Reg frowned as he looked at AJ. "In my experience, men like that don't trade. They take."

"You're right, I suppose. When should we start trying the radio?"

They both stared at the VHF as though it had an answer for them.

"When the GPS shows we're 20 miles off the coast, or they get really close to us," Reg replied. "No point clueing them in on what we're doing. If they hear a reply from the Coasties, it might scare them off, but if they know we're not getting a reply, they'll know we're all alone."

AJ nodded, and walked over to the ladder. "Get you anything Reg?"

"I'd love a coffee if you can fire up that little stove of yours," he said, managing a smile.

"Coming right up," AJ replied, and slid down the ladder to the deck.

Thomas was moving tanks around in the racks, getting them sorted for when they docked.

"Quit working, Thomas, we can do that in a jiffy when we get there," AJ said, grinning at him as she dropped into the little cabin and grabbed her stove.

"Making me anxious, just waiting, best I keep myself busy I reckon," he replied, clanking tanks as he switched them around.

"He's been explaining the different tanks to me," Nora said, sitting on the starboard bench. "I heard you talk about the different gas mixes, but I didn't know one from another. Now I know the skinny 40s are the oxygen and 50% nitrox, and the fat 80s are the others, all marked by the colour or the label." She patted the 40 cubic foot oxygen tanks behind her. "I need to keep busy too."

Thomas heaved the last of the heavy tanks into the racks, organised by gas, as AJ brought the stove up and set it on the bench. She filled the stainless-steel container with water and used a barbecue-style butane lighter to spark the flame. She steadied the base of the stove with her hand against the heave and roll of the boat as it laboured on towards Grand Cayman.

"Did I hear you tell Reg you can see them again?" Nora asked.

"Yeah, they're back there. Hard to tell how far but they're gaining for sure."

They all looked off the stern and could make out the boat behind them when they rose over a swell.

"How long until we get in radio range?" Thomas asked.

"About half an hour still," AJ said. "Reg wants to wait to try the radio until we have a better chance of reaching the Coasties. If they hear us calling with no response it tells them we're on our own."

AJ jumped up. "Nora, hold the stove!"

Nora obliged and AJ vaulted up the ladder to the fly-bridge.

"Reg! They won't know we didn't get a reply. They're farther away than we are, they'll just think they're still out of range."

Reg looked at AJ. "Hmmm. Guess that might work. You'll have to respond like you received a reply, give 'em some theatrics."

AJ reached for the VHF radio handset.

"Mayday, mayday, mayday. This is Hazel's Odyssey, I repeat, Hazel's Odyssey. Mayday, this Hazel's Odyssey. Distance 30 miles north-west of West Bay. We are being pursued by suspected pirates, repeat, pursued by pirates. Request immediate, armed assistance. Over."

She released the microphone button and waited. Reg looked at her.

"You know, if it turns out they're fishermen who happened to be heading home, same way we are, we're gonna get billed a pretty penny for calling out the Coasties for no reason."

AJ cringed. "I know. Well, for now we're not reaching anyone, and by the time we can reach them, I have a feeling we'll know one way or the other," she said, nodding her head towards the stern where the boat behind them was noticeably closer. The radio was silent.

"Copy, Cayman Islands Coast Guard, this is Hazel's Odyssey confirming. We request immediate assistance. Over."

Reg frowned. "You're too good at this."

AJ chuckled. "I did manage to convince my school I was my mum calling one day. It was such a nice day, it seemed like a waste to spend it in school. Boy was she mad when she found out."

"See, what they didn't realise was that day was an important part of your education. Getting put to good use today," Reg said with a wry grin.

"Copy, Cayman Islands Coast Guard, this is Hazel's Odyssey. Confirming, twenty minutes ETA. Over."

Reg stopped grinning. "Course, if they don't have their VHF on behind us, don't make any difference."

42

CARIBBEAN SEA – JULY 31, 2020

Aldo and Tattoo both stared at the VHF radio on the instrument panel of the Contender. Ridley, still seated against the port side gunwale, reflexively looked up.

"What are they saying?" Tattoo asked, glancing at Aldo.

"They're calling the coastguard; apparently they think we're pirates," Aldo said slowly.

Ridley looked down again before they noticed he was listening. He figured it was good to know Tattoo clearly didn't speak much English, but Aldo must be fluent to understand the transmission. They had only conversed in Spanish, so he realised he hadn't known before. How that helped him, he had no idea, but anything he could learn made him feel like he was still engaged somehow. While he was still alive, and they hadn't caught the dive boat, there was still hope. The radio call lifted his spirits immensely. He didn't know the closing rate, or exactly how far they were behind, as he could only glean information from what the two men said, but if they could survive the next twenty minutes, help would be arriving.

"Shit, man, this little island can't have much in the way of police," Tattoo scoffed.

"I don't know what they have, but we haven't done anything wrong. It's not illegal to travel across international waters. We don't have to worry about their police or their coastguard, unless we enter Cayman waters," Aldo replied.

"Or unless we attack that dive boat," Tattoo said with a grin.

"Which apparently we need to do in less than twenty minutes," Aldo added, and nudged the throttles forward a little more. "But something doesn't seem right," he added thoughtfully. "We didn't hear a reply, not even a crackle like we're slightly out of range."

"What's the range of these radios?" Tattoo asked, looking at the unit in the console.

"Boat to boat, only five to ten miles I think, but farther to a land-based aerial if it's mounted up higher. But I don't know exactly. We're getting close to where they called from which is about thirty miles out. If they got reception from here, we should too."

Aldo reached over, took the handset off its hook, and pressed the microphone button.

"Hailing Grand Cayman, hailing Grand Cayman, this is 'Reels Up', do you copy, over."

"Who the hell is 'Reels Up'? Tattoo asked.

"Best I could come up with on the fly, sounds like a fishing boat at least," Aldo replied with a smile.

The radio was silent, so Aldo keyed it again.

"Hailing Grand Cayman, hailing Grand Cayman, this is 'Reels Up', requesting a fuel stop, do you copy, over."

They both stared at the radio which remained quiet for several moments. And then it came to life with the accented voice of an islander speaking English.

"'Reels Up', this is the Cayman Islands Port Authority, our borders are closed, I repeat, our borders are closed, please state your port of origin, and your current location. Over."

"Shit, I guess we are in range," Tattoo blurted. "What did he say?"

Aldo looked puzzled. "They want to know who and where we are."

Ridley was even more puzzled. He had figured they were out of radio range and it was the dive boat playing charades on the channel, but that sure sounded like the Cayman Islands Port Authority.

43

CARIBBEAN SEA – JULY 31, 2020

Thomas hung up the microphone. "Was that okay?"

"That was bloody brilliant," AJ exclaimed. "I never knew you had a serious, official voice."

Reg shook his head. "I'll never know whether I can believe any of you ever again, you're all too good at this acting malarkey."

They all turned and looked at the bright white Contender skimming the tops of the waves just a quarter of a mile behind them and bearing down fast.

"I don't think it worked," Thomas muttered.

"They think they have some time still, they sped up to catch us quicker," Nora said.

"Alright, listen up, this isn't negotiable," Reg said sternly. "Nora, hide in the cabin below, stay out of sight. You two, stay low and under the fly-bridge where you're most protected and listen for anything I yell down."

"What are you gonna do?" AJ asked.

He shrugged his shoulders. "Keep heading for the island. If they're after stopping us, then we'll see what they do. If they're not armed then they'll have to ram us before I'll back off. But my guess is they're armed, and our fibreglass boat can't protect us from bullets. I'll have to yield and try and talk our way out of it."

"Why don't I stay up here and keep trying the radio, Reg," AJ pleaded.

"I can use the radio, now get down there, all of you, and stay out of sight. They know there's more than me on the boat, but hopefully they don't know exactly how many. We can keep Nora hidden at least. Go on." He waved a hand at them. "Get down there."

The three scurried down the ladder and AJ tried to come down close to Nora, so perhaps they wouldn't pick her out if they had binoculars. Nora stepped down into the cramped cabin below and AJ went to close the short door and top hatch. Nora stopped her.

"It's not right, me hiding down here when I got all of you into this mess."

"Keep your ears open and stay hidden, maybe you'll be able to help if they don't know you're aboard. Trust Reg, he's the only one of us with military training, he'll get us out of this," AJ said and pulled the top hatch closed.

"What did he do in the army?" Nora asked.

AJ smiled sheepishly. "He was a diver in the navy. But he can be a hooligan when he needs to be."

She closed the little door and sat on the opposite bench to Thomas. They both looked back and watched the sleek boat close on their stern. It appeared to be going even faster now it was running in the smooth water in the Newton's wake.

44

CARIBBEAN SEA – JULY 31, 2020

Aldo listened to the VHF radio from which a new voice made the call.

"Mayday, mayday, mayday. This is Hazel's Odyssey, Hazel's Odyssey, Hazel's Odyssey. Mayday, this Hazel's Odyssey. Distance 23 miles north-west of West Bay. Being pursued by pirates, repeat, pursued by pirates. Request immediate assistance. Over."

Aldo slapped the console with his hand and grinned. "I knew it, I knew it was bullshit."

Tattoo stared at him. "What?"

"They never reached the coastguard, they were trying to trick us." He waved towards the stern. "Get ready up front, I'm going to pull alongside."

Tattoo made his way forward, clutching the railing for support as they surged through the water at nearly 50mph. He came around to the port side where the duffel bag lay on the deck. Ridley watched him unzip the bag and pulled out a handgun, which he tucked in the back of his trousers. He then took out an assault rifle, keeping it low so it couldn't be seen by the dive boat and placed it on the padded seat. Ridley didn't know one gun from the next; he had never been around firearms, or certainly ever fired one, but he had seen enough movies to know this was a serious weapon. A shiver ran through him as he thought of the look on Tattoo's face with the gaff in his hand – he dreaded to think how trigger happy he would be with an assault rifle.

Tattoo positioned himself on the padded seat over the cabin in the bow with the rifle under his hand at the ready. He nodded to Aldo, indicating he was ready. Aldo waved his own handgun at Ridley.

"Stay down. Any movement, any noise and I'm going to shoot you in the head. Understand?"

Ridley nodded, and doubted the man was kidding. His expression had changed, his jaw looked tight and his eyes were cold and piercing. He had the steely focus of a game-time athlete, but in this case, his game was with people's lives. Ridley realised when Aldo had talked of adventure, this was what he had in mind.

The VHF radio blasted again with the same voice, making the same call. There was no response. Aldo pulled out across the wake of the dive boat and the Contender effortlessly carved through the chop. He eased the throttles back as they pulled level. Aldo tucked the gun in the back of his trousers and stood to the edge of the helm, making himself visible beyond the t-top. He held up a hand and yelled loudly in English.

"Stop the boat please. We would like to talk to you."

45

CARIBBEAN SEA – JULY 31, 2020

AJ couldn't hear what the man was shouting, but through the window of the half cabin she could see he held up a hand, indicating they should stop. The Newton didn't slow down, but turned to port, veering away from the expensive-looking centre console. She saw another, brute of a man sitting up front, looking back towards the helm. The pilot turned in pursuit and easily sped back up to reach the dive boat, as he signalled his man up front to stay put. She watched him shout again and hold his hand up towards the fly-bridge above them. This time Reg abruptly turned towards the Contender, which quickly steered away before they touched. AJ hung on and looked over at Thomas who was trying not to slide off the bench, his eyes wide. Bloody hell, Reg, she thought, nothing like offence is a good defence. When she turned back the man in the bow was now standing and pointing a vicious-looking military-style gun at the fly-bridge. She held her breath as the man tilted it slightly higher and the ear-splitting sound of fully automatic firing momentarily drowned out the boats' engines. The Newton began to slow and AJ leapt up, ready to race up top and check on Reg. Thomas grabbed her arm and pulled her back as a wave of nausea swept over her at the thought of her friend being shot. The short door to the cabin below swung open.

"I can't stay down here, what's happening? I heard gunfire," Nora babbled.

AJ reached out and batted the door to. "Stay the hell down there, it's fine, they're stopping us."

It didn't feel fine. AJ fought back the urge to charge out and do something. What stopped her was her complete loss of what that something might be. Guns versus dive gear wasn't a square fight in anyone's world. They were helplessly at the mercy of the pursuers. She breathed a sigh of relief as they slowed with the engines idling, and she heard Reg's voice.

"Who the hell are you people and what are you doing firing on us?" his voice bellowed from above.

AJ heard a man laugh and then reply in English, with a Hispanic accent.

"We are the people with the guns, right now that is all you need to concern yourself with. The people under the shelter should come out to the deck, and you can come down too. Shut off your engines please."

AJ and Thomas stood and stepped out from under the cover of the fly-bridge, as Reg did as asked and made his way down the ladder. AJ saw that the man at the helm, who she presumed was Trujillo, had a pistol in his hand. He looked at her.

"You, tie the boats together."

She took a line the burly man with the machine gun handed her, and after dropping a fender over the side, tied it to a cleat. She moved to the stern where Trujillo tossed her a line and she repeated the process. She moved back to the middle of the boat and anxiously wondered what would come next, as the man killed the outboards on the Contender. It was strangely quiet after the constant drone of engines and the excitement of the past few minutes.

Trujillo dropped the gun down to his waist and smiled at the three of them standing on the deck of Hazel's Odyssey.

"Let me establish how this will go. If you lie to me, I will kill you." He reached down and pulled a young man to his feet by his hair. He looked early twenties, lean build, medium height with a bloodied and bruised face. Blood stains streaked his tee-shirt and his hands were bound in front of him. AJ guessed she was looking at Ridley Hernandez.

"You probably don't know this guy, so to prove my point I will shoot him first."

Aldo lifted the gun to the side of Ridley's head and all three of them shouted for him to stop at the same time.

Aldo laughed. "Okay, okay, calm down." But he didn't take the gun away from Ridley's head.

Ridley looked over at AJ and she tried to read whatever message he was trying to send her. He blinked slowly and softly shook his head. She couldn't really tell what he meant, but she took it to mean 'don't worry about me'. Too late, she thought, even if we didn't know you were Nora's boyfriend, we're not going to sit by and watch these men kill you in cold blood.

"What is it you want?" Reg asked. "You can see we're not carrying anything of value, we're just divers."

Aldo pushed the gun harder against Ridley's head, tipping his chin down. Ridley closed his eyes.

"I think you're lying about that. Think carefully before you answer me. Did you find something of value on the plane at Sixty Mile Bank?"

AJ quickly replied. "Yes. Yes, we did."

She glanced over and saw Reg was nodding in agreement.

"I'd very much like to see what you brought up," Aldo said. "You." He waved the gun away from Ridley's head, and across the boats in AJ's direction. "What did you find, and where is it?"

AJ was standing directly opposite the evil-looking man with the machine gun, which was pointed directly at her. She forced her eyes away from him to look at Trujillo by the helm.

"Diamonds. There were diamonds hidden in the plane. I have them in the cabin."

He waved the gun towards the cabin. "Go ahead, slowly. Just you. Try anything and I'll shoot this kid, followed by the old man."

AJ carefully turned and walked towards the cabin door, which she noticed had swung open again. She wasn't sure if Trujillo could see her so she made her moves deliberate and obvious. She peered down and saw Nora squatted on the floor next to their camping gear. Nora held up the transparent, reusable plastic bag they had put the stones in. AJ took the bag and realised Nora had something else held against it in her hand. It was her stove lighter. AJ looked at her in puzzlement. Nora signalled for her to tuck it in her pocket. AJ did so, but was still confused. She backed out of the cabin and held the bag out in front of her as she walked towards the stern.

Aldo tucked the gun in the back of his pants and pushed Ridley down to his knees next to the helm station. He stepped close to the gunwale and reached out to take the bag. Seeing the man up close she was surprised he looked quite normal. He was a good-looking, middle-aged man with a well-groomed beard and neatly combed hair, despite the wind on the ocean. He smiled warmly as he took the diamonds from her. If they weren't being held at gunpoint in the middle of the Caribbean Sea, she would describe the man as pleasant. She looked down to her right at Ridley, who looked battered and exhausted. He winked at her and almost imperceptibly nodded his head towards the bow. Aldo was studying the contents of the bag so she stepped back and walked in front of Reg and Thomas to return to where she had been. It took everything she had not to react as she walked the few steps. Crawling around the edge of the half cabin under the fly-bridge was Nora. As AJ stood behind the bench and the tank racks, facing the big man with tattoos and a machine gun, Nora wriggled over her feet.

"What's in there?" Tattoo asked in Spanish, looking over at Aldo.

Ridley saw a female hand appear just above the gunwale, in front of the woman with the purple-streaked hair. The hand turned the knob of the dive tank as Aldo took a step towards Tattoo, holding the bag to show him the diamonds inside.

AJ looked down at Nora, who was twisting the black knob, opening the valve to the 40 cubic foot tank containing pure oxygen. She had chosen the second tank from the end as AJ could see the valve opening was facing directly away from the Newton. In her other hand was the can of brake cleaner from the tool tote, which she held behind the tank so it couldn't be seen from the Contender. Everything fell into place in AJ's mind, and she reached into her pocket. The hiss of the gas escaping the tank under 1,500 pounds per square inch of pressure made Aldo look up. Tattoo had lowered the assault rifle while he looked at the bag of diamonds, but hearing the hissing sound, he too looked up and began to raise his weapon. Their eyes widened as they both noticed something in AJ's hand as it swept in front of the row of tanks. Ridley lurched from his knees and buried his shoulders into Aldo's legs, sending him towards Tattoo. Nora moved the can of brake cleaner alongside the dive tank and pressed the button on the top, spraying a long stream of flammable fluid towards the other boat. AJ clicked the igniter, catching the brake cleaner alight, which sprayed through the flood of oxygen creating a powerful blast of flame. Tattoo lurched to his right just as Aldo fell into his henchman and the burst of fire hit them both. Tattoo screamed and his finger instinctively pulled the trigger, hammering bullets into the torso of his boss as the two fell to the deck. Nora released the button on the can and the flame instantly died. AJ cranked the oxygen cylinder knob closed as Thomas vaulted over to the Contender where Tattoo lay screaming in pain under Aldo's body, his rifle trapped between them. Thomas pulled the handgun from the back of Aldo's trousers and pointed it at the charred face writhing on the floor before him.

Ridley staggered to his feet and leaned on the railing atop the gunwale of the Contender. AJ helped Nora up from the deck of Hazel's Odyssey and watched her burst into tears when she saw him. Nora climbed over the rails and wrapped her arms around him. Ridley winced as she squeezed against his ribs, but he didn't mind the pain.

Reg took the gun from Thomas, who had been holding it as

though it was red hot. He had never held a gun before in his life and wasn't sure quite what to do with it once it was in his hand. Reg, on the other hand, did know, and he kept it carefully aimed at Tattoo while they pulled Aldo's bloodied body away. Tattoo was in no shape to resist or think about trying. His shirt was burnt away and the skin from his waist to his forehead was red and blistering. He curled up and moaned on the deck while they took his handgun away, and a knife they found strapped to his ankle.

AJ ran up the ladder to the fly-bridge when she heard the VHF radio crackle to life.

"This is the Royal Cayman Islands Police Service hailing Hazel's Odyssey, do you read? Over."

She snatched up the handset. "RCIPS, this is Hazel's Odyssey, I read you, over."

"This is the Royal Cayman Islands Police Service, can you confirm your mayday call, over."

"RCIPS, this is Hazel's Odyssey, requesting immediate assistance, we need medical help, I repeat, we need medical help. We're about 23 miles north-west of West Bay. Over."

There was a brief pause and AJ looked up when she heard a faint thumping sound. In the distance she could make out something in the sky towards the island.

"This is the Royal Cayman Islands Police Service, we see you Hazel's Odyssey, tied to another boat. Confirm. Over."

AJ waved frantically. "RCIPS, this is Hazel's Odyssey, confirm, two boats tied together, no immediate threat but require medical help as soon as possible. Over."

AJ replaced the handset and breathed a long sigh of relief. She looked down from the fly-bridge at the carnage below. How the hell are we going to explain this to Whittaker, she thought. Thomas was gathering up the stones that had scattered when the flame burnt the plastic bag to pieces. It had done a good job of cleaning a lot of the muck off of them too, as they sparkled on the deck. Thomas held them all in his hand and took them to Ridley who was sitting with Nora on the bench seat behind the helm station. The helicopter arrived overhead and hailed her to switch to another channel. She walked back to the radio and sat down heavily in the helm chair. Maybe one of those diamonds could go towards Nora's upcoming court costs, AJ mused to herself. And then again, she remembered, she might need some help herself after harbouring an illegal alien… and lying to a policeman… and diving under the restrictions.

"RCIPS, this is Hazel's Odyssey, we were attacked by pirates, I repeat we were attacked by pirates. One of the attackers is dead, I repeat, one fatality. The second is badly burned and needs medical assistance. Over."

The helicopter hovered above the two boats, causing ripples to roll out across the water in widening circles.

"This is RCIPS helicopter, confirm one for transport. We'll lower a basket and an officer to assist. Over."

AJ opened the mic. "Roger, RCIPS. Be aware there was also a kidnap victim aboard…" She released the button and thought for a moment. "I repeat, there were two kidnap victims aboard the pirate boat. Both are safe and secure, one has minor injuries. Over."

46

GRAND CAYMAN – AUGUST 1, 2020

AJ slept in later than she could ever remember. At least since she was a child. She finally slid out of bed and poured herself some coffee at 9:45am. She would have stayed under the covers longer, but she was expecting company at 10. She had wrapped herself around a pillow and drifted in and out of sleep for hours, thinking about Jackson. She had three more days to wait until their weekly video call and she desperately wanted to talk to him. To share what had happened.

They had waited a while for the marine police boat to reach them after the helicopter had hauled Tattoo away. Ridley had explained he had nicknamed the man as he never actually heard his real name. He had looked at AJ's arms and blushed, which had made her laugh. As there had been a fatality, the police had to secure the scene, which was the two boats tied together, and make sure any forensic evidence was preserved. All their stories matched, including how AJ had managed to get the can of brake cleaner and lighter from the tool tote when she retrieved the diamonds – Nora and Ridley having been on the Contender all along.

They were all brought back to the island on the police boat, while the Newton and the Contender were towed in later by more police craft. Ridley was taken to the hospital under police escort and the others spent the rest of the afternoon, and most of the evening, giving written statements and repeating their stories multiple times. Whittaker had sat with AJ, and when she told him Nora had been on the boat that came from Mexico, he grew quiet and looked at her for a long time. She had managed to keep it together, and when she was finally released to go home at a little after 11pm, Whittaker admitted they had found no trace of DNA on the sailboat. Not even a hair. As the owner of the dive boat, who was supposed to be fishing and not diving, he did charge her a fine for their violation of the island's lockdown rules.

Tattoo, whose real name turned out to be Manuel Pineda, wasn't saying much, mainly because he was pumped full of painkillers for the burns, but he did repeat multiple times in Spanish that he didn't know Ridley or Nora. He was out fishing with his buddy, Aldo, and has no recollection of what happened. Whittaker didn't believe a word, and charged him with piracy and attempted murder.

The wreck of Dingo Doyle's plane, Queen of the Island Skies, would be registered later that day. AJ had arranged to go to the port office with Reg after lunch. They were placed under self-quarantine, as they had left Cayman waters and interacted with foreign nationals, but Whittaker gave them a waiver to button up the official paperwork. The formality of locating the rightful heirs and owners would be easy, as he was going with them. The wreck was in international waters, so no country could lay any claim, and Ridley would get to keep the diamonds.

The two weeks of quarantine also gave Ridley and Nora an opportunity to figure out where they would go. He had work papers in Tortola, but she didn't have legal papers to be anywhere except Norway. With the world slowly recovering from lockdown, their options were limited, and flights few and far between. AJ knew an immigration lawyer who occasionally went diving with her and Thomas, so she planned to pass her name on to Ridley and

Nora. Maybe they could find a loophole to remain on Cayman until things found their way back towards normal around the planet.

Her bagel popped up in the toaster as she poured her second cup of coffee. She was glad she had summoned the energy to throw on shorts and a tank top, as a knock at the door told her Reg had arrived early with Ridley and Nora. She opened the door, still chewing a bite of her breakfast, and waved Nora and Ridley inside. Reg waved from across the garden as he headed back home. He and Pearl had a spare room, which beat sleeping on AJ's pull-out sofa bed, so they had won the two of them for their quarantine period. Pearl loved it. Reg pretended to tolerate it, but actually loved it too.

Nora looked nervous.

"Want some breakfast? Coffee?" AJ offered.

"No, no, Pearl fed us like we were never going to eat again. We're stuffed," Ridley replied.

He held his ribs as he talked, but his face looked a little better cleaned up, although he still had a shiner on his cheek.

"I can take a walk while you do this," he said, looking between the two women.

"Maybe for a few minutes, but don't go too far. I'll probably call you back inside," Nora said.

He nodded, leaned over and kissed her, then headed out into the garden.

AJ sat down at her tiny dining table and Nora took the seat opposite. She woke up her laptop computer and opened her Internet video calling software she used to talk to Jackson. She thought of him again. Why telling him would somehow relieve her of some of the burden of their traumatic few days, she didn't know. But it would, and she needed to see his face. She spun the laptop around and showed Nora where to enter the contact email to make a connection, and then she rose to leave. Nora grabbed her hand.

"Don't leave. Please."

AJ nodded and sat back down.

Nora slowly typed in the email address and paused for a deep breath, before hitting the connect icon. A synthesised ring tone sounded before a scratchy sound followed by a woman's voice.

"God ettermiddag, hvem ringer? Nora! Er det deg?"

"Hei mamma."

The two women burst into tears and Nora reached up to touch the screen.

AJ stood, and quietly walked out to join Ridley in the garden.

ACKNOWLEDGMENTS

Sincere thanks…

…as always to my amazing wife, dive buddy and partner in crime, Cheryl.

…to my lovely mum, and my older brother… I say older like I have other siblings… I don't, I just like reminding him he's older. – Michael, Jo, Ben and Sophie.

…to my great friend James Guthrie who keeps me in line with his detailed critique, and enthusiastic support.

…hugs, and love to my fake kids and real grandkids. I love you all and am blessed to have you in my life. – Lindsey & Dave and Andy, Rachel, Ethan & Kira.

…to Andrew Chapman, my tireless editor, who optimistically believes I'll learn how to use apostrophes… Fortunately, the final touch to my books is in his caring and capable hands. He can be found at PrepareToPublish.

…to Drew McArthur for his tech diving advice as well as his stunning photography gracing the cover of this book.

…to Jo at the wonderful Divetech Grand Cayman for the use of their Newton 36 dive boat in the original cover shot.

…to my growing advanced reader copy (ARC) group, whose input and feedback is invaluable. This book in particular has benefitted from a good deal of guidance in the aeroplane and deep diving scenes. Any inaccuracies or artistic licence are solely on me! It truly is a pleasure to work with all of you and my stories are better because of you.

...to Mike Polson who told me his father, Doc Polson, would be touched and excited to be mentioned in these pages - which made my day.

...to the marine conservation organisation Sea Shepherd for all that they do – yup, Sea Sentry is my not very subtle way of plugging them. Check them out at www.seashepherd.org

Above all, I thank you, the readers: it is your kind words and loyal purchases that have opened the door to more adventures for AJ Bailey, and allowed me to fulfil a lifelong goal of being an author.

LET'S STAY IN TOUCH!

To buy merchandise, find more info or join my Newsletter, visit my website at
www.HarveyBooks.com

If you enjoyed this novel I'd be incredibly grateful if you'd consider leaving a review on Amazon.com
Find eBook deals and follow me on BookBub.com

Visit Amazon.com for more books in the
AJ Bailey Adventure Series,
Nora Sommer Caribbean Suspense Series,
and collaborative works;
Graceless - A Tropical Authors Novella
Angels of the Deep - A Tropical Christmas Novella

ABOUT THE AUTHOR

Nicholas Harvey's life has been anything but ordinary. Race car driver, mountaineer, divemaster, and since 2019 a full-time novelist. Raised in England, Nick now lives next to the ocean in Key Largo with his amazing wife, Cheryl.

Motorsports may have taken him all over the world, both behind the wheel and later as a Race Engineer and Team Manager, but diving inspires his destinations these days – and there's no better diving than in Grand Cayman where Nick's *AJ Bailey Adventure* and *Nora Sommer Caribbean Suspense* series are based.

Printed in Great Britain
by Amazon